M000048268

Hell is the CEO
A novel by Mark Mettler

Acknowledgement

I always thought it was a sign of confidence and a positive outlook to speak big dreams and ambitions out loud. Writing a novel some day was both of those things to me. When I finally got around to doing it, I couldn't imagine anyone shattering those dreams by declining to publish it. I didn't seek out writer's groups because I didn't want to be discouraged and intimidated by better writers. I figured I could find an editor at the end to correct my spelling and punctuation placement and self-publish. I took it on alone. In short, I didn't do most of the things aspiring writers would be wise to do.

The editor I eventually found did far more for this story than find the misspells, however. She shaped the deeper meaning in real time, led me to uncover its core, and helped me to see the story the way I wanted readers to see it. It took longer as a result, but for me, it was worth the wait.

My editor is my daughter, Maxie Mettler, and this book is more than I imagined it would be because she inspires me every day to find my true self underneath the years of self-applied veneer.

This is a work of fiction. Names, characters, businesses, places, events, locales, and incidents are either the products of the author's imagination or used in a fictitious manner. Any resemblance to actual persons, living or dead, or actual events is purely coincidental.

Copyright 2019

Prologue

To really understand a song, to pull the meaning from it, you have to know the words, the lyrics. They are the poetry, and poetry has meaning, right? Adding the music was a brilliant way to get people to at least hear the words, but why bother with the whole enterprise if those words weren't important? If they didn't have a message? Tom could understand why people liked instrumental music, even jazz and classical, neither of which he could appreciate very much, but he could understand it. He could even understand music meant to do nothing more than get you up and dancing, though disco was its own particular scourge. Tom understood the many slices of the musical spectrum, but there was only one that saved his life.

For Tom, it had to be about the lyrics. The musicians carried the weight of the words out of the depths of existence from which they came and made them easier to wash down, like a cup of water for a pill. The music was the flower opening up to the world, but the lyrics were the nectar. At a time in his life when he felt alone and defeated, Tom discovered the incredible healing effects of lyric-driven music that spoke to him, that he chose. It was his religion when he rejected the one he was given. It was his haven when he had no friends.

In the spring of 1974, Tom Cooper's faith anointed him a man. For nearly a year he'd practiced chanting a long passage from the Torah that he delivered to a large gathering of his family. It was music with lyrics in a way, but most definitely not ones he could relate to. When he was finished, and he'd stuffed the breast pocket of his blue blazer with envelopes full of checks, he told his parents he was done with going to Temple. He didn't tell them that while they may think he was now a man, the kids at school were challenging him to live up to it daily. He didn't tell them they were cruel to him. He didn't tell them they were physical too. He didn't tell them they used Tom's religion as one of many excuses to isolate and bully him. He didn't tell them a world that had once seemed bountiful and endless had come to feel small and oppressive. He didn't have those words, but he discovered there was music that did. He heard a multitude of voices describing life the way he saw it – unjust, unequal, unfair. The voices resonated inside Tom, giving him something to cling to. A sense of hope born in the discovery of kindred spirits. A vein of humanity searching for meaning beyond life, struggle, and death.

Tom soon became obsessed with the music of the 1960's, still dominating radio airplay. As the agony of his adolescence dragged on, Tom discovered what those early years of his childhood meant through the eyes of his musical heroes, and he could compare it to the world he was now inhabiting. If the 60's were about freedom and breaking through boundaries to new frontiers, the 70's were a black hole into which those romantic notions had collapsed. Tom's father lost a family business to the oil-shock recession in '73. That's why they were in this new town where all the kids sucked. Tom had the feeling he'd narrowly missed out on something special he should have been a part of. By the time he was 15, he was in danger of falling to the dark side of nihilism. So many of his new heroes, the saints behind the lyrics, were dead. The abuse at school marched on. The world had no meaning, life itself, no purpose.

And yet, he found positive messages in the music that sustained him. So he carried on. And he made it through. Just in time to face up to the reality of choosing a college and a career. Tom had not had time to process what kind of work might be meaningful to him for a lifetime. His parents had made it abundantly clear he needed to study something that would lead to a good job when he got out. They got his grandparents to agree to pay his way. He would owe the debt of being successful. Undergraduate business school seemed like the way to go.

There wasn't much debate about the meaning of things in business school. Something was either a profit or a loss, a credit or a debit, an asset or a liability. It made it easy to learn. Black and white. Data-driven. Logical. Even marketing was way more scientific than Tom had imagined. The one subject that tried to get underneath all that crushing logic and explain it was economics. Tom gravitated to it. Instead of understanding how one business goes about its work and makes money, economics tried to make sense of how all of humanity acted, alone and in relation to each other.

Economic thought in 1983, Tom's graduation year, was heavily shaped by Milton Friedman, an advisor to both Ronald Reagan and Margaret Thatcher. Friedman famously wrote that "there is one and only one social responsibility of business—to use its resources and engage in activities designed to increase its profits." Anything else, he argued, was "unadulterated socialism." And then there were these two professors whose names Tom had long forgotten, who wrote an article about how the CEOs of public companies ought to be paid. In a nutshell, they argued that the best way to ensure that corporations acted exactly the way Friedman described they should would be to align the interests of top management with those of the shareholders. The way they argued it should be done? Tie their pay to the stock price. What's good for the stock price is good for the investors, and therefore the right course for the company. It made sense to Tom. The one in charge would have the fate of all the shareholders in their hands. They would have the most power to influence results. Of course, those results should drive their pay. It seemed like a virtuous circle to Tom. A team with everyone on the same page was usually a winning team.

Tom's economics professor was quite enamored with this article and told them that these ideas were finding their way into the banking and investing worlds and would change Wall Street forever. He described it as the perfect opportunity for smart, undergrad business majors like Tom and his classmates to dream about the kind of riches that in the not so distant past would only accrue to visionary company founders or be inherited from daddy. 'It was capitalism getting aligned with democracy' Professor Thompsonville nearly shouted, when they discussed the article as a class. Anyone with enough talent could eventually run a public company in America and if they did right by the shareholders, they themselves could get rich beyond their wildest imaginations.

As he contemplated that idea, Tom could hear Pink Floyd singing 'Money, so they say, is the root of all evil today'. It made him smile. There was a lyric for everything, and his rule was simple - if a line popped into his head, it's meaning must be considered. Tom thought about all the stress the lack of money had caused his parents. He thought of all the good that could be done with a lot of money. The root of all evil was not money, but the lack thereof, wasn't it?

Tom graduated a few weeks later. He got engaged to a girl he met at a party in his freshman year. That became his meaning. He landed a seat in an executive training program. That became his path.

July 26, 2015

It was still early on a Sunday morning, but Tom could already feel the weight of the work week on his shoulders. On Monday, the pain would begin again, the ache of seeing dead people walking. Not zombies, flesh-eaters with hollowed out eyes and blood-breath. These were real men and women, mid-career and later, active, engaged, scurrying to and from meetings, carrying on their corporate work. They were all responsible for something, had a title they had to explain over and over again to their mother. They cared about what they did, if for nothing else than that they spent so much of their lives doing it. They told people they met that they liked their job, without going into the details of their frustrations, because everybody had them. They shrugged a little when they said it, to let people know there were definitely some frustrations. That's what having a career was all about, frustration alternating with accomplishment, highs and lows, achievements and disappointments. And they liked having a career as opposed to a job. There was continuity to a career, a certain permanence. An era in your own life. All those people were real people, with real careers. They just did not know that very soon, very suddenly, those careers would be rudely interrupted. They had mostly been identified, and Tom knew a bunch of them, and suspected others. They were dead people all right – dead to the future corporation that would move forward in a re-organized fashion that did not include them.

Tom knew because they needed him to know. His organization was going to be eliminated as it now existed, subsumed by another, the work dispersed to new leaders. Most of the people would be alright for now. The first phase was aimed at Directors and up. The company was profitable but not growing. The last few years had been marked by fits and starts for new initiatives and growth vehicles while core business units had begun to stagnate or decline. A consultant's grand design for an efficient organization to support the future, which cost the company millions in fees, had failed to deliver any visible benefit. All the things that were promised by the little boys and girls in their Brooks Brothers business casual togs - clarity of roles, faster decision-making, smoother work streams – had failed to materialize over the 18 months since its implementation. Now the company was going to reorganize the CEO's way – lop off about 20% of the most expensive part of the workforce and figure out how to make do with less.

In 32 years of corporate life, Tom had seen this movie many times. In this version, he was sworn to secrecy, and while not promised anything, led to believe he would be part of the new organization going forward. He knew it was coming, because the current design, cooked up in that fucking consultant's witches' brew, was just plain dumb. He knew it when he took his role those scant 18 months ago, and it was true today, and he already knew the role was going away. It had been time well spent for Tom. In the company's "split and focus" design, Tom got a chance to run his own little fiefdom inside a business unit that was the only one hitting its' numbers. He'd escaped the unit run by the loathsome Dutch

Bagley, for whom Tom had developed an unhealthy level of hatred, a hatred so deep he wasn't even sure himself where the intensity of the emotion was coming from. Or if hate was even an emotion, or just a disease. His boss going forward, assuming he did make the cut, would most likely be Mark Stover, who'd come to the company in the last reorg. Mark didn't know shit about what Tom's business unit did, or how they did it. Even though they collaborated on work often, Mark showed no interest in digging into what Tom was responsible for, which Tom immediately recognized could be a survival leverage point someday, and that day had come. The company needed him. His team did too much important shit. It was specialized knowledge. 'How could they be integrated with the other business unit?' 'We'll need to have Tom's help.' 'Is Tom a keeper?' 'Dutch doesn't think so.' 'How about Patton, the CEO?' 'Always been on the fence.' 'Bailey and Moran, his boss, and his boss's boss?' 'They say he's indispensable.' 'Well that does it then, he stays.' That's how Tom was sure it went, when HR was talking to itself about him. That's how he got his double secret security clearance. And that's how the dead people he now saw walking came to be his problem as much as anyone's. He knew the ones he'd already marked in his mind, and depending on how deep the final blows would cut, there were others he was chewing over in his mind, getting prepared to be asked. Hey sniper, pick out a couple more targets. We're short of quota.

Tom had always tried to wall himself off from his direct reports emotionally. It was so crystal clear to him early on in a career of managing others that these people would make or break him. How could he do what he had to do – ensure he had the very best people on his team – if he became too attached to average performers? Better to treat them professionally, hold them all to high standards, coach them up the best you can. The day will always come when someone will ask you to stack-rank them, and they will ask that with bad intent. The bottom 10% will be laid off. The bottom 25% will be put on warning. The bottom 33% will have their bonus reduced by a factor of two. The bottom 40% will get a pay freeze. All manner of beastly creations cooked up in the HR kitchen, with the math courtesy of finance. It would be arbitrary, and Tom's people would be reduced to numbers anyway, so better to let them stay as two dimensional as possible, as people. But funny thing about people. They're generally likeable. They can give you hard work and loyalty and a willingness to be coached, and the next thing you know, you appreciate them, and not just the stars, who are easy to like, but all of them, to some degree or another. You appreciate all of them.

But then that inevitable day rolls around and the next thing you know, some of them are going to get shot. Every other time, Tom had been ready. He'd kept the average performers in particular at bay. He'd been cool and calculating and had regularly thinned his own herd without being asked, as a good executive should. He'd sat down thoughtfully to reassess his organizations and offered up ways to cut jobs and survive the headcount loss. He'd played his parts, all the juicy roles. But over these last several years, these nearly eight, long, puzzling years that kicked off with the worst economic disaster of Tom's lifetime, it started to get blurry. Where did Tom start and where did he end? He couldn't stop liking people and he started to want to be liked. In the past he only cared about being appreciated at work - by anyone – his peers, his people, his boss. Being liked, or even loved? That wasn't a goal for strangers. Workmates. Coworkers. Colleagues. Cellmates. Fellow travelers. They were characters in his life, important to his life, but the relationships didn't need to be cozy. He could try to remember how many kids they had and their general ages. He could try to remember their spouses' names if they had a habit of using them in conversation. About half the time he remembered to ask if people had a nice weekend, but the other half of the time he probably left someone with the impression he didn't give a shit about them. But over the years they'd begun to flesh out more, round out, become human. Tom started to feel an obligation to them. None of them deserved to be among the walking dead. Even the average ones were such good people, so good to their own people, so loyal and hardworking, that it was killing him that there could be pressure to cut a couple of them.

There it was, the emotion that used to be turned off with a half twist of a knob as Tom dialed in the cold killer, stuck on. The dead people walking were crawling on his skin this time, and he didn't appreciate the feeling. It made him really angry at Patton, thinking you should just shake everything up to send a message, get rid of a bunch of senior people. People who had suffered already with the shitty performance on his watch, and people with the most to lose, at the stage of life where the kids and the parents are sucking the marrow out of their bones. And would Patton be touched? Would the CEO cough up 20% of his direct reports to the guillotine? Which of his direct reports should go? 20% is 20%. Well of course, if it was Tom, Dutch Bagley would be the no brainer, but Tom knew he shouldn't, couldn't, expect to see that. It was a hopeful thought that got him through some days, but life never worked out that perfectly for him. No, Patton probably would not have to look anyone in the eye and tell them they're fired. Just say some hard goodbyes after the deed was done by others.

July 27, 2015

On Monday, Tom took a call from HR. Funny how a single functional area, staffed by individual human beings, was so often reduced to a faceless two-letter acronym, often spat out in disgust. As if the people who worked in HR - *Human Resources* for God's sake! - weren't actually human. They were a monolith, and a feared one at that. An unexpected call from HR? No thank you. It was the *resource* part you had to fear. That's what took people and put them on a par with raw materials, office supplies, toilet paper, gasoline, and electricity. *Human* becomes a much less complex adjective when placed in front of *Resources*. Just another input. When output goes down, inputs must be reduced, in order for the books to balance, for the profit to remain the same, because only with profit can the company remain a company. And only with growing profit can a public company's stock price rise. And everyone understands that's the only mission. No one questions what it means to be human when the adjective is used so simply. Everyone understands it means head count. Resources. Lower revenues? Lower costs. Balance. Fewer resources? Harder work. Balance. The company's fate hangs in the balance. Trap doors will swing open, and people will hang.

In this case, HR was a woman around Tom's age, someone he'd never met prior to a few weeks ago. She supported the division that Tom's group was slated to fold into. This would be their third meeting, and almost certainly not their last. Like Tom, it was necessary to include her in, to manage the process of identifying who would go and who would stay. Donna, that was her name, Tom had to remind himself as he somewhat surreptitiously headed to her office on the fifth floor. Not HR. Donna.

Donna had an assignment for Tom. While most of the names on the list of potential layoffs had been solidified by now – the dead people, as Tom called them – it was still necessary to complete an assessment worksheet, so the company would have some documentation on file in case of a wrongful termination lawsuit. People who performed the same job would be compared to each other, ranked, and theoretically, the worst performers would be the ones that were let go. Like most things in corporate life, this was not going to turn out to be entirely true. The real deal was that there were targets, no matter how good the people were. There were 60 vice presidents in the building. There would be 45 when it was over. 15 was the target. There were 240 directors. 48 - 48! - was the target.

Tom grimaced to himself on his way over, fighting the sight of dead people with grim humor, with bad puns, with hallucinations. The company had a target, and therefore the dead people walking had been targeted, and now Tom saw them not just as goners, but goners wearing outsized archery targets like sandwich boards. And that was a funny thing to imagine, funny-sad of course, but what were you gonna do when fucking HR called and you had to go sneaking up to their office? To her office. To Donna's.

Donna presented Tom the materials he would use to rate his 8 direct reports, but the metrics were quite different from the traditional factors the company weighed in their annual performance review process. There were just three big words against which everyone was to be evaluated. Tom looked down at the page at the bolded terms. **AGILITY. DISRUPTIVE. VISIONARY.** Fucking Christ, here we go. There were bullet points under each, in small type, with little dashes in front of them, but Tom wasn't reading, he was seeing. A trapeze artist, a tumbling gymnast, a crying, spoiled brat, a drunk douchebag at the bar, a street corner preacher, a fortune teller. HR had been drinking again. Wonder who cooked up this Koolaid mix?

On closer inspection, people with **agility** were defined as able to anticipate future consequences and trends, able to quickly make decisions, adaptable to changing situations and demands, and relentless and versatile learners. The best people would also be **disruptive** – drivers of change, comfortable with ambiguity, risk, and uncertainty, with broad-ranging personal and business interests. And finally, as **visionaries**, they'd be able to see connections among data and events, to operate with clarity without the need for certainty (whatever the fuck that meant), and able to identify viable ways to move forward in the midst of confusion. In other words, Tom thought, once we finish the layoffs and mash all the pieces together in a new organizational structure, it's going be a shit-storm and a cluster-fuck rolled into one, and it's going to take people who are comfortable with that kind of environment to survive and hopefully move the company forward to better results.

This meant Tom would also be rated on these words. Hallelujah. Another chance to be judged. Tom had had a lifetime of it. His parents. His teachers. The kids in the new town. The bullies. As time continued on, his wife Michelle, his sister, his children. His mother in law. Every boss he'd ever had. His own people, in something called a 360-degree review. His peers, in the same way. So much feedback, so many judgements. How was a man to know who he was anymore? Whose opinion should he trust? Does his boss Bailey consider him a **visionary**? Is he agile enough? He knows it probably doesn't matter. He's staying. Even if he's not totally sure he should, or wants to. They need him, they've been pretty clear.

Tom Cooper was a senior vice-president at a Fortune 100 company. Well, at least it was one a couple years earlier. Now they were 117th, and falling. But the point is, he knew what the fuck he was doing. If they didn't think he did, he'd be gone by now. Yet HR spares no one the annual review process. For most, it should be a thoughtful time to hear feedback, to reflect on one's year, to be open to suggestions to improve. But at the senior level, there's not much time for niceties. The last four bosses Tom had, at two companies, since he first made VP, employed a very simple thumbs up/thumbs down scale. They barely bothered to tell him anything constructive, as earlier bosses had. He felt like he was now in the deep end of the pool, where they really only needed to come around every once in a while and make sure you could still tread water. They could probably get it over with faster with a simple scale. You're either totally fucking brilliant, or you get shit done, or you need to get your shit together. If you're one of the first two, life goes on. Tom was in the get shit done bucket. Let the brilliant ones fight about who's more agile or disruptive. Yeah, let them fight over the CEO's chair too. As long as Tom got shit done, most of the time he got left alone to do his thing.

From time to time over the years he was lumped in with the stars, passed his talent management tests with glowing reviews, the secret meetings where young leaders are discussed in terms beyond the black and white numbers, the places where words like Visionary live. In the corporate world he'd navigated, you couldn't get this far without that occasional boost, from a supportive, enthusiastic boss. But Tom had never made it all the way through. He was heading into his middle fifties, the dangerous years, the years when people disappear if they don't break through into the executive suite. He still got shit done, always did. But that's now what he was. Who he was. So he didn't give a shit anymore where his boss would rate him on the new flavors, the words of the day, of this cut down day to come. He was staying. He knew what the fuck he was doing. They didn't even understand half of what he did. They needed him.

For his own people, Tom would do his best to rate them accurately on the scale of expectations, from far exceeds to fails to meet. But back in his office, reading the definitions of the skills and then trying to marry them to the ratings, Tom found himself just shaking his head and rubbing the part of his forehead just above the bridge of his nose. It was a stress-release mechanism for him that also seemed to work on live lobsters about to go into a pot of boiling water. He'd never stopped to consider whether his people met his expectations or not when it came to 'staying in close touch with the external environment and bringing this perspective in'. It was hard enough navigating a course through the ever-mutating goals and strategies of the internal environment, let alone trying to figure out how a wild, rapidly changing world would impact the company. In the end, Tom decided it didn't really matter. He knew he could rank his people in order from 1 to 8 in terms of their value to the company, so he made sure the assessment scores totaled up to match his ranking. No one would ever look at them or challenge them, or share them with the associates. They would sit in an electronic file, and corporate life would go on, either with or without all of Tom's people.

July 31, 2015

By Friday of that same week, after several more meetings with Donna, there was a fairly clear definition in place around Tom's future role with the company, and which of his people would fill what new boxes, either in Tom's organizational chart, or someone else's. Or so he thought. Donna sent him an email with what had by now become their cryptic shorthand – "do you have a few minutes?" "can you come up?" As soon as he was able, Tom trundled back to the fifth floor. Donna was waiting with some org charts splayed out on her little conference table. She greeted Tom with a wry smile and a weary sigh that signaled this was no more enjoyable for her than it was for Tom. Despite her involvement in the process for Tom's division, and the division he was folding into, she was unclear if she would still have a job when the layoffs were announced in the coming weeks. HR was not immune to the targets either.

"I have a little bit of bad news for you, unfortunately", Donna began hesitantly. "We need you to cut one more person from your organization".

"One more box on the chart, or one more actual person from my current org?"

"One more person."

"But then I'll have an empty box. Who's going to do that job?"

Donna stared at him blankly. "I don't know."

"Okay, see this is why this is hard for me – I'm not getting enough visibility into the full scope of the new organization – is there someone else available for this job if I eliminate one more person? Is John Larsson available?"

"No." There was a half beat pause. "But, we can go into the level 12's and they'll count toward the target too." She said this like a small child discovering an extra candy bar in the bottom of her Halloween bag. Like many big companies, Tom's employer used a leveling system not unlike the Federal Government's, where numbers identified people across disparate jobs and functions that would be paid the same because their jobs were considered comparable. In Tom's company, level 12's could be directors or they could be individual contributors whose accountabilities were considered as important as a director. Technically, to be called a director, you have to have people who work for you whom you direct, thus the term 'individual contributor' was created for those who did not manage others. Corporate life was nothing if not literal, and in this case, that desire to be both literal and equitable was putting some of those individual contributors in the danger zone. Be careful of the company you keep. Donna pushed a sheet of paper across the table with six names on it.

"These are your level 12's that are not directors. Is there someone here you could cut?"

"Are we not going to put them through the assessment tool?"

"Unfortunately, we don't have time".

Tom looked at the list. He knew all of them well. Therefore, he quickly knew who would have to go. Yep. He was the least agile, the least visionary, and fuck, disruptive in a way that Tom had never appreciated anyway. It took about 22 seconds to shift the fortunes of two souls, and only one of them would ever know about the decision. That's the power vested in Tom by his position, by his background and experiences, by his willingness, by his culpability. Someone he needed, someone who should never have been part of any layoff anyway, had been saved. And someone he tolerated, who contributed a lot over the years but was no star, had just been consigned to the dust bin.

From Tom Cooper's private journal. October 2001. Age 40.
Employer 4.

The proof of my duplicity was a matter of public record, a graph on a Powerpoint slide shown at an analysts' meeting and broadcast live on the internet. 3,600 salaried positions in the field would be eliminated over the next 18 months. 3,600 people I just spent 8 years of my life working shoulder to shoulder with would lose their jobs. And I felt guilt as I remembered my role in their slaughter, the role of a mid-level executive with aspirations.

There were in fact, six of us, eventually pared to three, that worked closely with a platoon of outside consultants to identify the work redundancies and unnecessary complexities that emboldened the consultants to recommend the slashing of 3,600 jobs. We were sold a half-truth, and like good merchants would, we marked it up to a full lie. In the post mortem we will be remembered as the most vile embodiment of the classic field put-down of headquarters staff, "Hi, I'm from the home office, and I'm here to help." Buttered up like pig-wrestlers at the county fair ("you've been hand-picked for a critical assignment"), we were sent out to 16 sites to gather the evidence that would be used to develop a profit improvement plan. Our boilerplate speech was that this was a golden opportunity for people to tell us all the things wrong with our company, the things that make their jobs too complex, too demanding. This was not about cost reduction, but about freeing people up to do more important work.

Yeah, sure. All of those people we spoke to, the store managers, department managers, district staff people, region staff people, field HR support, trainers; they are hearing our strong, kind voices telling them that senior management finally realized that the reason our stores were difficult to run was because we'd given them far too tough a task to accomplish. We took the onus off them – "It's not that you lack ability or dedication to hard work" - and now that it's all said and done, we're whacking off their arms and legs anyway and asking them in the future to do even better, with less. Oh I'm certain they're burning with rage right now, thinking about how we made them feel special to be part of this vital project. Just as we were told, as we received our hoods and axes, how honored we should be to be chosen. How could we not know those were executioner's tools we were holding?

But of course we knew. Not even strongly suspected. We knew deep down. After all, we didn't reach this point in our careers because momma drowned the smart ones. We knew the likely end game, and though we were sincere in a lot of what we said, we also knew that even our own job titles were in jeopardy, and better to be on the team figuring it out than just a marcher in the rank and file. I've learned that there's a particular layer of middle management that is very useful to senior management in assignments like this. We didn't need the mercenaries fighting this war against expense for us. We knew without asking that we had to take about $300m of people cost out of the field. But first we had to figure out how to run the business with fewer people, and to disguise that as a sacred mission to simplify life for everyone and give the *customer a better experience. So senior management can stand back and say, 'We didn't set out to eliminate jobs, those were the recommendations of the team. We put some of our best talent on the project to work with some outside consultants, and this is the outcome.'*

So occasionally, there are barbed roses to be picked on the way to the promised land for those mid-level executives that make up that "best talent". There are dirty missions to be carried out for the good of the cause, and if you succeed, there are vague, unwritten promises that bigger jobs, bigger paychecks, lie ahead. Even perhaps, the potential to be one of the controlling circle, a senior executive yourself. No less in the line of fire, mind you, but at least partially insulated. And extremely well-compensated. Is that really what I want?

I know that I want the money. And I do want to be challenged to think critically and strategically in the regular course of my work. I just resent this dance they;re doing with me. Telling me how strategic I am, and holding out that carrot of bigger jobs in the future where I'll get to exercise that skill. And while I'm working to get there, they're showering me with this love - I've got a mentor now, a senior VP of marketing - and a new level of stock option grants that I'm supposed to keep secret because they're being awarded as part of a special talent management program. And of course I got that special high-visibility assignment. I got the hood and the axe. I got to be the executioner.

Friends, forgive me my duplicity, but I am but a pawn in a Machiavellian game. I've been played as clearly as you have, and while you may lose your job, I've lost the last of my innocence. What a terrible curse, to lose all your honest belief in goodness and fairness by the age of 40.

August 25, 2015

One week after a second quarter earnings announcement that fell 2 cents a share short of street consensus, and during which the CEO reduced his guidance for the full year by upwards of 10 cents a share, a meeting notice appeared on Tom's calendar from his boss, John Bailey The meeting notice had no topic, but included the rest of the leadership team for his business unit. It seemed too early to be an announcement about the cuts – that was at least a week away, after the Labor Day holiday, based on the inside information Tom had.   The only speculation at a time like this was bad speculation, so Tom hoped Bailey wasn't about to announce he was leaving the company or retiring. As bosses go, he was a good one – and at Tom's level, it's not always easy to say that, given how close those jobs are to being the CEO, to catching that CEO infection, that virus that seems to destroy the capacity for empathy. Even though Tom knew he'd soon be moved under a new executive, he didn't want to see Bailey, an ally, gone from the company.

As it turned out, the timing of the meeting was driven by a surprise request from Patton to speak at every business unit head's next staff meeting, as long as that could be arranged this week, to suit his schedule and his needs. In this case, his needs were apparently to celebrate a corporate version of Festivus, an occasion for the head of the organization to let those closest to him know the many ways they've disappointed him in the quarter just finished. Tom was already in the room and had just heard Bailey explain to his team why they'd been pulled together when Patton came through the door just as the second hand on the wall clock swept past ten a.m. on the dot. Caleb Patton was a trim man of average height, with thinning hair going silver at the temples. He had a uniform of gray slacks, white shirts, and various shades of sportcoats. Even now, in the summer, when the casual workplace really earned its keep, he was never out of uniform. Tom felt Patton did this to remind everyone his job was just a little more important than the rest of theirs, and also to show that he is making sacrifices for the massive CEO package he earns. Patton nodded as he entered, took a seat, and without preamble, said what he wanted to say.

"I have to tell you that last week was not a good week for me. Do you know what I hate more than almost anything in the world? Reporting poor results." Patton paused to slowly scan the collective faces in the room to make sure everyone's eyes were on him and they were receiving his message. "When I say 'almost' I mean the only thing that could make it worse is if I also have to reduce our outlook." Patton let that one hang out there for a beat as he again quickly scanned the eyes of the five people in the room. "Can you imagine what our big institutional investors' reaction was? I don't have to imagine it, because I spent the rest of the week taking their angry calls."

Tom knew that the company and its CEO had just committed the cardinal sin of Wall Street - missing on the down side without warning. He was not surprised Patton had decided to come in and eviscerate them personally over it.

They always say shit runs downhill, and the CEO was flushing his right on top of the people he considered most responsible for ruining his summer. Tom wasn't so sure he wouldn't do the same thing, if his people had told him one thing and then two months later delivered something totally different. That was the problem with CEO's, they were usually fucking right. And they were like ancient royalty as long as they served - free from owning the guilt as long as loyal subjects could be found to assign it to. Only the board could fire the CEO, and they weren't here every day to question his methods.

"I don't think the people in this building are feeling the same heat I am. I don't think there's enough recognition that if we don't get moving on transforming this company we could be bankrupt in five years. Maybe I'm old school, but I'm tired of seeing people walk into this building at 10:30 like their job is an entitlement. I know you're all smart people, and I think you're working on the right things – at least it all sounds good when you lay it out for me – but we've got to perform a lot better than we are, and we've got to deliver on what we say we will. Maybe you're working on too many things, maybe I just don't have the right people. I don't have all the answers, but I do know something's got to change around here."

Tom's boss did what a good boss does – he stood up for the team and took accountability for his business unit's results. He agreed with the CEO that they needed to be better at delivering what they'd forecasted, and committed that they would do just that, moving forward. Tom was burning inside at the 10:30 comment while Bailey was talking. Just a week ago, that was about what time he came in because he had a dentist's appointment at nine. Tom and most of his peers in senior leadership routinely put in 60 hour weeks and took work home with them on top of that. They had to fit the rest of their lives around this massive commitment to their company and their careers. Of course Patton knows that, he gets his fucking teeth cleaned too, doesn't he? Did he really have to be an asshole all the time?

This was the typical argument that raged in Tom's head whenever he was in the presence of the CEO. The CEO was necessary in this world - someone had to have ultimate responsibility for the collective work of the enterprise. One hand to shake on big deals, one throat to choke when things are going shitty. Someone had to lead them, set the vision, approve the strategies. No. The CEO was only another role player. No enterprise of scale, with thousands of workers, could be run by one person successfully. The CEO should organize, encourage collaboration, coach the team, bring good ideas up from the people doing the work and use them to make the whole thing better. In the argument, Tom allowed the all-powerful CEO to call it like it is and deliver beatings like the one Patton was giving them today, because he was right, and therefore the beating was richly deserved. And on the other side of the debate, in this circumstance, the CEO was just another fallible human being like the rest of them, and he had no fucking right to come in here and berate them for results he is equally responsible for.

Patton next asked what help the team needed from him – what obstacles could he clear? What was getting in the way? Tom recognized the question as one he'd heard from other CEOs over the years. It was probably on page one of the CEO handbook. He was casting for blame, and like a patient fly fisherman, he kept putting that bait out there until Bailey finally took it and threw the Chief Information Officer under the bus – needed IT projects were constantly late, cost too much, and invariably fell short of supporting the business. That seemed to satisfy Patton – Tom could almost see him opening a mental to-do list and adding 'kick the CIO's ass' to it. He moved on to the next message he wanted to deliver.

"Next week we're going to have a headcount reduction in this building. A lot of people who have been with us for a long time are going to lose their jobs. You're all terrific people, but there are just too many of you. Maybe when it's done we'll get to decisions faster and maybe be a little less bureaucratic and act with a little more urgency. Our business is on a burning platform and maybe when we're done with this people will realize that a little better than they do today." He coolly looked each person around the table in the eyes as he delivered this news, which he knew wasn't entirely a surprise to any of them, to varying degrees. Then he got up from the table.

"Well, I don't want to take up any more of your time than I have to, so unless there's something else, I'll let you get back to your meeting." There was nothing else. The CEO left the room.

September 9, 2015

On cut down day, Tom conducted his one difficult exit discussion at nine. It was with The Last Man Out. The level 12 that he coughed up on the spot. It was time to clean up that mess. There was nothing to say beyond what every jilted lover has heard – it's not you, it's us. You've performed well, and contributed much, for a long time, but the company is in a difficult transition and needs to cut costs to fund investment in the turnaround plan. This is your notification that your job has been eliminated. Very simple, unemotional, final. Tom had come to believe his role in senior management was a succession of characters in a play – he could easily lose himself in a role like a trained method actor, and deliver lines with the gravity and integrity the author intended, whether or not the actual words had any meaning for him. And Tom knew ultimately, deeply, who the author was, even if he didn't write the words himself. It was the CEO. It was Patton. This was his cut down. No one put a gun to his head. Not the board, not the big institutional shareholders. He raised his hand and said he could cut costs faster than sales were shrinking. He could address the imbalance, see-saw it the other way, to even more profit. Over-correct, over-cut, over-deliver. Sometimes when you're chasing it the other way too long…not cutting fast enough as sales come out…you over-lurch in the other direction. You jump out in front of it. This was Patton's way.

Throughout the building, the little assassinations took place, all perfectly scripted. 15 vice-presidents and above, 48 directors, and some untold number of those pesky job grade 12's. People flying high in their careers, picked out of flight by hunters that could not miss. Hunters who had done the evaluations and identified the targets. Hunters who knew right where to catch them flapping by. HR was on the ground, a Labrador ready to pick the bird up gently in its mouth. Take it back and lay it at the feet of the hunter. Give it the papers that explained what happened next. Now that you've been shot out of the sky, here's what we're going to do for you. And the severance would be explained, the benefits, the timeline. The process was effective in its commitment to secrecy, because little shockwaves of surprise rippled along phone lines spreading the word of who had been let go. Surprises abounded – people others would perceive as top talent, including many with long tenures with the company, were on the list.

John Larsson showed up in Tom's doorway around 11. He was the guy Tom asked about when he thought he had an empty box to fill. He was one of Tom's direct reports when he first came to the company eight years ago and even then, the word was out that John was possibly a blocker. A blocker was an executive who was generally competent in their role, but maxed out. Not capable of further advancement. Would fail at the next level. And yet they're sitting in a great chair. They're squatting in a job that could be a development opportunity for younger talent. Doing the job, but doing a job someone better should be doing. Not because they would do the job better. But because they had more headroom, more runway, more steps to take, bigger shoes to wear. If one of those types was in the job, the company would still get the job done, but it would also get an executive ready for bigger and better things. Which means they're always on the lookout for potential blockers. You can't allow your talent to be blocked, so when you know where the talent is, the next step is to put it where the blockers are. Those blockers need to be moved over or moved out if they can't be moved up. Tom always feared one day becoming a blocker, had heard the word in one of the first talent management meetings he ever attended. Knew instantly what it was, and why top management kept an eye out for it. There was nothing good about it. Even on a football field the blocker is an anonymous contributor, a big fat guy with a number in the 70's on his back, plowing into other fat guys, down after down, trying to free one of the skill players for a big play. Same thing in business – the blocker needs to free up space for the faster talent. Only thing is, he often has to be sacrificed to do it. Shot.

Tom understood, and he knew that there were such things as blockers, but he also felt that many people who delivered consistently better results the longer they stayed in a role should not be considered blockers, but rather, strong contributors. Trusted professionals. Steady Eddies if this was still his mother's generation. Tom was able to successfully advocate for John Larsson on those terms, for several years, until an earlier, more minor shake up, when they were separated. He was sure nothing had changed in John's performance in those ensuing years. That's the best part about trusted contributors, professionals. They're consistent. Just not consistently valued. And so here he was, standing in Tom's doorway, looking like a man who'd just witnessed his dog get hit by a truck. His dismissal had come as a total shock. He didn't have to say a word. Tom knew what had happened.

What do you say to someone you care about, someone who worked hard for you, someone who delivered for you, when they're standing in front of you a step removed from blunt force trauma and on their way to the grief of loss? Someone who's only begun to process what has just happened to their self-esteem, what they're going to say to their spouse, to their parents, to their friends? Someone who's losing a great paying job just as his oldest is starting college, with two more still behind? Someone who's over 50 who will have to go on job interviews and explain why his former company decided 80% of its leadership team was more talented than him?

Tom tried to look shocked, but he probably managed surprised and sad at best. He stood up awkwardly from behind his desk.

"Oh shit, they didn't....John, please, come on in, sit down." They moved to the chairs around Tom's conference table and John sat heavily, his eyes searching Tom's for more help with the "why" behind what had just happened. Tom signalled more empathy with the most versatile word he knew, but one which he rarely spoke in the workplace. "Fuck."

"So, I take it you're all right?" John asked.

Tom hadn't considered that some may be surprised he was still here, though this wasn't really why John was asking. If he was shocked at his own dismissal, then certainly he could be shocked again.

"Yeah, yeah, I'm still here. I can't believe they're letting you go John, but I'll admit I was worried. I'd asked for you in my organization going forward and was told I couldn't have you. But I really didn't know what that meant for you. I was working on things in a vacuum. I'm really sorry. It's a bad decision for the company. A bad day for the company." Tom was showing real empathy now. That was the first rule he broke. HR's rule. The CEO's rule. The lawyer's rule. But Tom had not directly had to let John go, so fuck that rule.

"Yeah, I'm shocked. And I'm sure you heard about Leon." Leon was John's boss the last couple years. He was one of the shocker names earlier in the day, but not so much for Tom, as his first thing in the morning meeting was with HIS new boss, Mark Stover, and there he found that he was picking up several of the responsibilities of one Leon Panera, a peer who had been with the company for 24 years. The picture had become clear then, and when a call came with a whispered voice asking if he'd heard Leon had been let go, Tom had already envisioned the conversation he was having right now.

"Yeah, I know."

"What are they thinking Tom? What's Patton doing?"

"The fucker is slicing heads at the top very deliberately. It's your misfortune to have a vice-president title, because there were definitely targets by job grade. That's really clear to me now." Truthful, but another rule broken. Was Tom trying to open up a lawsuit hole big enough for a truckful of lawyers?

"But I don't get why, Tom. We're not doing that bad. I mean I know Q2 kinda sucked, but for the year, in our forecast at least, we're okay. And this seems just so random".

"This was Patton throwing a fucking hissy fit over second quarter earnings and this is his way of sending the organization a message – no one's safe. It was a highly imperfect process, obviously." Tom looked sympathetically at John as he waved his hand in his direction, palm upturned, offering John up as an example of yet another senseless reduction in force.

"The timing is shitty too. It's September already. People stay in place this time of year. All the movement doesn't usually start until January." John was already thinking ahead to the job search. That was good.

"John, listen, if there's anything I can do for you, references, conversations, emails, whatever you need. Feel free to list me as a reference with anyone, and I'll speak to anyone who wants to ask about you." Yet another taboo abused. The company preferred to simply verify employment, and stay silent on why an associate left, or how they performed when they were here. Fuck them on that too.

"I appreciate that. I'm sure I'll be taking you up on that."

Tom glanced up at the clock on his wall. It was an impulse born of awkward pauses in awkward conversations. But it was also that Tom knew in the back of his mind that there were indeed, several more conversations he needed to conduct, with the survivors on his team, some of whom were moving out of his organization to other jobs, and some taking on new roles on Tom's new team.

"So I take it at your level, this is your last day? Did they tell you they were going to walk you out?" Often in these stealth attack reductions, senior people are caught unprepared and haven't thought about the confidential company data they might like to squirrel out the door with them. By design of course. And if the company was particularly paranoid, security personnel would accompany fired executives to their offices to make sure they didn't access files and send them to their home emails, or grab mountains of paper out of drawers and stuff them in their executive backpacks. In most cases, in Tom's long experience, any vp and above fired would be expected to leave the building that day. Two week notices were for voluntary resignations only.

"They said I could take my time, but yes, today is my last official day. I might just go home now, or go for a drive and deal with my office tomorrow. They said I could do that." John had seen Tom's glance at the clock, recognized it well from their time together. He stood up. And then Tom stood up and shook hands with a man who would slowly become just a fond memory of a part of his life that had passed and would never be recaptured. The next phase of Tom's career and life would begin the next day, in another new role in a changed and chastened company, and all energies would be needed to pick up the pieces and move forward.

September 30, 2015

When a CEO does what Tom's just did - take a hard whack at leadership ranks - the aftershocks take a little while to settle in. Tom had been a party to this restructuring, but as a subcontractor, working his own little piece but not quite certain what the plan for the building looked like. As he put exceptional care into his contribution, ensuring critical work, and workers, would be protected, he expected the same of his new boss, the somewhat inscrutable Mark Stover, and everyone else in the C-suite. And while there is no such thing as a perfect organizational structure, Tom had come to set high standards for the thin layer of management between him and the CEO. If he was capable of getting as far as here, and there were only a dozen or so people with bigger titles in the company, then he was qualified to judge their performance and expect competence and inspiration in equal doses. He expected them to have spent as much time designing the new structure as they did on deciding who would go and who would stay, although he should have known better, given how quickly things were changing at the end. He expected, perhaps too altruistically, that the stated purposes of the downsizing – enabling faster decision making through less bureaucracy and pushing accountability down in the organization, empowering lower levels to make decisions – would be honored in the new organizational design and in revised processes and behaviors.

Christ, his own brain was feeding him thoughts in Powerpoint bullets. No, all of that fancy-named shit wasn't actually going to occur. Within days of the cut-down, it was clear that those expectations would be shattered. The new structure was still highly matrixed, with shared accountabilities and blurred lines of responsibility. Meeting cadences did not change. The cultural need to push all decisions as high as possible to eliminate the risk of being second-guessed persisted. In short, people were acting like nothing happened.

Part of what Tom was feeling was his own fault. If a bunch of leaders were going to be sent home, someone had to take on extra work. Since he was an insider and part of the process, Tom had manipulated it to the best of his ability to architect his own role to be that guy. It was a bit of a power play. Keep the big shit he did on his plate, the shit that was why they were keeping him, and take on some extra shit, just to keep the good shit. When it was done, and Tom folded into Stover's organization, he had two peers in the new structure who each had smaller portfolios of responsibility than Tom. Tom liked it that way. They were hotshots. 10 years younger than him. Consulting backgrounds. Blue-chip MBA's. Ivy League undergrad chops. Strong functional resumes (albeit, with very short stints in lots of different chairs). All the CEO markers. They would be the guys that Tom could be construed one day to be blocking, but for now, there were three seats, enough for everyone. And they were perfectly fine co-workers. Tom liked working with smart younger people. It kept him alert. Reminded him of what he once was, and how he once hoped. And then came more aftershocks.

Within a week of the announced new structure, with dust still flying, one of the hotshots bailed. He'd been working on an exit all along, and just coincidentally, got a chance to hold two futures in his hand at the same time and pick one. And incredibly, the other went a week after that, for a C-suite job in a well-funded startup. This is what happens to companies. When they're successful, they attract talent like Pooh to a honey pot. Struggle, and they bleed that same best talent out. Hit the team with a downsizing and the future darkens. When talented people start to flee an organization, the impact rolls to every level. Survivors question what the smart folks saw that made them leave these great high-paying jobs. People like Tom, suddenly sitting next to two empty boxes on an org chart, begin to ask themselves whether being the one still here is a sign of commitment or stupidity. And since stupidity would have got him fired, where's the appreciation for the commitment?

The pressure in the building, in Tom's ears, in his brain, in his lungs, in the back of his throat, in the hollows behind his eyes, was a constant thrum. Everything had changed, and yet nothing had changed. The calendar flipped over, the work day started with almost 100 leaders gone, results continued to suck. Of course, that was the one certainty – that results would continue to suck in the near term. Suck in a relative way of course. John Larsson was right, internal forecasts to budgets suggested things weren't so bad. But compared to the expectations in the C-suite they sucked. And those forecasts? Spit-shined by Dutch Bagley himself, to reflect a future brighter than the team really believed. So the same pressure as before, with far fewer vessels to pour it into. Each vessel accepting what it always had, a river up to the top of its banks, and then the world keeps pouring. The worst of it, the source of Tom's searing anger in those first couple weeks, through the aftershocks, was the C-suite. His own boss was part of it, and while he seemed to get it, he had no power alone to change the pounding pace of meetings, driven by the insane need of the most senior people in the company to dig up the fucking tulip bulbs every other day to see if they're sprouting yet. Ten fucking minutes after uttering the words, 'After the re-org we're going to have to do things differently around here,' they just got right back to business as usual, which included unending opportunities to inflict pain on others in one meeting setting after another, weekly, monthly, quarterly, rinse, wash, repeat.

Tom recognized that this was a time for him to show leadership. Intellectually, he knew what that meant to his boss. Stay strong for people. Be calm. Try to remove obstacles. Help people get past their anger and anxiety and get back to work moving the company forward. But Tom had more protective ideas about what his leadership needed to be. His people needed to be freed up from bullshit and some of it, only Tom could remove for them. He felt for the orphans — the people who'd worked for his dearly departed peers. While the company began a search for replacements and interim arrangements were made, Tom felt it was up to him, as Stover's top lieutenant, as the most experienced, shit, just say it, as the oldest, to be willing to call bullshit whenever and wherever and from whomever it appeared. Take the bullets that might come, but stand up for the people. Tom was a survivor for the umpteenth time and he needed to lead the survivors of the second swing of the axe and new org structure in less than two years.

They deserved a champion. Didn't he fit the bill? Tom had always been the picture of calm, the level head, the true professional. He could pull off manufactured anger, but his demeanor on the whole had always been a quiet pond in the woods. It was a big part of his package, his carefully constructed suit that had stayed his skin for 31 years. The demeanor set the tone for the interpersonal relationships Tom developed, always respectful if a little reserved and antiseptic. And they set the tone for his leadership style. He gave his people space. Let them speak at meetings without filters. He gave them professional respect and the benefit of the doubt, without being afraid to challenge them to do better. He asked them to have a purpose that was based on facts and evidence over emotion. It was easier to stay calm when focused on facts. The demeanor became so much a part of Tom at work that no one expected to see him frustrated, upset, enraged. Like his hot emotions were permanently controlled by an internal air conditioning unit. Of course this was the man who could be, should be, the people's champion. He just had to continue to control the boiling frustration, the furnace, a coal-burning furnace, black heat. He had to use his best acting skills. He had to use the cool-skin. Balance out the inferno.

At the birth of his career, the first day, sitting in a big conference room with 70 other executive trainees, Tom began this construct of creating a persona for himself. It was as if he knew right away he couldn't just be Tom Cooper, because the truth was that he didn't belong there. To meet the expectations of others, to rise to the CEO's chair, Tom would have to craft a vision of the person he was expected to be, and then fulfill the requirements of the role. Tom had loved acting as a child. He was in school plays every year until the 8th grade, after they'd moved to the new town and things went sideways. He'd picked it up again in college. He could lose himself in a role, get away from the constant pressure of being himself and just play a part. In some ways, it was easier on the soul that way.

Tom quickly realized that other functions in the company did not understand how much more difficult the new structure was for the team, for his team and the orphans too, and how they had to adjust some of their processes and expectations to a new reality. He would instruct those other functions. He would correct them. He would get on his stump and make the hard speeches. He would explain what had changed, and what it meant. He even gave it a name. The Stamp Out Stupidity Campaign. He loved the phrase so much he actually spoke it out loud to people, missing the unintentional irony of that completely. In any meeting, any venue, any hallway conversation, any face to face casual encounter just three steps back from the mens' room sink, any chance meeting in the salad bar line in the café, he took it upon himself to educate others, to adjust their behavior to match the new reality. But the campaign was failing miserably. The matrixed corporate structure was so disturbingly dysfunctional that the mission continually ran into walls.

And then Stover sat him down two weeks into the campaign. In truth, it was a regularly scheduled touch-base, but Tom's mind always looked for the truth one layer lower, and as soon as Stover began to speak, he converted the meaning of their meeting to a 'sitting down and talking to'.

"Tom." Whenever someone walked into his office, Stover did the same thing, looked right at them, and said their name, like he was exhaling a cigarette, little smoke rings with names.

"Mark." Tom knew how to join a club.

"Come in, sit down." Tom was on his way to a chair at the conference table anyway.

"So. How's it going?" Stover smiled and pushed back in his chair a bit, getting comfortable. Tom considered a multitude of possible responses, all various shades of the truth, depending on how he wanted to interpret the question.

"Shitty as expected, I guess."

"Yeah, it's a little crazy around here."

"You think?" Tom smiled, to let Stover know he was okay, capable of dealing with shit, and crazy, in heaps as high as anyone wanted to dump them.

"I know it's rough right now. But I'm hearing from people that you're just killing them."

"How do you mean?" Tom's protective armor and cool suit both activated. His brain kicked up a notch in processing speed.

"It's one thing to rightly point out what we need to do better, and another to just complain. Or be argumentative. I've heard the word 'disrespectful' used more than once."

Tom stared at Stover as he spoke. He had been presented with negative feedback from time to time in his career. He had a process to accept it. The words came in and he tried them on, looked at himself in the mirror of his mind, got outside himself and imagined others looking in. Had his behavior created the image he wanted others to see? Sure. He was angry. A lot of the time. The place was fucked up beyond repair right now and he couldn't be the only one who saw that. But he also couldn't lead his team if he was the only boss making a ruckus. He guessed he was acting like an ass a lot lately. But didn't somebody need to? Fucking people in other parts of the organization were clueless. He had to wake them the fuck up. In his mind he felt that needed to be the way to get through to people – to shock them into understanding everything was now different. Obviously it wasn't working.

"I guess I can see how some people could see me that way. I'm frustrated, Mark. Our organization is in a completely new world, and it seems like other parts of the corporation don't care, don't want to hear it, don't want to adjust. As a company, we just don't know how to stop getting in each other's way."

"Oh, I get it. Trust me, I get it very well." Stover stopped. He was slowly nodding, slowly pushing himself back into his chair, and then forward again, like an old man in a rocker on a porch. One of his inscrutable silences. Tom was good at silence too. He waited. "I have a tremendous amount of respect for what you're doing for the company Tom. I really do. You took on more than anyone, and with Dowd and Sanders gone, until I replace them, I can't tell you how much I need you to keep doing it. You just have to lighten up on people we have to work with. Every org went through some reduction. Did we get whacked hardest? You bet. This was a two-year target, and I wanted to just rip the band-aid off now and get most of it done. I didn't want to have to come back next year and take another 10% out. Is the total organization perfect? No, it's not. So we have to deal with those things. I know you can do this."

Of course Tom knew he could do it. He could take his professional senior leader character and plug him into this situation and he'd handle it beautifully. He'd stand figuratively tall and be a role model of cooperation, a voice of reason, a team player. But if he did, wouldn't most of his direct reports know he was lying through his clenched teeth? They were smart, too, aggravated themselves by how things were unfolding, afraid for the future, with the company still listing in rough seas. Rumors of mergers and buyouts and going private swirling. And for many of them, a belief that the re\org just five weeks old now had set the place back, not put it on a path forward. Tom knew what Stover was looking for in a response, so he gave it.

"Of course I can do it Mark. And I will. And I'm glad you understand how fucked up things are. I just hope we can find a way to do things better than we're doing them right now, or people are going to keep walking." Tom had that going for him. They really needed him now that the hotshots had bailed. Sanders and Dowd. Where were the future stars now that the sky was dark? Somewhere else. Stover really needed Tom. It gave him more leeway to be brutally honest, as long as he still came across as loyal and wanting to be part of the solution. That was a good place to be, power-wise. Hard to think about firing the pack mule who trudges along with the heavy load, even if he occasionally brays out a complaint. And Stover was being reasonable. He didn't act the high school principal, explaining to Tom all the ways his recent petulant behavior was hurting the team's performance. He just shared what he'd heard and asked him to pull back a little. They seemed to understand each other pretty well, even if Tom strongly smelled the CEO-jones all over his new boss. Maybe he'd be a different sort if he got all the way there. Maybe he'd never get there. Tom wasn't sure whether to root for him or not.

"Alright." Stover put two fingers up to his eyes, and then pointed them both at Tom's eyes and waggled them. "We're getting each other here."

Tom left the meeting a half hour later, after they turned the time back into a touch-base with a rapid fire back and forth on a wide range of business issues. The real substance of the meeting had come before that, and Tom went back there in his mind. He knew what he told Stover, but he seriously wondered if he could pull it off. Doubt in his abilities had never been much of an issue for Tom, even as doubt in his meaning and mission in life had run rampant. One of those abilities had always been to control himself, to control the narrative about himself, to quickly react to feedback about what was expected of him and adopt the new persona so quickly that as few people as possible saw the Tom that wasn't welcome. But even though he promised to do just that, he wasn't so sure he could do it this time. He had begun to lose confidence in that particular talent. For the first time in a long time, he was stumped. He felt un-tethered. All those years walking in space but always with a ground wire, a touchstone, a path back to the capsule. Over and over, telling himself all that mattered was his health, his family, his friends. Any mountain of bullshit could be scaled. Any heaping of abuse could be absorbed. Any internal heat could be extinguished. He always knew what he had to do, knew it really deep down in his bones and right on the surface where logic sits. But now he was cartwheeling slowly through space. He felt like anything could happen and he'd just go with it.

They could fire him tomorrow; not likely given the circumstances, but he wouldn't give a shit if they did. Stover and Dutch Bagley could both get fired, one of the other C-suite execs who thought more highly of Tom could end up in charge, and Tom could get promoted to Stover's job. Also not likely, and Tom really didn't want to get promoted. Not at this company. No way. Too big a mess. But his people were great. Weren't they? They deserved his best. Not just his protection and advocacy, but his attention to them, and the things they needed to be challenged to do better, to achieve what they wanted to achieve. Did he still have it in him to do that? And for some of them, even that gallant effort might be seen as a man just kidding himself, and not willing to admit to them that they were all fucked. For a solid day after the feedback session with Stover, Tom just drifted. And then he made a decision. He bucked up. There was a role that needed to be played here, and Tom knew he could play it. He would just suck it up one more time and go for it.

He would be the leader as wise patriarch, calmly dispensing a story supported by positive facts that painted a picture both inspirational and believable. In tough times people always look for leadership and one of the hallmarks of Tom's career progression had been this ability and willingness to step up and be positive, to embrace change, to keep his people well-informed and constantly exposed to the more uplifting aspects of the company's performance and outlook. In some ways, this was Tom emulating what he wanted from his CEOs over the years and did not generally get. It was like a quaintly old-fashioned wish for what CEOs should be; kind, professorial, wise; as opposed to biting, pragmatic, relentless. Given his own weariness and waning belief in the mission and meaning of corporate life in general, if he successfully pulled it off, he should be nominated for an Academy Award.

From Tom Cooper's private journal. April 1995. Age 34.
Employer 3.

I used to think I understood capitalism, but if this is it, what I'm experiencing now, I'm starting to have my doubts. I watch the stock market and I'm seeing companies announcing massive layoffs in the name of restructuring, and instead of their stock prices getting hammered, they're going UP on the news. You'd think a company doing shitty enough to have to lay off thousands of employees would see its stock price go down. Nope. It's technology replacing jobs in many cases, and good paying jobs at that. The stock market likes that. The top end of the pyramid is doing great. CEOs and top management are getting outsized bonuses tied to those stock prices going up. They're outsourcing stuff overseas, like call centers, taking away full time jobs with benefits from people here. Real wages for the middle class and working class have stagnated, while the rich keep getting richer. And even though things are going great for them, the rich want even lower taxes, less regulation, smaller government, and have a disdain for social welfare, much of which we have because of how bad it got the last time Capitalism went off the rails.

I should be happy, right? I'm on my way to being one of the privileged. I'm perfectly constructed to benefit – white, educated, competitive. Shit, I've got the job I do now because the company offered early retirement to a whole generation of overpaid, underperforming managers, in order to hire newer, younger, less expensive talent like me. But if I submit to the system, don't I risk one day becoming that overpaid talent? Indeed. I should have known better than to come to a company that just had to push a bunch of long-serving people out, and sure enough, now just under two years in, they're reorganizing again. The messaging and the benefits have changed a lot in those two years. The one that eased my entry in was generous in part to 'acknowledge the tremendous accomplishments and efforts' of those being sent into early retirement, and to send a message to the entire corporation that though it was a necessary business decision, it could be done with compassion and a recognition of the human toll it was taking. This time the messaging is a desire to 'weed out those managers who are unwilling to transform themselves to the new model of performance leadership that this company needs to move forward'. And what does that new model of performance leadership look like? The CEO was quoted in the Wall Street Journal thusly:

"A compelling place to work does not mean a nice place to work. We expect our people to feel a degree of stress and anxiety."

So the rules of engagement for me have been set. I cannot be comfortable in the American Capitalist system of 1995. I must feel a degree of stress and anxiety every day in order to compete, to provide for my family, to survive. And in doing so, I seem destined to lose a little of my humanity, a little of my compassion, a little of my tolerance for those less skilled, or less advantaged. And if I feel that, and others feel it, and we all act on it, where does that lead us, or leave us? Can we keep the fabric of society from fraying at the edges if at the center we are getting colder and tougher? Facing job insecurity every day, will we bring ever-increasing waves of negative energy to our interactions with others? If we do, are we contributing to a meaner, less accepting society? And won't that invite backlash from those who suffer in this environment? And dare I go so far to ask, are we at risk of driving class divisions along economic and educational fault lines that could really imperil the future of Capitalism yet again?

I don't hate Capitalism. It comes with freedom. It seems inherent in us. But it doesn't have to be this unbalanced and out of whack. It doesn't have to be mean. And when we've let it get that way, we've snapped back. We got labor laws, a work week with two days off, unemployment insurance and social security, all because the system wasn't working for enough people. Hopefully, if it gets any crazier than it already seems, we'll snap-back again.

October 8, 2015

Tom's commitment to the role of strong-but-cuddly wisdom-dispenser lasted about a week. Really, all it took was one of Dutch Bagley's quarterly all-day team meetings to blow it to bits. At the core of the hatred burning a hole in his chest was this meeting itself, which Tom considered to be the Mona Lisa of corporate life, capturing the absurdity so perfectly all other portraits paled in comparison. After the reorg, Dutch Bagley was now responsible for everything that happened in North America. He was at least the 4th most powerful person in the company, and by some inexplicable warp in the universe, he was still considered by some to be in a 3-person scrum to be the next CEO, whenever Patton released his death grip on the role. To Tom, who had worked for Dutch somewhere in his empire for all but 18 months of the last 8 years, he was a unicorn. He was the rare leader, the only one, in Tom's 30+ years of corporate life, to have broken through the Peter Principle barrier and then risen to another level beyond it, with the recent increase in his responsibilities. The Peter Principle was coined in 1968 by a 27-year old academic who theorized that "In a hierarchy every employee tends to rise to his level of incompetence ... in time every post tends to be occupied by an employee who is incompetent to carry out its duties ... Work is accomplished by those employees who have not yet reached their level of incompetence." In today's world, most people think the Peter Principle is in play when a person is in one job bigger than they probably should ever have been given.

And then there was Dutch Bagley. In Tom's mind, the last job Dutch held was already a full level beyond what he should ever have been able to achieve. And now he was another step over that line. And some still said he could replace Patton and run the whole thing in the not too distant future. Tom didn't understand it. Dutch had seemingly had it in for him from the start. Someone had sold him on the idea that Tom was in the 'brilliant as shit' talent bucket before he started, but when Tom had turned out to be more of a 'gets shit done' executive it seemed to sour Dutch on every idea Tom had ever put forth. For Tom, to have his hard work rejected when you consider the source to be a gets-nothing-done imbecile had been hard to take and hard to manage through. And since the CEO and the board seemed to be missing what Tom could see, he'd kept his incredulity about Dutch mostly to himself. And now, after 18 crazy but tolerable months away, Tom was back in Dutch's organization, because after all, he now ran everything in North America. And therefore, he was back at the quarterly circus known as "Dutch's All-day".

Dutch Bagley had 11 direct reports after the restructuring, including a couple who sat on the executive committee of the corporation with him, including Mark Stover. Those 11 executives had 29 senior vice-presidents and vice-presidents and directors reporting to them. These 40 people, plus Dutch and his caddie, squeezed themselves into the company board room that was designed to hold 32. Dutch's caddie was a woman named Connie who was not his admin (Dutch had one of those as well), but more of a chief of staff. Connie went everywhere Dutch went. She pulled the reports he liked, and carried them for him when they traveled. She wrote all his speeches, and she kept religious notes of everything Dutch said, to whom he said it, and what follow-up Dutch expected from the verbal exchange. She literally took those notes and put them in a giant excel spreadsheet and followed up on hundreds of comments with a tracking system and weekly emails to the 40 people who were in Dutch's sphere of control. It was beyond painful.

And then there was the surrealistic experience of a Dutch All-day itself. Each meeting's agenda was structured exactly the same. At 9:00 am, Dutch welcomed his knights to the round table, which in actuality was a giant egg with its narrow end flat-topped. Dutch and Connie occupied the two seats at the narrow end, though Dutch, with his ample girth, took up ⅔ of the actual space. Connie sat in his shadow, looking like a court stenographer.

For the first 45 minutes of the agenda, Dutch would hold forth on whatever topics or themes he cared to hear himself talk about. When he was done, which was never shorter than the allotted time and often over, he handed off to his finance chief, who ran through numbers for half an hour. Dutch assumed the role of color-man during this otherwise depressing and dire reading of the declining sales figures, deleveraging profit, and other woes besetting the organization. The rest of the day was blocked out into topics and presenters chosen by Dutch. His stated goal was to make sure his team was one team, that they all understood every aspect of the company's business. Each topic would last 30 minutes. The presenter would have the first 15, then time for Q&A. Most of the Q's came from Dutch, and sometimes, oftentimes, they weren't really questions at all, just more pontificating and lots of judging. And then, mercifully, the day would run out of half hour blocks, and Dutch would have his wrap-up time, because he never tired of the sound of his own voice.

The shape of the table in the board room seemed to be designed to make sure no one could hide in plain sight, and yet it had now become common to bring laptops to the meeting, under the guise of becoming digital. Years ago, Dutch tried to set ground rules prohibiting phone usage, wanting to command everyone's full attention. People surreptitiously viewed messages and emails on their Blackberries in their lap under the level of the table. Now, after several new executives had come to the company from faster-paced, more digital environments, it would be seen as archaic to disallow full electronic device access 24/7, even in the emperor's chambers, and Gasp! During the emperor's own speeches! So now it was possible to hide while sitting at the table, as long as you were pretending to take notes of what was being said, rather than catching up on the endless polluted stream of email or booking a trip to Cancun.

In the animal kingdom, when the lion catches an antelope and begins the process of devouring it, the rest of the antelopes don't stop to gather around and watch. But at a Dutch All-day, the rest of the herd has nowhere to run. So while each half hour topic inevitably turned into an evisceration of one kind or another for the presenter, 39 people had no option but to listen, watch, and await their turn, on that day's agenda or another. And of course, one person, Connie, would be furiously typing, capturing every Dutch insult that could be rephrased into a question that required follow-up. It was worse than absurdity. It was criminal, tiresome, and infuriating, and now here Tom was, back in a place he'd thought he'd escaped forever, 37 days after the downsizing.

As a bonus prize for his first meeting 'back in the fold', Tom was on the agenda after lunch to talk about one of his businesses. He grabbed a spot at the bottom of the egg, to the side, as far from Dutch as he could get. As the rest of the room settled in, Dutch arrived and began shuffling his papers and whispering to Connie while surveilling the room. Tom watched Dutch watching them. He was looking for the tell-tale signs of what the opening Dutch sequence might bring, like a baseball coach trying to read a pitcher's body language to see if he's tipping off his pitches. There were two Dutches - Tom called them Good Dutch and Bad Dutch for simplicity's sake. Bad Dutch glowers without knowing it, simply by not smiling. When Bad Dutch scans the room, his eyes look dark and lidden, a hawk scanning the ground for the slow rodent that will become his next meal. Good Dutch can be a magnetic, slap you on the back kind of guy, and if he were there, he'd be working the room and rubbing people on the shoulder. Tom could tell in seconds who'd shown up, and no surprise given the company's continued challenges, it was Bad Dutch.

The opening was an all-time classic.

"First of all, never, ever, in the history of this company, have I seen a performance like we delivered in the second quarter. Missing by as much as we missed was inexcusable in my mind. It was particularly frustrating to me that most of the miss came in the last three weeks of the quarter, like you were all lying to me for ten weeks, and then you fessed up and said it's going to be a disaster. Unacceptable. This income statement, look at the numbers! Pardon my French but they suck. I'm embarrassed to be responsible for them. I'm embarrassed for this team, for this room of people. You seem incapable of fixing our income statement. It's all there in black and white for you. Some of you control marketing, some of you have operations, some of you have revenue and margin. You have to work together, do you understand that? The income statement doesn't create itself, but if it did, it would look like this one. A good P and L is made by a good team, and this team is not doing it, man, it's just not doing it. I know, I know, you're all working incredibly hard. But it's not happening. It's just not. The guy down the hall, you saw his reaction, although to be fair the downsizing was in the works well before the quarter ended, but the timing was no accident, I'm sure you're all smart enough to know that. We have to get serious guys. We have absolutely no good new ideas. None. We're terrible at innovation. And let me say one more thing, if I may. Over the last few weeks I've heard some disturbing things from people in the organization, lower level people. They say things like, 'I didn't do this because I heard you don't like it'. You know what that's called? That's called blaming the boss. That's people, maybe people in this room, dropping my name as an excuse for not doing their jobs. And I don't like it, and I'm not going to stand for it."

There was a pregnant pause where you could feel the whole room lean in a little to see if maybe this was the end. It was not.

"Our business is a burning platform. I want to be very clear about that. We have core businesses that are under attack and we don't have enough new businesses that are performing. We can sit here and say 'woe is me, the CEO just cut my head count,' and bicker and spin our wheels and blame the boss all we want. And we'll be dead. Dead. We have a whole day to talk about initiatives to turn this thing around, but if you're going to just do what you're doing now, working in your silos, keeping your head down, or complaining in whispers in the hallways, none of it's going to matter my friends. None of it's going to matter. The competition will eat us alive. Because they're good. They're not messing around. We've got to bring our A game. I'm not seeing a lot of A games right now. Here's what good teams do, you see. They look at the toughest times as the times you get to show what you're really made of. They pull together. They work on problems together. You people complained we did this meeting too often so we went to quarterly, but that means you have to talk to each other in between! One hand has to know what the other one is doing. It drives me crazy when we get in this room, and you're looking at each other like you've never heard what the person is saying, like you never talk to each other outside this room." Another pause. Dutch scanned the room with his best brooding glare. He had to be done, right? Not right.

"Let me say one more thing about the downsizing. I know there were some very long-serving associates who were let go. Some of them your good friends maybe. There was no joy on this floor in doing that. No joy whatsoever. But that's an example of how we have to manage our business. For 7 years running now, we're not growing. But we never stopped adding people. That just doesn't work. That's how your P and L gets turned upside down. We had to do what we had to do, but there was no joy in it whatsoever. Some very good people had to go home. I hope I never have to be part of something like that again in my career, but it depends on the numbers. Let's not lose sight of that. There they are in black and white. We share them with you because you're professionals and you need to understand them. You ARE the numbers. As a team you own them, and I need you to work as a team because that's why you're still here. You're the best team we have right now, but you have to deliver. This year is quickly turning into a catastrophe. I will not tolerate missed forecasts from this point on. We've missed forecast month after month after month. It stops now. If you can't deliver the revenue and margin, I'll just slash the expense line to shreds. That's easy for me. Very easy. We're good at that. Not what I want to be known for, people. Not what I want to be good at, but I can do it with the best of them. All right?" He glanced up at the clock. He was still only half way through his 45 minute opening monologue. He continued.

"You know I spend a lot of my time out in the field and I see so many things we could be doing better, and I don't think enough of you in this room get out of this building and talk to real people, talk to some customers, talk to our people. I seem to be the only person who understands what's going on…."

Tom's phone lit up with a text from a friend across the room. "Did I die this morning? Because this is purgatory." Tom suppressed his urge to smile. Dutch liked to look around the room and stare people down while he spoke and to smile in the face of his diatribe would be highly inadvisable. Tom had stopped listening to whatever Dutch was rambling on about. He could already summarize the message in thirty seconds, even if it was going to take Dutch 45 minutes to deliver it.

Tom knew Dutch was right about the teamwork, but who the fuck's fault was that? If the ship is a drifting and rudderless mess, is it the crew's fault or the captain's? And when did beating a team with a stick ever inspire them to come together? Dutch was neither conniving enough nor stupid enough to believe that by setting himself up as a common enemy he could unite the team. He just sincerely felt they sucked and needed to hear it. He also had the illusion that in general, he was beloved, despite his occasional foul moods and rambling verbal explosions. Good Dutch was liked, and sure, some long time folks who'd come up the ranks with him were mostly spared the whippings and supported him wholeheartedly. But to think that he was immune to the impact of bringing Bad Dutch to the room so often was ridiculously narcissistic. Tom certainly had exhausted an arsenal of ways in which he imagined telling Dutch to fuck himself, that had all died before ever reaching a vocal chord. But that taste didn't go away so easily.

The meeting got more depressing after that fabulous start, with the numbers marched before their eyes on slide after slide looking like the weak German soldiers surrendering at Stalingrad in those History Channel documentaries Tom watched to fall asleep at night. The company had so many issues, like every company Tom ever worked for. Or at least it seemed that way to him. Did he just pick the wrong company four times in a row? Was he betrayed by the bad luck of incompetent CEO's in their seats at the wrong time in their company's history? Or was all work, everywhere, in every company that was public and trying to meet the expectations of shareholders, a continual grind? Was it truly a game of 'see how high the monkey can jump'? Keep holding the banana higher and higher in the air, just out of grasp, constantly challenging people to hit heights they don't know how to hit? Tom could see how at first it would seem to be a trick that inspired effort and even gradual improvement. But in the end, if you never can reach the banana, isn't it guaranteed to frustrate?

Dutch liked to manage by complaining. Tom had never heard a bold, original, exciting idea tumble from his lips, unless it was hair on fire unrealistic. That's what he was good at. That was his job. Real innovation that could work and turn the game around? That was the team's job. His job was to judge and criticize the team's ideas. And complain. And that's what the rest of the day's agenda looked like – each of the half hour presentations and discussions were around different ideas people were working on, giving them a chance to educate the entire team and Dutch an opportunity to share the stage with them, to share with the rest of the team what he thought of every one of those ideas or initiatives or business updates. But mostly, to complain. Ideas presented to Dutch generally fell into one of four categories, each with its own particular set of Dutch mannerisms in response. The most common complaint – "too small" – was accompanied by a crossing of his arms, a leaning back in his chair, and an air sniffing, chin up dismissiveness as he said the words. "Boring" kept the crossed arms, but there was no regal preening in his facial expression, just a dull, monotone utterance, with an exaggerated slow closing and opening of his eyes. "Dumb" came with a slight smile like he was the first one to get a weak joke, and the rest of the group still wasn't getting it, causing a slow shaking of the head, and quite often a "you just don't get it" follow up. "Unoriginal", was sponsored by a grimace and a quick head shake, followed by an extended palm and a "but if you want to do it, it's a perfectly fine idea, it's just been done before, that's all."

Tom awaited his turn. How would Dutch welcome him back to the fold? Go easy on him the first meeting back? Give him the benefit of the doubt? What good comes from being doubted? The hell with that, just give me the benefit of listening. Of believing. Of trusting. Much better than doubting. Some hard decisions have to be made. Tom didn't want to come back next year and lay more people off. He wanted to be part of the solution, the generator of new sales, new profit, new growth. But it required some pivoting, some belief in new ideas, and Tom wanted to show some urgency. 37 days, that's all it'd been. 37 days of craziness and bullshit and nobody changing and the failed Stamp Out Stupidity Campaign, and yet Tom still had managed to pull together a plan that took bold action, cut away some pieces in order for the whole to come back stronger. In order for the team and company to focus on the best opportunity. He was ready to move on it, had his team fired up. Stover had bought in. Tom had found out he's a risk-tolerant boss. Now he'd find out if he was a 'got your back' boss as well. Dutch had been prepped on the plan. He wasn't fully bought in. That's why Tom was on the agenda. So Dutch could air his disagreements and displeasures in front of forty other people. This is how Dutch would welcome him back, indeed.

When the time came, Tom jumped into a set-up of key facts about the business, and why he wanted to execute his plan. He barely got through half of those facts before Dutch jumped in.

"I completely disagree with your thesis. I've read the deck, and I don't like this at all. You're giving up on a business we should be able to dominate."

"No, that's not what I'm proposing or saying – but it's not a business we can dominate. We've shown that. It's just not."

"I think you have the wrong product. I'm so disappointed in how we've managed this business for probably 10 years now."

"Dutch, I can walk you through the numbers, even the best product, the best set of services, won't give us the return we need on the investment."

"It's giving up, plain and simple."

"No, it's a repositioning, with a plan to recapture dollars by placing bets in other areas and supporting them with resources."

"You can call it what you want, but I know what it is, and I don't know what you people don't understand about what's happening to this company, but you can't keep quitting on businesses because they get a little tough...." Dutch got going on a ramble that was not now only about Tom, but about Stover, and Tom's departed peers, excoriated in absentia, and eventually the entire team, which apparently had its collective head up one colossal ass. During the rant Tom's phone lit up with another message from his friend across the room. "You're doing great".

The only good thing about a Dutch rant was that it was quite literally like sitting on a chair between rounds of a heavyweight fight. While he bombastically plowed his way through a litany of common complaints about quitters, Tom had a chance to breathe, get a drink of water, and collect his thoughts. He also had a chance to stare at Dutch with eyes he hoped Dutch would notice were black with ill intention. He wanted Dutch to see that somebody hated him, that this was not the way to win friends and influence people, and certainly no way to run a company. He also wondered when Stover might step in and offer some backing. What signals about how tenuous Stover's footing was with Dutch could he glean from his silence so far? Always so much to process at once in an encounter with Dutch.

The "you're giving up" complaint had its own particular Dutch mannerism of course, in this case a move Tom called the "Mussolini" – chin thrust forward and tilted up, lips pursed, that chin moving toward the offending servant, invading their space, if not physically, then certainly mentally, with a certain amount of intended menace. Tom tried to puncture the face with more facts, and to try to garner some excitement for the part of his plan that involved growing the adjacent businesses….but of course each of those tactics came with the risk of being declared 'too small', 'boring', 'dumb', or 'unoriginal', and sure enough, given Dutch's position going in, there was more than enough of that to go around, until Tom's allotted time was declared over. He knew this because Connie had been holding up flash cards from the other end of the table with a countdown. "Ten minutes". "Five minutes." "Two minutes". As if Tom was the one on the clock, with some actual control of the pace and direction of the conversation. Stover did eventually jump in here and there with support, but this was a Bad Dutch All-day, and nothing was going to go well.

When it was over, Tom was seething. How could he keep doing this? He was a grown-ass fucking man and he was tired of revisiting high school, and wedgies in the boy's locker room. Dutch was a classic bully, and Tom had gotten rid of the last of those in his life nearly 40 years ago by kicking his ass.

But this wasn't the first time since then, that he was faced with someone who deserved that ass-kicking but good. Felony assault is the phrase for it if you're wearing a nice shirt and you're at work, so Tom had never acted on the impulse. Instead, he sat blankly staring, mustering up his best far-away look. He knew Dutch would swing his gaze to him soon, as part of his normal scanning of the room, and he wanted him to feel a little shiver of uncertainty, a what-the-fuck-is-that moment. He was sure Dutch would expect him to be banging out a resignation email to Stover, or whispering to the person next to him, and what he wanted him to see was a vacant building. A death stare. He wanted him to try to make eye contact and lock in on nothing but the eyes themselves, no flicker of light, no twitch of the brow, no subtle nod of the head. He'd have to quickly move on with some sudden butterfly of uneasiness he wouldn't quite be able to put his finger on. Tom knew it would only be fleeting, this little victory of non-violent protest, this little ripple he anticipated causing in Dutch's psyche, before his mind just said, 'fuck him', and moved on to other victims. Tom's churning mind was a good thing right now, part of the weaponry, part of what made the death stare so real.

At the end of the day, when Tom was back behind his desk, trying to blast through a couple dozen waiting emails and delete a hundred more, Stover poked his head into his office, leaning against the doorway as if waiting for an invitation to enter.

"So. How would you describe today's Dutch All-day?"

"Let's see. As a team, we suck. When it comes to forecasting, we can't find our ass with our hands. We've nearly destroyed the P and L, and the fact that we don't have a plan to fix it is completely irresponsible. We have no imagination and no good ideas. Does that about sum it up?"

"That about does it, yeah." Stover laughed. It was all they could do.

"But wait, there's more! If only we had good ideas, all our problems would be solved, because Dutch has unlimited funds to support good ideas, but as long as he says we don't have those ideas, he's just going to cut marketing and cut people and say no to virtually everything anybody says they need." They both laughed.

"Par for the course, right? Can I come in?" Stover assumed the yes and closed the door behind him. He sat down at Tom's conference table, and Tom came over to sit across from him.

Stover continued, "So? Where's your head right now?"

"Other than on my neck, what are you really asking?"

"How do you feel about the company, about the reorg, working for me, working for Dutch again?"

Tom didn't waste time thinking about how he should spin his response or analyzing what his boss might be fishing for or not saying to him yet. They just talked about this at the end of the Stamp Out Stupidity Campaign barely more than a week ago. He just spoke his truth again.

"I'm on the fence to be honest with you. Part of me believes there is a way to make this business work and we're doing enough of the right things to get there. Then I do the math and I have a harder time getting there – any further erosion of the core than we're banking on and it all falls apart. And then I think about Patton, and Dutch, and as long as they're still here, we're definitely fucked. We'll never get there. So I figure the board has to recognize that at some point and get rid of both of them, and then maybe this would be an interesting place to work."

Stover slowly let a grin touch his face as Tom spoke.

"You and I see things much more similarly than you might believe. I don't mind telling you I'm at my wit's end with Dutch. He's a blowhard and a buffoon, and I can't believe I have to report to him. I'm still trying to figure the board out; the few times they've let me have access to them. I agree, I don't know how Patton, who's not stupid, doesn't see the damage the guy does and keeps promoting him."

Stover stopped talking and Tom considered what he'd just heard – his boss is absolutely in a tough spot with Dutch, and he wasn't afraid to tell a fairly new direct report exactly how he felt about him. That was interesting. That smelled like more change to come. More turmoil. The kind of environment Tom had always thrived in – like a master class surfer who wants to ride the biggest waves. Stover spoke again.

"So what are you going to do about Dutch?"

"What do you mean?"

"It's not going to be easy for you if you can't figure out a way to work with him."

Tom added ice to his eye contact as he very calmly replied, "I've decided I'm just going to make the best decisions for this company, for the things I'm responsible for, and if you or anyone else doesn't think I'm adding value on the whole, then feel free to fire me. I really don't care, to tell you the truth." Stover held Tom's gaze, his own eyes a bit of a mystery still, before standing up while saying,

"Fair enough then." He extended his hand, which Tom, also standing then, shook. "I'm glad we both know where we stand."

From Tom Cooper's private journal. January 1991. Age 29. Employer 2.

I'm so glad I came to this fabulously stable company. After just a year, I've completely figured out their human resource strategy: hire the most aggressive, competitive people you can find, pay them just enough above the industry average that it's hard for them to leave, let them fight viciously among themselves for recognition, fire the bottom 10 percent every year, promote the top 10 percent, and mercilessly beat the shit out of the middle 80% for the rest of their miserable careers. I'd heard the rumors, but I thought I'd always be in the top 10 percent, and this would be a great place to make some real money. For sure, now that I'm here a year I can join their very lucrative profit-sharing program, since God knows they will always grow profit, since they always have, even if it takes breaking the back of every manager to do it. I guess by signing up, I'm signing up for my fair share of abuse, to get a share of the profit. And abuse there is, nearly every day. We fight with each other, we bicker, we feel the tension the company wants us to feel. Well, fuck 'em. Every day must end, every week must pass, I have love to come home to, and a son to watch grow. Good health and youth are still on my side. I will be a human being to other human beings, and survive in my soul these foolish corporate battles.

I have to. Michelle and I just brought a helpless infant into this world. It's my responsibility to build a safety net for them, and hopefully, for the next child to come. That's more than 20 years of responsibility ahead. I need to provide a cushion against the pitfalls that life might bring. I need to keep opening doors to bigger jobs and more money, because they equal more security. It's my mission.

And my happiness? Shame if it can't be found in the 60 hours a week or more of career time I'm devoting. Shame be, if humanity in corporate wars is weakness. I have my other hours, with my family. And I'll try to be true to my soul at work, and to find the humor to accept the indignity of this corporate salaried slavery I've signed up for.

October 8, 2015 (later)

Tom had let his anger morph into a solemn silence by the time he walked in the door from the garage that night and gave Michelle a lifeless little peck on the lips as she stood over a head of lettuce, shredding it into a bowl. All he had focused on for the balance of the day was the little tidbit from his conversation with Stover, 'it's not going to be easy for you if you can't figure out a way to work with him'. Of course it wasn't going to be easy, it was never easy, and that wasn't the point. It was that it was going to be miserable. It was that a fucking malevolent fool like Dutch Bagley had the power to make Tom miserable. A grown man with more than enough 'agency', as his daughter called it, to not let himself feel miserable. But if he actually had that agency, he wasn't ready or willing to exercise it yet, or in this case, didn't quite know how. Tom knew his passionless kiss would signal Michelle this had been a particularly bad day. He tried to be conscious of just unloading work shit every night as the only topic of their conversations, but Michelle didn't like stony silence either, so sometimes he needed to signal her to ask what's wrong, to make the conversation that followed her responsibility, if it was all about work. She didn't disappoint him this time.

"Not a good day back at the Dutch All-day?" She remembered.

"Oh, it was great. It was a full-on Bad Dutch day. Epic opening rant. He scorched me of course, on my plans."

"Uh-oh." Michelle was always alert to indications in Tom's work complaints that his job might actually be in jeopardy. She understood very clearly what their life was built on. She knew how big the mortgage was and how much college for two would ultimately cost. The decision to have her stay home these 20 something years with the kids was one they made together, and Tom never forgot to acknowledge his appreciation for her trust in his ability to be their sole financial support. He was thankful that she had not become like his mother - paralyzed with fear about her financial future, with no faith that Tom's father had control over what happened to them. If Michelle harbored any doubts it was only because Tom himself had placed them there. He talked about the dark side of corporate life often enough. Particularly the ease with which companies dispose of people like Tom.

"It was not unexpected. Just a reminder of how much better my life was the last couple years out from under that man."

"You did seem much happier under Bailey. He retired right?"

"Yeah, he announced after the reorg." Tom was impressed that Michelle remembered. They'd generally avoided socializing with the people Tom worked with, so keeping names and roles straight had to come mostly from retaining what Tom talked about at night, and Michelle admittedly had trouble tracking all the names and titles and reporting lines that wrapped around Tom like coiled barbed wire.

"So tell me again, Stover reports directly to Dutch, and Dutch reports to Patton, but Stover also reports to Patton?"

"No, Stover is on the executive committee for meeting purposes, but only because his job is so big it's convenient to have him right there for Patton to torture without having to do it through Dutch."

"And how does Stover do with Dutch?"

"Funny you should ask that. Apparently not very well, from what I learned today." Tom relayed Stover's 'blowhard and buffoon' comments.

"Oh my god. That's not good is it? I mean for you if Stover likes you?"

"I think Stover likes me. He's a little.." Tom held his hand out, fingers splayed and made a see-saw between his thumb and pinky while humming audibly in a slightly incredulous way.

"Hard to figure out?" Michelle finished the sentence knowingly.

"He's got some of that 'I want to be the CEO' crap sticking to him, but for the most part I can live with him and believe what he says. But he's playing a waiting game with Dutch, and I'm not sure he's going to survive that. And then yes, that's not good for me. I'm just, I just don't think I care."

"Well you have to care enough to keep your job. I mean, they kept you, so obviously Patton at least, thinks you're doing a good job. That's why I'm asking, can Dutch get rid of you on his own if he wanted to, so soon after they just did all those layoffs and kept you?"

"Of course he could. Particularly if I lost it and told him to go fuck himself." Tom purposely did not smile when he said this and looked directly at Michelle. She had begun to smile, but now looked more nervous that he wasn't smiling. Tom instantly regretted playing facial expression mindgames. It was hard to get back to normal human conduct so soon after work. Like talking to your spouse without trying to send veiled messages. Still, there was something he didn't know how to say.

"Oh, come on, you're not really at that point are you?" Michelle looked at him expectantly.

Tom considered the question and the purposely serious expression he'd used to accompany his answer. He'd met Michelle when he was barely 18 years old. The moment he knew he was in love was a morning her eyes locked on his and poured so much warmth and love his way he could literally feel it fill up his body. He had never felt adored. He wanted to hold onto the feeling forever. That's when he knew he couldn't fully tell her about his town, what happened to him there. He told her his high school was full of cliques, and she shared hers was as well. He told her he didn't really fit in with the jocks or the freaks, and he didn't want to be one of the nerds, so he mostly just kept to himself. She was a pastor's kid and felt similarly disenfranchised from the available social groups. It was something they bonded over, re-inventing themselves in college as a popular couple with lots of friends. He never went back and corrected the narrative with detail. He didn't talk about what it felt like to have your entire high school hate you. He didn't tell her how often he tried to hide next to the coach's office in gym class to avoid losing another pair of underwear to a ripped waist band. He didn't confess the many days he purposely missed the bus and walked four miles home alone, a good ninety minutes to contemplate the mean-spirited nature of others. How could he explain to Michelle now? How could he tell her he'd never lost the hate for his tormentors that he'd balled up and swallowed when the abuse finally ended, if she didn't know about the torment? When Tom spent time with Dutch that little ball of hate turned on like a 100 watt bulb. He was everything Tom knew about bullies. He had inexplicable power that was not earned. Feeling powerless is the worst part of bullying for the victim. It fuels the belief that there may be no end to it. Dutch made Tom feel like he hadn't in decades. His shadow filled up every doorway. How could he explain that to Michelle? 'Remember when I said I hated my high school? Well, it was kind of worse than that.'

"I don't know, Michelle. I might just be at that point." He looked at her beautiful blue eyes and accepted the warmth they now bestowed upon him when he did so. It was not the full-on heat he once felt. He sometimes thought she loved him less now that time had revealed his flaws, and he longed to feel the full-on adulation that was so empowering and reassuring once again. He didn't let himself blame her for what he was missing. He vaguely knew it had to do with walling off his soul from the rest of the world. Once those barriers are up, even magic keys have a hard time opening the door. And one of those barriers was the untold story of bullying and abuse. How could he explain his issues with Dutch without it?

Michelle pursed her lips and smiled grimly, while slowly shaking her head. It was her sympathetic expression when Tom appeared to be in a mood that would not be easily fixed by anything else she could say. He didn't know how to tell her that she was particularly beautiful to him when she did that. Michelle had more love in her than Tom could take in, and he envied how much she had left to bestow on the kids, and to devote to a daily outlook that was kind and caring.

Somehow that little pursing of lips that were still turned up at the corners in a smile revealed the power of empathy to lift you up and push you forward. It was a face that said 'it doesn't matter to me what you're going through, but I care about you and I can see it's troubling you.'

"I'm gonna go change." Tom turned and walked out of the kitchen.

October 15, 2015

During the org structure work, Tom had seen an opportunity to claim some martyr status, and also, to build a power base that would make it difficult for the company to dislodge him. He willingly took on essentially what was a job and a half, in order to maintain those key responsibilities that were important to a particular executive in the C-suite, Mike Moran, the vice-chairman, with whom Tom had developed a mutual admiration. He could keep Dutch from torching Tom without a discussion, and Tom took every opportunity to spend time on the parts of his responsibility that took him out of Dutch's direct fire. It was using the too-fucked-up-to-work matrixed organizational structure to his advantage. If he had meeting overlap that involved Dutch and Moran, he did everything in his power to get a delegate to the Dutch meeting so Tom could go to the Moran meeting. This was Tom's latest plan to stay sane. The Stamp Out Stupidity Campaign had just made him crazier. And apparently meaner. Driving change in a positive way? Dutch just slapped him around over his best laid plans. Maybe there was a third way, a do-no-harm way. He could simply try to live in the moment and, as much as possible, disappear in plain sight.

Even at the level Tom was operating, it was easier than one would think to do that in a corporate headquarters building of over 4,000 people. Even if he was doing a job and a half.

For starters, he was quite cognizant of when he might be missed. He knew when his boss was traveling without him, and that basically just left Dutch and Patton to truly worry about. Tom's admin was plugged into the admins in the C-suite. She had a loud phone voice. Tom could mention he 'might need to speak to Dutch later', and his admin would soon be checking if he was in that day, just in case. If there was an out of town board meeting, Tom knew there was no one that would miss him if he wasn't in his office. The entire C-suite would be gone. His own people were mostly self-sufficient, so they wouldn't miss him either. Virtually the only thing Tom needed to do when he wasn't in meetings was respond to emails. And he could do that anywhere. Truth is, Tom had been preparing for this disappearing act for some time. It was well-researched and practiced. And now he could envision an almost zen-like positioning for himself in which he was highly paid and titled, but had no one who particularly needed him. Stover and the senior guys would always hold him accountable primarily for his results – and as long as he delivered they wouldn't have a lot of questions for him. Even Dutch had had to concede more than once over the last 8 years that Tom seemed to find a way to deliver when he had to. If it wasn't always everything he was looking for, it was generally better than his peers. No one in the C-suite needed Tom to explain to them what he was doing or create strategies for them. As the most senior member of his new boss's team, Tom knew he would be trusted to just do his job while Stover focused on filling his holes and keeping any more good young talent from leaving. And because Tom had hired, trained, and retained a strong group of direct reports, he didn't need to do a lot of hand-holding and they didn't need to run to him for validation of every decision. If he really wanted to, Tom could show up every day and play the role of an empty casual Friday outfit – a pair of Dockers and a Brooks Brothers striped oxford making a half-mill answering emails and sitting in meetings. Or he could cut out early and preserve his sanity for another day. Either way, the only stressor was that pesky need to deliver the results. And that was the existential threat to Tom's plan to hide in plain sight – the company's business sucked. And while he was still adept at running faster than the other potential bear snacks, the race was too close for comfort. So there would be an element of high risk for Tom in slowly ebbing away from his responsibilities.

And yet, here was the idea of it taking shape in his head. It wasn't really a plan so much as a reality he had to find a way to deal with. He just couldn't muster the give-a-fuck for 60 hours anymore. Nor even 50. If he couldn't deliver the goods in his diminished motivational state then he deserved whatever fate they wanted to impose, didn't he? They would find him out, wouldn't they? Not just Stover or Patton or Dutch, but his peers and his people too. No one could keep up appearances and throttle back for sanity and drive better results all at the same time, could they? Shouldn't Tom just do the honorable thing and leave? Not the way the other guys did, the hot shots, for greener pastures, but in acknowledgement that his heart was no longer in it, and it was a disservice to the company and his team to continue on.

But Tom couldn't really just walk away, could he? Or accept getting fired for poor performance? It would be stupid. In a little over a year he'd be 55. Soon after, he'd reach ten years of service too. That would meet the 'rule of 65', making Tom eligible to receive retirement benefits early, without penalty, should there be a change of control or a layoff that impacted him. Sticking around and hoping one of those events occurred would be the smart move. Leave on his own or get shit-canned before then? Nothing but vacation time owed. So Tom had to stick it out, didn't he? For the money? For the pay, for the stock grants, for the annual bonus, for the three-year long-term incentive plan annual pay-out.

If he could cocoon, if he go on autopilot, if he could hide in plain sight, it wouldn't be so bad would it? Tom could easily rationalize that he was just as effective as ever. He was an expert at only spending time on what really mattered, and because his people were so good, they would handle the day to day beautifully. He could fake engagement with his eyes wide open in any interaction with senior leadership. He could have them believing he was just like them – spending his off hours obsessing about the job – wondering how to beat his competitors, how to get more out of his people, what game-changing moves he could make to improve the business, when in fact he was not giving work even a passing thought once he walked out the door each night . But could Tom really keep fooling himself? Tom was a circus performer. He'd come to accept that. For years, his job in the show was keeping his balance while standing on a giant rubber ball while juggling. Now he was thinking about re-assigning himself to walking a tightrope at the top of the tent. Spectacular falls await.

But if this was to become a waiting game, there was still the issue that the day to day had become close to unbearable. The really awful impacts of the matrix were guaranteed to drive conflict. Crossed reporting lines. Shared responsibilities but misaligned accountabilities. Mini-fiefdoms created out of survival instinct. And at the levels where the work gets done – by people who were still competent in their posts – there was conflict galore. Tom put aside those dreams of fading away like the Cheshire cat's smile. They lasted 20 minutes in the middle of another bad day. Fuck that, not giving up yet, change is coming, it has to come, be patient, don't do dumb.

Tom went back to trying to find his cool skin, his wise leader. He religiously practiced common sense on a daily basis. He could always do this. He could always rise above. He'd survived everything to this point, hadn't he? Couldn't he do it again for his team? For his family? For his survival? The company headquarters had become a war zone, and the noise and dust of battle was everywhere. He heard the collective angst of his team as if it were a real sound, emanating from his now six direct reports and the eighty or so people they managed, rumbling up through the floor, seeping in through the walls, going home with him at night. Their frustrations, their loss of faith, their fears, when stacked and bound together, made a monster, and no matter how hard he tried, that monster became his companion throughout the workday and when they went to certain meetings together, the monster became one with Tom, and he continued to walk a fine line between being the voice of reason making the most sense in the room and being a petulant ass when the room still wouldn't move to do anything differently. He could see his once formidable diplomatic skills ebbing, and yet he just couldn't bring himself to do something about it. The anger just kept bubbling to the surface and getting in the way.

Tom knew what the real problem was. He just didn't believe the company was a winning company any more. The swagger he felt a part of when he first arrived, of a company that had just figured out the winning formula, had quickly waned. Things started going sideways almost immediately upon his arrival, with the entire economy collapsing, and then, in the long, slow recovery, an absolute revolution in the way the world works, with everything and everyone on their way to being wirelessly connected. Big companies that have made big bets in one direction have a hard time slamming on the brakes and heading off the other way. Smaller disruptive companies were changing the world faster than Tom's company could move, and now some of them were achieving scale as well. Their situation was ripe for a strategic repositioning, which meant they were ripe for consumption by consultants. They had to change but they didn't know how. Smarter people, people with more context, could help them. So in they came, through an open door.

The consultant process is always the same. Two or three salt and pepper partners come in and dazzle you with their sheer brilliance, promise you they'll be devoting at least 27% of their weekly brainpower to your problems, and then introduce you to the engagement partner, just turned 30 with no salt in sight, whom you will see every day as a reminder of just how much fucking money this is costing you. The engagement manager will arrive with a small flock of kids that could be Tom's own children, who will proceed to spend 8 weeks building a fact base, essentially interviewing everybody on the org chart and then spitting back in Powerpoint form what they collectively said. They will create slides for the Powerpoint deck that they fall in love with and they will appear in every subsequent deck, building on each other, until the final deck exceeds 100 pages before the appendix, and the appendix will always by definition be longer still. The deck will be delivered to senior management toward the end of the three months, and a sweeping set of recommendations, which often require follow up billable hours for implementation and execution, will be presented. Tom could count 8 times in 8+ years the process had unfolded to attack one part of the company or another, or at times, the whole damn thing, and of all the new ideas the company had implemented as a result, he considered one successful. One out of eight. A batting average of .125. A lot of misery, disruption, and firings. What a waste. .125 was a very bad batting average in baseball, get you demoted bad, get you told to find a life outside of baseball bad. But the consultants who cooked up those 7 misfires got paid every time, and some of the same ones came back multiple times. And the CEO and the other leaders who signed off on the ideas are all still here, through all those failures. Tom was betting and hoping they were out of strikes.

That Tom was still there at all, beyond his formidable survival skills, was a testament to the power of home. Six moves in just the last twenty-four years, southwest, midwest, southeast, and now home again, where it all began, and at his age there would be no more going away. He was thrilled to get the offer after an arduous vetting process that lasted nearly six months. It was a promotion, at work and at home. He had one more chance to find a place he could plug into, contribute, feel great about, become a leader within and an ambassador without. In his hometown. In his wife's hometown. It seemed too good to be true. And as usual, it was.

Now, after eight full years and counting, Tom had survived but not thrived, a bumpy ride to be sure. It would have been easy to jump off the horse when he realized it was unbreakable, but that would have meant chasing the next high level job at some broken company that's looking outside because their shit is messed up internally – and moving the family again. So Tom had stayed. Tried his best to lead. Stayed focused on taking care of the people who did good work for him and the company. Put just enough wins on the board over the years to stay ahead of the axe. And yes, endured the occasional Dutch Bagley beat down, only to rise and shower and come back to work early the next morning. There was college tuition to pay and pay and pay again. The family was home. Tom had to balance that. He was close to clearing the first hurdle, getting the kids through school. There'd be more options after that. He could address his own happiness then, the happiness that comes from finding joy in all the hours of life, not just those spent away from work.

Work/life balance meant different things to different people. Everybody had to find what it was to them. Tom wished he could feel that rush of being part of something successful, the emotion he'd felt in his college theater days, holding hands with his cast mates and taking bows to enthusiastic applause at the conclusion of a play.

Those first few years of his career, long ago, when senior leaders seemed to have the answers, and the company he worked for had a swagger that a young recruit could feel in his bones just walking in the door. That feeling of being on a winning team, the confidence it breeds and the strong sense of camaraderie. That experience had sadly eluded Tom for most of his career, so his balance was not about making room for two essential but distinctly different sets of responsibilities, both of them vital to his being. It was about how much he could endure at work, how long he could stand the pressure of always playing from behind, putting up with the Dutches of the world, in order to take care of that other world, where the love of his wife and the health of his family and close friends was all he needed to be happy. In fact, there was no balancing point at all, simply a wall with a door. As Tom left home for work, he grabbed whatever face off the wall was required that day – tough bastard, wise mentor, demanding manager, ruthless negotiator, and a couple hundred more – and left whatever was left of who he was at home behind. It was getting harder and harder to find himself when he got back. It hadn't always been this way, but at this hoped-for last stop, it's what it had become.

From Tom Cooper's private journal. May 2002. 41 years old. Employer 4.

It was late in the day – yet another seemingly endless meeting was dragging on toward 6 pm. Twenty miles away, a baseball game had just begun, my son's game, his reason for being at the beautiful age of 11. I remember with brilliant detail that feeling myself, the anticipation of a ball hit my way, of the pitch that I will hit hard, fair, and uncatchable. I want to be there with him every game, to see him enjoy it as I had, to share a little of that feeling again. I glanced at the clock on the wall. Time was slowing down and speeding up simultaneously. The meeting seemed to have no end, as if time had been suspended, and yet as I calculated the distance I had to drive to get to the game, I felt time rushing forward: for each meeting minute, I lost two minutes of the game.

This was not a meaningless meeting. We were heavily involved in mapping out a strategy to revive our business. My livelihood and the welfare of my family are tied up in the success of this business, as were those of the other twenty people in the room. And I was far from a passive participant. This was my business, the one listed on my business card and half the room were my direct reports, looking to me for leadership. But as the hour grew late, my engagement in the process waned, and all I wanted to do was get in my car and drive those twenty miles to watch a ball game that meant nothing, but then again, everything.

Finally, at six, the meeting was over. A grown man of 41 years ran with his briefcase through hallways of cubicles, down a staircase, across a parking lot. Twenty miles in drive-time traffic to get to the game, all the while time moving faster, the game moving forward, moments I was missing. When I finally arrived it was the bottom of the sixth of a seven inning game. Our team was behind. David had been 0 for 1 with a walk. He told me if the team got the lead back he was going to pitch the 7th. The meeting, the strategic planning, the business I needed to fix, was all behind me. It was out of my mind entirely. The top of the 7th was beginning. We were down by five runs.

What happened next was wonderful. The boys rallied. One after another came to the plate and coaxed a walk or stroked a hit. The runs began to pile up. In the middle of the inning my son smashed a long fly down the right field line and raced to his first double of the season. This season that will mean everything to him, until next year, when another one will begin. We took a three run lead to the bottom of the 7th, and David took the mound and delivered a one-two-three inning to close out the game. I had missed six innings, but I had missed nothing. As soon as it was over, my thoughts turned quickly back to that last meeting of the day. The temporary oasis of the game, as embodied by the flush of excitement and pre-teen ecstasy on my son's face, gave way quickly to the harsh reality of my business responsibilities and the next day of work that would begin barely ten hours later.

On the way home, I thought about our company in baseball terms. It feels like our 'last ups', just like my son's team faced in the bottom of the sixth. I knew when I came here it would be an uphill climb, but there was a chance to be part of a heroic business comeback. It's looking pretty dicey right now. But rallies happen in baseball, in life, and yes, even in business. I had just witnessed one in baseball, and I feel like I have it in me to be part of one at work. All the anxiety I'd felt as that clock ticked toward six, as I'd rushed through traffic, because I believed I was missing something important, ended up being misplaced. I'd arrived in time to see all there was to be seen in that one last inning. Maybe that's still ahead for me, and for the company. Maybe I'll even be on the mound when we win, or be part of the go ahead rally at least. Maybe my anxiety about the future will prove to have been misplaced. A lot can happen when the game is on the line. There's always one last chance.

October 19. 2015

It was now 40 days since the reorg. Tom began to feel the same way he had before it had all begun over the summer. A typical day started with enough on his to-do list to keep him focused, the energy of getting shit done pushing him along toward noon. As the hunger of mid-day began calling it reminded Tom how un-pleasurable work really was. Even eating a salad, accompanied as it was by self-denial, was a highlight of the day compared to everything that had come before it, and that was the good part of the day. In the afternoon, Tom's attention began to wither, and as another day went by, with the continuing bullshit, the continuing pressures, the continuing misery, his sense of detachment from it all slid along a rail to anger. He left work pissed off and sad.

Maybe if Tom had thought about it more, this routine that had taken hold, he would have scheduled his next call for earlier in the day. But as it was, it came after lunch. It was an arranged call with the president of one of his suppliers, to discuss a cost increase. There was a time when cost increases weren't a big deal – inflation ran 3-5% a year across so many commodities, and companies could pass increases to customers and keep everything in balance, keep the profit rolling, maybe even tack on a little extra profit along the way from the factory to the customer. From the dirt to the table. From the ground to the pump. From the hen to the frying pan. So many hands touching everything along the way, and a little bit of profit has to stick to every hand, or no one would lift a finger. Cost increases made everyone feel like their enterprise was growing. But economic shocks had wrung inflation's neck, markets became even more about supply and demand, and professional killers, aka consultants, aka MBA's, aka CFO's, aka CEO's, now insisted that cost increases be fought with every last breath in your body. Sometimes the increases would be legitimate, but they would fight them anyway. Somewhere along the line they would be stopped. Some company would fight it to death. The others would jump in and help tear apart the prey. The source, if legitimately faced with higher costs, would have no choice but to find a place to cut, to stay in balance, to keep their share of the value chain. People would lose. Factories would move. Everything was about power now. Negotiating power. Bargaining power. Market power.

Tom guzzled an extra strength energy shot. He had sleep apnea that he refused to treat with a mask, so to make up for the restless nighttime hours, he loaded up on caffeine throughout the day. It also fired him up a little, he had to admit, and he was feeling a need to get fired up for this call. Terry Simmons was a total prick. Pure penis. Tom had worked with his firm for several years and found him entirely odious. He was a tall, athletic man seemingly created to confirm one's assumptions of what a senior executive looked like. Crisp suits still, even as the world went casual, silver hair so perfect it was like every strand was measured, snipped, and carefully laid into place beside the others. He spoke looking straight ahead, so if you weren't six foot four, he never looked you in the eye. He was serious to a fault unless the conversation turned to his alma mater's college basketball team, which was perennially good, which gave him an opportunity to show his lighter side by viciously gloating about his school's success. As if, by attending it 35 years ago, he was still delivering victories. As if his success in business, in his career, reflected glory back to the school so that they became entwined in their successes. As if that made him superior to virtually everyone he met, and all would chuckle good-naturedly at his boasting in acquiescence of their inferiority. God, Tom hated this fucking guy. And now, like he had each of the last 4 years, he had announced a cost increase. He considered his company a premium supplier. Their products could command virtually any price. It had nothing to do with inflation at the source. It was purely about greed.

Tom had no problem taking on greed. The relentlessness it took to fight everything, every cost increase, every concession sought, tooth and nail, no matter how just the justification, had rubbed him raw. He was just tired of the eternal flame of battle. He wanted the pilot light to go out. But he still enjoyed summoning the energy to fight the real villains. The pricks. The ones looking to tip the balance in their favor. Tip it so far all the cups and plates slide off the table. All the chips in one direction. Tom had acquired a lot of skills along the way, to help re-tip those tables. He'd been schooled in negotiating tactics. He had his cool demeanor, his coat of arms. The one constant. Smooth professionalism. Facts. Calm. Tom was a classic stone-faced poker player. Part of that was the persona. The cool. The calm. Almost serene. Factual. Truthful. Calm. Calm, because really, fighting over the cost of nuts and bolts, pen and ink, socks and shoes, salt and pepper, what would any of that really mean? As long as there was a home to go to at the end of the day, a place to be human, with your loved ones, shouldn't you be able to be civil when all you're really talking about is nuts and bolts?

The call had been precipitated by a snarky but calmly and beautifully written email that Tom had crafted to start the cost negotiation process. Tom had decided that this year he would simply accept the supplier's annual increase with the humility of a servant bowing obsequiously to a royal, and then peer up from his stooped, submissive position, and calmly threaten to cut the royal's balls off with anything and everything he had handy that was remotely sharp enough to do the trick. He couldn't say where, he wouldn't say when, he wouldn't commit to how. But, oh, it would happen. Circumstances demanded it. Thank you sir, may I have another, and then you can wait and wonder when the payback will come. The email captured that sentiment perfectly, Tom felt. It was quite nearly a masterpiece. It got a chilly response from Terry Simmons, who tersely requested a one to one call to discuss. They put it on calendar, and this was the designated time for Terry to call Tom.

"Terry, how are you?" Tom's voice was friendly but authoritative. Calm.

"I'm fine Tom, can't complain."

"I'm glad we could get on a call, thank you for finding the time".

"No thank you, I know how crazy it must be there." A little dig from Simmons at the tough performance lately and the recent reorg.

"Listen, I know you have some concerns about my email, so I'm all ears, and happy to discuss."

"Well, sometimes words in an email can be construed in different ways, so why don't you go ahead and walk me through your thinking."

"No, please, if it's not really questions you have, but a response, why don't you go ahead first?" It was Chip and Dale, overly polite chipmunks, each bowing to the other, you first, no after you, no you please, I insist.

"Tom, you clearly have a point of view, so why don't you start?" Tom clearly did, and he was ready to deliver his rationale.

"Okay, sure. You've come to us for the fourth consecutive year with a cost increase of at least 3%. There's no justification for it, in my view. Raw materials costs are down, actually, for most of what you make. Labor costs are not rising as quickly as you've been raising your prices. When we've asked you for justification in the past, you've generally listed a variety of market conditions and cost pressures that we haven't seen to the same degree, but this time, you've basically said your justification is that you can. And while I appreciate your honesty this time around, I still can't stomach the premise." Tom was cool, calm, measured, restrained. Conversational. Matters of fact, recited. He continued.

"What I said in my email was simply factual. We have other options for what you sell us. At some point, they become so much cheaper than you do, that we have to seriously consider moving some of our business. Some meaning all the way up to all." Still calm, but this was clearly a hostile statement, which Tom loved to deliver as coolly as he possibly could. He was breaking down his email for Simmons line by line. To give the meaning, to explain the veiled threats, to make the case for no cost increase, because this was what he had to do, what he was paid the most to do, to get other people's money-grubbing paws off his company's profits. With this more overtly threatening meaning now tumbling out of Tom's mouth, Terry Simmons interrupted.

"I know I said I'd let you start, but I've got to stop you right there. What you just said, and what you put in your email, tells me that you just don't understand our industry. You don't know the difference between a premium supplier and a commodity supplier. In fact, I showed your email to my CEO and he was incensed. He said the person who wrote it was obviously clueless, and if this was the person we had to deal with at your company, then we had to get a meeting ASAP with Patton and Stover." His voice and pace rose as he spoke, and Tom could sense this was just the beginning of a longer lecture, and he couldn't believe he'd been interrupted so soon, and was now being attacked. He felt a burning at the bottom of his rib cage like the gas flame on a stove top, and his heart sat on top of that flame, jumping to another level at the first lick of the fire. He could feel a tingle shoot directly from his chest to his brain, which just exploded in light, and the light flooded down to his vocal chords, and he knew there was no stopping whatever was going to come out, which ended up as:

"ARE YOU FUCKING KIDDING ME TERRY? AFTER 30 YEARS IN THIS BUSINESS YOU'RE TELLING ME I DON'T KNOW THE FUCKING DIFFERENCE BETWEEN A PREMIUM SUPPLIER AND A COMMODITY SUPPLIER? YOU KNOW WHAT THAT IS? THAT'S FUCKING BULLSHIT! WE'RE DONE HERE!" And he slammed the phone down so hard his hand rang with vibration, as if the disconnection of the call was a punch that connected with a jaw. Tom's entire body was on fire, and he immediately stood up from his chair, put his hands on his hips and looked around the room as if he were seeing it for the first time. What the hell just happened? Did he really just f-bomb the president of a major supplier and slam the phone down in his ear? That could have repercussions. That wasn't smart business. That wasn't cool Tom. But that fucker called him clueless. CLUELESS!!! He deserved everything he just got and more. Much, much more. Tom opened the door to his office and wandered out into the open space outside, out amongst the cubicles and the people working in them. He was sweating a little, everywhere. He felt giddy. Almost insanely happy. But he had just broken his cool for the first time in over 30 years. Broken the professional code. Lost his shit over nuts and bolts. But not over nuts and bolts. Over insults. Over injustice. Over a privileged prick who deserved to have shit thrown in his face every day for the rest of his life. And then Tom remembered the last time he felt this way.

It was the beginning of his junior year in high school. After the summer he finally went through puberty and shot up to his final adult height of five feet, seven and a half inches. After he started lifting weights so maybe the bullies would finally leave him alone. Stop making him the mark upon whom assholes broke their cherries. Stop the random kids from firing punches into his shoulder just passing in the hall. Stop the kids in gym class from competing to rip the elastic band on his underwear while trying to pull it over his head from behind. Stop the kids on the bus from spitting at him. Big mucus-filled loogies. But a different body did not deter some young d-bag, a sophomore hockey player trying to impress the upperclassmen on the team, from taunting him in the hallway. Christ, Tom barely even knew the kid, what did he have against him? He was about Tom's height, burlier. Tom had no idea if he was an experienced fighter, if he fought in the hockey games that Tom did not go to. He stopped when he saw Tom at his open locker. Came over and slammed it shut, just as Tom quickly withdrew his hand. Had some kids behind him beginning to egg him on. Put his right fist in the air and showed it to Tom. Tom hadn't fought since 7th grade. When he first fought back against the bullies. When they formed a circle like a human boxing ring, and found other victims for Tom to fight – the weakest bully quickly becoming just another target for their amusement. But as the other kids grew, and Tom stayed small, pre-pubescent, he stopped fighting back. Just took it. He hadn't thrown a punch in four years.

The kid put his clenched right fist slowly up against the left side of Tom's face, and just pushed a little, sending Tom's head back. And then everything just kind of went white. Tom remembered later his antagonizer's face seemingly floating in the air, disembodied, at eye level to Tom's. He remembered throwing punches, rights and lefts, in order, like a windmill. First right, then left, then right, then left, rightleft, rightleft, rightleft, rightleft. He didn't recall playing defense. Didn't recall getting hit himself, barely remembers the feeling of his fists connecting with the face, but seeming to feel as if every punch did connect, rightleft, rightleft, rightleft. And then someone was hugging him from behind, holding his arms down to his side. It was his best and only friend, Seaver. His eyes refocused. His tormenter was still in front of him, also being held around the arms. The assistant principal was coming, the shouts of 'fight, fight' like a 9-1-1 call reverberating down the hallway. Tom looked at the bully's face and there was blood streaming from his nose, one of his eyes was swelling, and the middle of his bottom lip was split open. His handlers turned him around and hustled him into the boy's bathroom. He heard someone yell. "Man, that last shot blew up his nose!" Tom felt a small trickle of blood from his own nose, a swipe of his right hand confirming it was blood, the right hand with cuts on every knuckle that Tom did not feel. He felt no pain at all. He felt elation. He felt fear. He felt he was suddenly capable of anything. He felt powerful. No one at school ever bothered him again.

That was exactly how Tom felt now. Standing outside his office, his hand still a little tingly from slamming down the receiver, his head a little tingly from the adrenaline. But good. No, great. Fuck them all. I'm a grown-ass fucking man, and if you deal with me, that's how you have to treat me. And don't think I won't defend myself. Don't think I won't fight you. Tom knew this wasn't really good. Certainly not great. For business. For the company. Relationship building was important. But wasn't the company under siege? Hadn't they just fired a bunch of people? Wasn't the ship still in peril? And this asshole wants to raise our costs? Put us out of balance? Don't I have the high-level clearance to discharge my weapons? Tom took a deep breath and headed down the hall to speak with his boss. He had to assume the next call from the supplier would go there. Tom was unprofessional. We can't work with Tom anymore. This was a serious breach. Our CEO is incensed. We need a meeting. A top to top. Without Cooper. Well, who the fuck cared anymore? For maybe the first time in his life, at a very deep level, Tom realized the only person he really needed to ask that question of was himself. And in this case, he decided he didn't give a fuck. He could get through what was left of his career without having to repair the damage he just did, because he had no interest in repairing it.

He poked his head into Stover's office.

"Got a sec?"

"Sure, come on in."

"Just want to give you a heads up you might get a call from Terry Simmons at Atlas. I can honestly say that for the first time in my career I completely lost my shit with a vendor." Stover smiled. Tom had noticed throughout his career that his bosses seemed to enjoy when Tom showed some emotion other than cool. As if calm was underwhelming. Calm was suspicious. Calm wasn't human enough. Calm was disinterested in the mission.

"What happened?"

Tom went through the set-up, the fourth straight cost increase, the lack of justification for it, his factual but snarky email. He gave the short phone call nearly verbatim from both sides. It was the truth. Surely Stover would see that Simmons deserved to be lit up. He would have Tom's back. And in fact, he did.

"Hey, I've been there. It happens to all of us."

"Yeah, but I've never been that way. I can do manufactured anger for negotiation effect, but I never lost my shit for real until this call. 31 years."

Stover smiled and leaned back in his chair.

"Welcome to the club."

Tom instinctively smiled, because that's what you do when your boss intentionally tries to be funny, when he's smiling too, to let you know it's a soft moment between you. Tom smiled, but inside he was struck with an uneasy thought. If calm was a veneer created to serve him at work, had it ever really been him? Was it always a lie, now revealed? Did he slip into the cool skin because it felt right, it fit him, it was him? Or because it was who he thought he should be, to win, to get to the top? Didn't everyone want a calm hand on the tiller? But he was calm everywhere, not just at work. He rarely raised a voice at home, to his wife or his kids. That was just him, wasn't it? Always under control. No fuss, no muss. Undisturbed. Once upon a time, he was sure of it, people would have called him 'happy go lucky'. A man who knew he had it all. Good health, nice wife, couple of kids, good job, lots of friends. Who could muster up anger over cost increases when you had all that going for you? Calm was serenity, calm was confidence, calm was happiness. When did it become just quiet? When did it become suspicious? What new club did his boss just tell him he joined? The club where people have two sides? Where they only occasionally flash white hot anger? Or the club where the members are angry all the time? Or just the club where people show emotion of all kinds? Highs and lows. Laughter and tears. Ecstasy and agony. All of it on the surface for the world to see. Tom was floating outside the capsule again, spinning in space. Trying to piece together what the fuck was going on. Who the fuck he really was. Undisturbed, as always? Or now, quite clearly disturbed?

From Tom Cooper's private journal. July 2003. Age 42.
Employer 4.

I am on the other side of the world for the first time, on a multi-million dollar yacht in Hong Kong harbor. The owner of the yacht is a man I just met, but all night he has been treating me like a long-lost friend, clapping me on the back, rubbing my shoulders, complimenting me on the firmness of my muscles. We have just finished a fantastically fresh seafood dinner on an island in the harbor, and he is now sharing his life story with me. A British engineer, working for an industrial company in Hong Kong, he invented a cool new power tool in his spare time, lined up a local factory to make them, and found an American company to market them. That was my company, a long time ago. The man is now chairman of a global company listed on the Hong Kong exchange at a value that makes him a paper billionaire, though it's obvious from the yacht that not all of the money is tied up in paper.

What a great American success story! Except none of the Americans in the story has seen the wealth this man has seen, from this great partnership we struck with him. I'm just one of a long line of salarymen who has had to endure the bloated ego, the insincere expressions of affection, and the shoulder rubs. It's clear to me my mission in life must be to pick his overstuffed pockets for as much economic value as I can muster for my company. I endured a long dinner conversation with his obnoxious 27-year old son, who could only talk about wine, women, and where, in the entire world that is his oyster, he should vacation this year. As I listen to his father's life story as his yacht cuts through the dark water, all I can think about is where we are at the moment, at my company – pensions just cut, headcount reduced. I don't begrudge this man his wealth because I still believe in Capitalism. But as I smile and nod at his stories, I can only think of one thing. We're not getting nearly enough margin selling this man's products, and we need to beat his executives hard to get some of that money back.

It's hot in the metal-bending plant in Tennessee, despite the big overhead fans blowing the dry air around. Five hundred American workers are building big silver boxes that people in the trades mount in the back of their pickup trucks. The company's been building boxes of some kind or another in this factory for over 70 years, and making the big silver boxes for us for 40. The quality is great, we sell them for a good value, and the customers have rewarded us with massive market share. I'm proud to walk in the shoes of the people before me who built up this business, who partnered with the people that own this plant, but there is an uneasy undercurrent to my visit. I'm here to compare the efficiency and processes to other metal bending plants I will walk in China this fall. Just in case we find that we can build the exact same quality for a lot less by moving production offshore, where this labor-intensive work can be done so cheaply.

Our business with this factory had been done all these years on a handshake, mostly on amicable and mutually beneficial terms. A few years ago, this company was bought by a much larger conglomerate, active in at least a dozen disparate industries, that imposed rigid return on capital metrics, which had begun to drive some friction over costs of goods. And now here I am, implicitly threatening to end this 40-year relationship, and abandon these 500 workers. It's a pretty simple concept, what I do. The customer only will pay so much for something. I get some because I sold it, and the vendor gets some because they made it. All that's left to decide is who gets what share. And that's where the dance starts, and it doesn't always end in a graceful dip. This conglomerate is a big public company like mine. I can read their reports. They minted money last year, their stock is way up. Not so much for us.

I walk the plant in my sportcoat and I'm sweating, but then so are the men and women, many of them wearing American flag bandanas, building the boxes. They don't know that their local management has to deliver that minimum return on investment at all costs, including being willing to just throw this business away.

October 20, 2015

Caleb Patton was the 7th CEO that Tom had worked for over the years. When Tom was just a young trainee, he could barely remember the name of his CEO, stationed as he was in a division that operated far from corporate headquarters. But with each promotion he'd come closer and closer to that flame, and he'd been on a first name basis with his last three. The CEO was an ideal in Tom's mind - he entered corporate life determined to be one, and as quickly as possible. When he first started, he told himself to think and act as if he were the CEO of the company, within the confines of his own role. He discovered quickly that his bosses considered this approach to be a predictor of future success, and like a prized calf, he was branded with the phrase "strategic thinker", and it opened doors early for him. This early success only convinced Tom further that becoming the CEO was his destiny. If he could think like one, why not get paid like one? There was a relentless logic to the CEO's role that Tom appreciated – just make every decision based on what's best for the company's long term success, and don't get blinded or distracted by short-term problems. The CEO made sense of it all. The CEO knew the meaning. The CEO was rational. The CEO was cool-headed. The CEO was calm. Tom could handle that. And this was the real world now. Time to stop sliding through school on smarts alone, having a good time and failing to maximize his potential. Time to kick some ass. It was sanctioned in the business world. You were expected to take out competitors. Both internal and external. He could win with his brain. No brute strength required. Tom saw the corporate ladder as a visceral, living being. A shimmering shaft of light leading from the Earth to the clouds. His place was in the clouds, and he knew the climb was intended for him.

But about halfway up the ladder, or perhaps more accurately, down the rat hole, Tom had realized that he was wrong. There was a level of existence above his consciousness, above his capability, a door he couldn't unlock, that the CEOs got to. He knew there were people smarter than him in the world. Of course there were, there always were. But Tom thought they mostly found their way into medical research, or academia, or high technology. Rocket scientists, brain surgeons, theoreticians. If brains like that settled for business, they went to Wall Street, founded hedge funds, became venture capitalists. Tom always knew he was not in that class. But a grubby business like making stuff and selling it? Squeezing suppliers, cutting costs, cheating the customer on quality? Surely the ex-jocks and the fuck-offs and the dopers and the band camp kids would end up there, and Tom could rise to the top of a scrum like that, with his brain and some hard work. He could be the CEO of an outfit like that, couldn't he?

And to be clear, Tom did climb that ladder. He did rise. He had his opportunities, he had his champions ready to anoint him. But all the way to CEO? There was no way it was going to happen. Even if the external world didn't know it. There was something missing in Tom. The want-to. The ambition.

He admired logic and understood strategy. But all the time? With no consideration to other realities? No consideration of the toll? It took a special mind to focus on something so single-mindedly. Tom started to pick out those who might make it. They would find the biggest jobs. They would get the keys. They would get the chance to leap from salary man to multi-millionaire, simply by running a public company. They would leave Tom in the dust. And they would leave him cold.

Tom had come to the conclusion that while strategic thinking ability may be a door opener and getting shit done might be an enabler, there was only one quality that marked every one of Tom's CEOs in a way he knew in his heart he did not possess. The best word he could put to it was relentless. There was no balance for them. Every moment was spent in service to winning in business. A special form of consciousness. They appeared to be living the role twenty-four hours a day. Their sense of humor, despite vastly different personalities and styles otherwise, was somehow always extra dry. Always grim-tinged. Tom kept looking for joy, and all he saw was the occasional ego-driven basking in reporting results during the good times. Always bracketed with some kind of warning about complacency or resting on one's laurels. Never just pure joy.

Over the years, Tom came to think of the CEO as his own personal 'other'. He closely observed the ones he worked for and read articles about the leaders of other companies. But it was deeper than just trying to gain an understanding of expectations. Even when he'd given up on the idea of being one himself, Tom felt like their presence; the things he knows they would want him to do were with him constantly. They were the other voice in his head for every hour of his working

life. Tom had always loved Jean Paul Sartre's "No Exit", where
three characters are damned to spend their time in hell locked
in a room together, each of them serving as one of the other's
personal torturers for all of eternity. As long as Tom stayed in
corporate life, clung to his spot on the ladder, reached for
another rung, his tormenter would be beside him. The CEO.
In every meeting, every decision, every interaction with his
people, and eventually, coming home with him at night to
become the unwelcome relative visiting his family.

It didn't matter that seven different actors had played
the role, they were all the same once they crawled into Tom's
brain. It was not their personal characteristics, their actions,
their decisions, that mattered, it was their underlying intent.
That sense of inevitability, the single course always predictably
chosen, the robotic response to everything, driven by that
simplistic intent. The CEO IS the shareholder, they're all that
matters, he serves at their pleasure, he represents them, he's
their avatar. And they always want the most money they can
wring from their investments. Of course they do. Who
wouldn't? And so Tom lived every minute of his own hell
with the CEO poking him, provoking him, reminding him he
knows what to do. Tom's a strategic thinker, he gets it. He can
be trusted to do the right thing. He gets shit done. Now go do
it Tom. Humans are resources, costs have to be in balance with
revenues. The quarterly earnings have to hit forecast. The
bottom 20% have to go. Tom learned to stop waiting for
direction and just take the action demanded so clearly by the
other in his head. The CEO. The awful choices one must
make in hell.

But this wasn't the real thing, was it?. Capital H,
capital E, capital double hockey sticks? This was not

damnation for eternity. This was not "No Exit". This was not Hell. This was Hell, Inc. And Hell, Inc. could be quit. Right? There was always an exit door. It was generally held open gladly, because once you'd lost the desire to be there, you were of no use anyway. Tom had looked at the red exit signs throughout the building for a few years now, the ones instructing people where to go in case of a fire. As if there were any real fires in Hell, Inc. There was just the one word, EXIT, a constant reminder there really was a choice. Even before you turned 55. Even before your last one finished college. Even before your mom started losing her mind. Even before paying off the $700,000 mortgage. EXIT? Was there really a choice? The CEO, the valet, the one who welcomed him, laughed the evil laugh of feudal superiority and said, 'You're mine until I say it's time.' Sure. There was no need for real fires in Hell, Inc. No physical torture. As Garcin said at the end of No Exit, "There's no need for red-hot pokers. HELL IS OTHER PEOPLE!"

And Patton? Patton might be the most evil he'd ever worked for. He liked to affect a folksy, backwoods commonsense persona, even though everyone knew he was a Harvard B-school grad and a broad thinker. When he was addressing a group, even the top 30 leaders, he was usually straightforward but engaging. He liked to start with a little cartoon that fit the theme of the meeting, like the one titled 'our corporate strategy', with the New Yorker-style drawing of a big man in a suit pounding his desk and shouting 'we will crush you'. Arid. But in an operating review, Patton could be a real bastard, slicing up key executives in front of others, threatening to fire them, always in a polite, folksy way of course, cushioned with the phrase 'maybe I should'. Often, if the results being covered were not good, and that was often, unfortunately, Patton would stand up and walk over to the windows of the boardroom and stare out the sixth floor window at the view of highways and office parks and malls and tight neighborhoods of McMansions. He would stand with his back to the room for as long as fifteen minutes, not saying a word, as his lieutenants droned on about the business and what they were doing about it. In those long stretches, the CFO and the vice-Chairman would fill the role of questioning the presenter. When Tom first began attending these meetings, a year into his tenure, he was amazed at the rudeness of the tactic. After a while, he just turned it into a game. He would go through the deck and put a little note "right here", where he predicted Patton would stand up and walk over to the window. Then at the meeting, when Patton inevitably made his move, Tom would mark the deck with an "actually here".

Ignoring people was a classic passive aggressive tactic, a behavior that Patton had truly mastered. He always came to the operating reviews with a large stack of emails his admin had printed for him. He would place the deck being covered, on which he'd already made his notes, to his left, and the giant stack of emails to his right. If presenters were drifting through pages of the deck that were clean of notes, Patton turned to his email stack and read them, turning them over as he finished each one, making no pretense that he was not multitasking, signaling his complete disregard for the speaker and what they were saying.

Over the last few months, since just before the reorg, Tom had taken to sitting right next to Patton at the boardroom table during the operating reviews, to see if he could steal a glance at some of the emails, maybe learn something he needed to be prepared for. Tom was not above treating self-preservation as his number one priority in times of trouble, and there had been plenty of times of trouble in his career. There was an ethical line, Tom was sure of it, and sure that he knew where it was, but he didn't always like to press himself on the finer details, or examine his behavior too closely. If there was a chance for a restructuring, Tom wanted in on it. He never wanted to be blindsided. He wanted a chance to think about what it could mean for him and begin to feel out the right mentors about future opportunities, or sniff out whether he might be in danger. He purposely didn't gossip about people, so that people trusted him with information about events, about serious shit. Peers generally considered him thoughtful and strategic. They liked bouncing things off him to get his take. That they also perceived him to be a good secret-keeper made it easier to learn the secrets they knew. Tom liked to know who was in the know, and then work to extract that knowledge. Knowledge wasn't absolute power in corporate America, but as a tool for self-preservation, it was irreplaceable.

So in the name of survival, in a way that might be seen as counter-instinctual to that survival, Tom continued to choose the seat next to Patton at the monthly operating review, in his new role. To steal his glances. Even if it was just the header of the email. The sender. The subject line. The font. The punctuation marks. So much could be gleaned from those face-up messages sent to Caleb Patton.

Forty-one days after the reduction and reorganization, at the monthly operating review, Tom settled into the seat that was inevitably available next to the CEO. It was to his right. To his left, the head of the egg-shaped table, the flat part, was where Dutch would sit. That was another little Patton trick. Everyone would expect the CEO to sit at the head of the table, but this was not Patton's meeting, this was each business unit head's time in the inquisition chamber. They could come in and sit at the head. They all wanted Patton's job anyway. Try the chair on. See how hot it is. So Tom knew that Patton would look away from him when he wanted to look at Dutch as he spoke. And Tom knew that the email stack sat to Patton's right. Tom was a strategic thinker, after all. His positioning to Patton's right would allow Tom to most easily shoot his eyes sideways, to scan, perhaps to read. They were there to review the same shitty numbers they reviewed at the Dutch all-day. Tom only needed to pay cursory attention to the presentation and discussion. It was basically a radio program and Tom had the deck in front of him, knew where his parts were, the pages highlighted and crib-noted, his story ready to be told. He had ample time to focus on his spying.

About an hour into the meeting, as Dutch droned on and on about accountability and responsibility while accepting both on behalf of the team, but none personally, Tom caught a name and subject line that chilled and thrilled him. The name was one of the board members, the sender. The subject line was Armistice White Paper. It was a short note, but before Tom could shift his eyes away to avoid detection, and then back, Patton had crisply turned the page over without so much as glancing at it. He knew what it said already. Had to have read that one from his actual inbox. Just in the printed pile out of habit. Tom vaguely knew the name Armistice as a hedge fund of some kind. A white paper from an outside investor? Were they a typical activist firm? Were they about to announce a stake? Is the company in play? Look at Patton. How calm he is. Even with this. That said it all. No blood whatsoever.

A white paper was originally a British term used to describe the authoritative study of an issue, a 'deep dive' in today's consultant speak, a scholarly addition to a public discussion, a useful tool of democracy. Some department of the government, or some academic body, would study a serious societal issue and propose solutions, inviting feedback and beginning that public dialog. In the hands of the modern day robber-barons, the hedge fund managers and the activist investors, the tool had become subverted. These firms, who might get a particular idea in their head that this or that publicly traded company was mismanaging its affairs, would indeed, do a deep dive into the company's financials, and come up with solutions to its problems. They then would often take a large stake in the target company, and use the white paper as a public communication tool to other current shareholders that they all could make some money on this stock, if the damn management knew what the fuck they were doing. Tom had once read a scathing white paper published by another firm, not Armistice, about one of his suppliers. So much of it rang true, but the solutions were not bold visionary strategies to put the company on a better track. They involved draconian cost cuts and essentially giving up on growth in order to funnel cash to shareholders. The kind of strategy that eventually puts declining companies into long slow death spirals. That white paper, to Tom's mind, also took a tone, a condescending, privileged voice that basically tarred every executive at the target company as either criminally malfeasant or simply delusional. It seemed a little over the top at the time.

To Tom, this was everything that was wrong with corporate America. Companies were living things, run and populated over time by different generations of leaders and employees. The big ones employed tens of thousands of people at any one time, a population that ebbed and flowed with retirements and new recruits and resignations and outside hires. The media had painted a story of the modern workforce that said loyalty was dead, the new generations were mobile, no one expected to stay at one company longer than a few years before moving on. Tom knew it was a lie. Every month he handed out service pins at his all-hands meetings. He'd given out 30 year pins and 25 year pins and 20 year pins and 10 year pins. He'd given the little curved piece of glass etched with congratulations on the first milestone, 5 years, many times over. To those young people, those millennials, who were so mobile and disloyal. People were loyal, if you treated them right, and gave them half a chance. If you actually earned it as an employer, and even if you didn't. People still gave meaningful portions of their lives to an enterprise, working alongside others for a common cause, learning to cooperate, team up, solve problems together. All while weaving this commitment into the rest of their lives, into their families, into their communities. "What do you do for work?" "Where do you work?" "What do you do for a living?" It's a common language, a common experience, because everyone has to work, right? It's the honest way to live, to give your hours in exchange for the means to eat, to shelter, to breathe in life with some sense of security that one's labors are the means to a comfortable journey. The collective efforts of all of these people could not be summed up neatly in a white paper. Yet the papers still got written. And while the content was focused on the sins and omissions of top leadership, they still damned the entire workforce with their invective, and reduced the collective efforts of the many to a futile exercise that is simply not creating enough wealth for the owners, for the shareholders. Diminishing the meaning of all their lives, all those hours spent trying to be part of something good.

Tom understood that public companies made their little deal with the devil of the marketplace when they chose to raise money by selling shares on an open exchange and allowing buyers and sellers to establish the value of the enterprise. And he understood that investors who buy shares in a company do so with the expectation that they will get a return on their investment. They can get it through dividends or they can get it through appreciation in the share price, or both. They can compare investment in one firm to investments in others, and are free to come and go as they please. Tom understood all of that well enough. But at what point did these investors earn the right to meddle in the company's business? To call out management as inept? To force themselves onto the board? To call for layoffs? To take money from long term strategic investments and funnel it to shareholders through stock buy-backs and dividend hikes? How does someone who had no interest, no stake whatsoever, yesterday, turn overnight into a critical decision maker? How do their "rights" at that moment possibly trump the tens of thousands of accumulated years of the people who work at the company? And when they walk away six months later, cashing out their stake with a quick 20% gain, leaving the pitted out company behind, they are once again nobody. They don't matter a whit to the new shareholders, the people they found to take their stake. They don't matter a whit, any more, to the employees and the management. They no longer need to be served. They gave up their rights when they sold. They are also not held accountable for the damage done to lives, the jobs lost, the families stressed. They have executed what capitalists are allowed to execute, and therefore, it must be good.

From Tom Cooper's private journal. September 1989. Age 27. Employer 1.

The corporate empire of which I am just a small cog is crumbling under the weight of excessive debt. One man, one fucking crazy man, has affected the lives and livelihoods of tens of thousands of people. Some have already lost their jobs, others probably will. Small companies dependent on our ability to pay them for the goods we've ordered may be forced out of business. So now we're selling out our long-term success to hit an EBIT number – an acronym we never learned just 6 years ago in business school – earnings before interest and taxes. In other words, the break-even cash needed to pay the interest on the debt and still run the business, to survive another day. I now understand high leverage very well. But I don't understand how management can't see that a more long-term thinking competitor, with a better balance sheet by far, is starting to eat our lunch. They're opening locations ripe for growth and outbidding us for the spots, if we're even able to bid at all. They're outspending us on advertising, driving our margins down with lower prices, and our need for EBIT is handcuffing us. I have to face it – they're a better financed, better managed company than we are. I have a warm feeling for most of our management – they're bright, kind, well-meaning people – but they think too much, talk too much, plan too much – and they don't execute shit. Mainly because of the fucking mountain of debt. I gotta get out.

October 26, 2015

Forty-seven days after the re-org, after Patton took his little action and sliced his pinky off, leaving him only four fingers to lead the company, forcing his hand to work the same way it always had despite being now 20% out of balance, the bomb dropped. Armistice Group announced it had accumulated 5.2% of the shares, and simultaneously published a white paper, 87 pages long, detailing in scathingly accurate and graphic language, virtually everything that was wrong with the company, with the possible single exception of failing to call out the insanity of promoting Dutch Bagley just over six weeks earlier.

The opening stated the case for change: "The company is losing its customers, its relevance, and its viability." Tom supposed that was true, although as a nitpicker, he would have put those things into a progression: starting first with the loss of relevancy, leading to the loss of customers, leading to the loss of viability, because there was no business without customers. And the company had lost customers. It had struggled to find enough new ones, or new things to sell the old ones.

Then the Armistice boys got down to the business of insulting the board, Patton, and the rest of the senior leadership team. Patton has "destroyed $6.7b of value in the last seven years". The management team was responsible for "significant and disastrous strategic and executional missteps". Current leadership was "incapable of delivering the kind of radical transformation that was required to rescue the company from its eventual demise" The company's "lagging margin productivity, combined with a non-scalable, negligently overspent infrastructure base, has resulted in consistently inferior financial performance". "Headcount is bloated". "Poorly thought out distribution network". "Failed to move deeply and fast enough on operating expense". "Current strategy has low likelihood of success".

The Armistice solution was then laid out in similarly graphic detail. Tom read the same words over and over and over again. "Streamline". "Consolidate" "Rationalize". "Optimize". "Reduce". "Eliminate". "Realign". "Restructure". So many negative verbs. All in the left hand column of virtually every slide in the presentation. But put them all together and they somehow lead to a positive outcome, driven by the right column verbs. "Develop". "Improve". "Increase". "Prioritize". "Drive". "Standardize" "Deliver". It all sounded so plausible. Any outsider looking in, and reading the publicly available information, might assume this was a slam-dunk opportunity. There was so much fucking wrong with this company, how could someone else possibly do worse given a chance to run it? And the solutions weren't game breaking. They all made sense. So much sense in fact, that the company already had most of them on its agenda. The entire document needed a "No Shit Sherlock" soundtrack to accompany the exhaustive read. If it was so fucking easy, don't you think we would have done it by now? Impossible to believe, but Armistice had Tom at the brink of defending Patton and Dutch and the board. The last recession was a fucking killer. It was all we could do to survive. Then the world changed, and we get it, we're working on it. We're a big fucking company. We can't turn on a dime. True, true, true, true, true. Excuse, excuse, excuse, excuse, excuse. Armistice was mostly saying what Tom was thinking. He knew it. And the change junkie in him began to sniff a riot of scents on the wind. The company was in play now. Vultures would circle, Patton would be distracted. The shit show would get worse. And shit would happen fast. "Urgent" was the other word used frequently in the paper. An urgent plan was needed. The company had to execute with urgency. The situation called for urgent action. And then came another torrent of verbs, all part of the urgent plan to move forward urgently: "Implement". "Create". "Design". "Deploy". "Develop". "Capture".

Tom wondered who they thought would do all of that creating and designing and developing and deploying after all of that cutting and optimizing and reducing and rationalizing was done. There were all sorts of good ideas, worthy goals, and possibilities with the right focus and leadership. And they tried to make it sound realistic, but the longer Tom read, the more it dawned on him what he was reading. Armistice's grand 100 day plan for his company was just an intellectual exercise. There was absolutely no way anyone was ever going to come close to implementing this plan. It was designed simply to signal to other shareholders that Armistice was smart as fuck and had done their homework. They had to be right, they had to be trusted. They knew the extent to which current leadership had failed, and they clearly knew what new leadership could do to deliver better value for shareholders. It was designed simply to put the company in play, to get other investors frothing at the mouth for the board and management to make changes, to do something, to make their stock price go up. Even if those changes wouldn't be the changes Armistice had laid out. Even if they did none of the glorious, magical things for the company's future Armistice suggested could be done. Whether Patton stayed and presided over more expense reduction and more cash to shareholders, or the board made a leadership change, or the company got acquired, or merged, or taken private, all of which had been rumored already, it wouldn't matter. As long as whatever happened made the stock go up by a factor of at least 20%, the aim will have been achieved. Armistice would take its quick profits and move on. And life in Hell, Inc. would go back to normal. Back to cluster-fuck city. That was right, wasn't it? Tom was right, wasn't he? Armistice wasn't asking for seats on the board, they weren't specifically calling for Patton's head. So this was just a signal. A kick-off. Put the ball in the air, see what happens. Armistice had just fired the starting gun The race to turn rumor into reality had begun.

Tom read the paper in skim, pause, dive in if interesting fashion on his phone sitting in the back of a 90 minute data dump meeting, then went back to his desk, creating his immediate to-do list in his head while he walked. First, he needed to do an accounting of his current internal standing. Who would support him, who would turn him into chum? Who mattered, or who would matter, if someone else was in here, kicking the tires, looking to buy? What would HR say about him? What's the official document record say about his performance? All those worthless reviews, ever more sparsely written, thumbs up or thumbs down, would they count for anything? Then, he needed to work the numbers again. What if the stock did get a 20% bump? What if something actually happened before the end of the year? It was late October. Fiscal year ended in March.. Tom would qualify for a couple bonuses, short of target though they were likely to be, they were still not chicken feed, so there'd be that to calculate again, make his guesses, usually accurate, as to where the payout would land. And then the restricted stock, the grants, the options. Check all the vesting dates, get out the little crib sheets from the bottom desk drawer. Check all those what-if's again, if he made it to April 1 , to the next big vesting date, if he kept all his current shares, if the stock hit 22, 24, 26. He would dream briefly about a bidding war for the company that somehow pushed the number to 32. Oh, 32 would be something. That would put long dead options back into play. Thousands and thousands of options. He'd work those numbers, just to dream for a moment, because it would definitely put him over the top, let him jump, let him figure out what would come next, let him breathe, let him rebuild, let him be.

Next, Tom would have to do some research. Who are the Armistice boys? What's their history? What's their typical progression? Wins and losses? Who have they tussled with in the past? Who else might come in if they're in the water at 5.2%? Anyone who goes above 5 has to show their head and call out their name. Marco? Polo! Tom knew who Marco was now, but who might Polo be? He needed to read what the pundits were saying, and also the nitwits. The Motley Fool, and the motley fools would all weigh in. Tom would study it all. He'd do it fast, right now, this afternoon, checking his phone as his pace quickened to get back to his office, he saw an hour blocked for the lunch he ate in 15 minutes sitting at his desk, a half-hour buffer after that which never got filled, and then a 1:30 call he could listen to on mute while he worked his list, and then a 2:00 he could bail on. That would be enough time. Tom felt a surge of excitement and a sense of purpose he hadn't felt in a long while, not for a great idea that would drive the business, not for a well-thought out strategy, not for anything related to the company's success. It was the immediacy of change that was more interesting than the change he was already in large matter rejecting. It was a belief that somehow he would make this good for himself and his family. He would be ridding himself of some demons soon, shaking off doom, regaining his balance. The adrenaline of positive energy turned his thoughts to the last item on his list, his team, his direct reports, the impact on them. Who did he need to teach survival to? Who would need some information from him to work the best plan for themselves? Who could he trust implicitly with any information that Tom should not, in normal course of business, be disclosing to them? A lot to think about, a lot to do.

From Tom Cooper's private journal. May 2004. Age 43.
Employer 4.

I thought nothing could be more mainstream than working for a big corporation in America, but I've become convinced that I'm involved in something far from it – in fact, I believe I'm trapped in a dangerous cult. Our supreme leader, the CEO, an alpha male, earns the lion's share of the profits of the cult, and holds the fate of all the rest of us in his hands. He does not serve as our elected servant, as our governmental leaders do. He is not beholden to our welfare, but rather to a shadowy Board of Directors, who represent the shareholders, an unseen group of owners who are primarily institutional investors. The CEO is supported by a select team of executives, usually ten to twelve (modeled on the Disciples?), and the bunch of them work clustered together in a specific location within corporate headquarters, usually the top floor. six in my case.

Location and office size play a big role in the cult. Up on six, there's upholstered furniture, big windows, nice views. Vice-presidents are scattered through the building but identifiable by their standardized spaces – cubicle walls that extend to the ceiling, a door that locks. As a Director, I get an oversized cubicle without walls to the ceiling or a door, large enough to squeeze in a conference table for four. Everyone else in the building has a cubicle just large enough to comfortably get work done, but small enough to make you understand you are nothing but a small cog in a giant wheel, and are not allowed to carry on a private phone conversation without being overheard by several co-workers. We know where we stand in the cult, not only by our titles, but by how much air we are given to breathe.

Like all cults, we have insidious ways to control the lives of our members. As you move up in the hierarchy, the more beholden you become to the senior leaders. Your loyalty is purchased with raises and longer-term incentive plans, and the more of it you get, the harder you are pressured to work. There is even a paraphrasing of the Bible used in my cult, "To whom much is given, much is expected," to drive home the point. Long hours of work and a devotion to the cause are clearly hallmarks of those who ascend to the inner circle. In fact, our CEO himself once responded to anonymous internal criticism of his outsized pay package by saying, "I have a substantial job and am rewarded accordingly." Inner sanctum level leaders, let's call them VP's, are also controlled through non-compete contracts that clearly feel un-American, but have held up in court under contract law. I'm not sure I understand how a free man could be prevented from working at what he's best at in this country for a whole year, but I suppose if one does not want that restriction, one does not have to sign the contract. Of course, after all those years in the cult, striving for the rewards that accrue to those VP's and above, it would be so hard to walk away over a silly little thing like indentured servitude, particularly since at that moment, you are being promoted and are not thinking about how unhappy you might be with the cult's direction someday.

And then there is the real scaling in corporate cults – the opportunity for ownership – stock options, restricted stock grants. Outright equity grants. These "buy-in" wealth builders really lock in cult membership for the elite, turning foot soldiers into multi-millionaires and sometimes billionaires, if they manage to become Cult Executive Officer. Think about that....the rewards for stock performance go disproportionately to the highest levels of leadership...and if the stock price goes up when expenses are cut, isn't that a sweet deal for leadership? When the CEO stands up and shouts, "We need to cut head count by 10%!" the rest of senior leadership might initially have misgivings about the impact on the remaining cult members, but are so handsomely rewarded when the stock reacts positively, they keep their mouths shut and cash the checks.

So, there I was, thinking nothing was more mainstream than navigating a career to the top in corporate America, a fine upstanding citizen in the land of the free, where all men are created equal. And here I am now, two-thirds of the way up the ladder, and there is neither freedom nor equality in the thing that is central to my life – the company/cult I work for. My fate is more directly in the hands of my immediate boss and my CEO than any government leader. I can achieve none of the financial goals I've set and the life experience I want to buy without their help. I serve as a director only by the good graces of the VP I report to. The higher education I want to provide for my kids, the comfortable retirement for my wife and me, are strongly predicated on how well the CEO steers this ship. I am in constant competition with other directors, as we race around the building playing beat the clock to get to our next meetings, currying favor with the higher-ups, trying desperately just to survive, while giving the appearance that what we really are doing is making the corporation better. I spend far more of my waking hours with these cult members than I do with my family.

No, this cannot be the American mainstream. It's just another splinter group, corporate America. A small slice of the population that works for the biggest 1,000 companies or so who choose to live this unnatural life, who get trapped by the trappings and can't escape its unnatural grip. I fully admit I'm addicted to the financial rewards, and they do give me three weeks of paid vacation to recover from my wounds and spend time with my family....so I stay. But I can't believe THIS is my center of gravity.

October 27, 2015

The good-guy, bad-guy list. It had to start there. Tom had to
determine two things, in his mind, two things immediately.
The first was whether the change that would come could
possibly be good for him, and in what way? If new owners
came in, if they went private, who would the buyers keep?
Who would they torch? How would that list match up to
Tom's good-guy, bad-guy card? What if they got rid of most
of the bad guys and some of the good guys got bigger jobs?
Could Tom re-energize? Could he be part of the solution, an
historic comeback, a big team win? Could he reap a big
financial score, work five to ten more years and be set for life?
That did sound appealing. The set for life part, at least. Or
maybe it would be good for him in other ways, a short-term
stock bump, maybe a generous change of control severance
package.

The second determination was the reverse. What if the
bad guys won? What if nobody came in and took the
company? What if the board and Patton gave up on everything
and just cranked out shareholder value? Every dime of profit,
paid out in dividends or used to buy back shares. Not a single
investment in growth, not a penny. And as the top line
contracted, shrunk, withered, so too would the expense base,
the resources to even run the business, the human resources
that would slowly be squeezed out, like the last sticky lumps

of ketchup in a bottle on the way to the trash. How could Tom's life get worse? That's how. What would he do if faced with that? The numbers, running those share price what-if's, that would tell him the risk, the downside, but that was just the money end. He knew he had other issues, nagging issues.

And outsiders? Couldn't there be outsiders that were even worse than Patton and the rest of the bad guys on his list? They could cut even deeper or faster. But then again, there was that change of control opportunity, that chance the new bad guys would be perfectly happy to send high-priced talent like Tom packing, even if it did cost them a little package. Packing, package, get it? A pun chuckle, and then Tom's brain moved on. The new bad guys could change Tom's title, diminish it, diminish him. And he could exercise his own rights under change of control, decide the new role wasn't enough, and take the severance and go. Then again, just like the current crop, they could see Tom's value, his necessity, and keep him plugged into the machine, give him no choice, keep him whole, give no legal reason he could grab that severance and run. The sorting of the key people in Tom's life into buckets, the people in his corporate life, the people whose titles and names Michelle could barely keep straight, despite the overwhelming and out of proportion influence they played in her husband's life, was only the start. Next he needed to learn about the outsiders, the Armistice guys, the rumored hedge fund circlers, the potential PE buyers, the long-shot acquirers. Tom would be prepared for whatever came, and as he crossed his office threshold he felt again the little buzz of aniticipation that comes with the potential for real change in his life.

The first name on the bad guy list had to be Patton. Tom did not have the same personal animosity for Patton that he did for Dutch Bagley, number two on his list with a bullet. But Patton was his tormentor deep inside, so surgically and methodically logical, so relentless in the pursuit of profit, so capable of damning Tom when he dared propose an idea that was about the long term at the expense of the short.. Patton just didn't have the imagination to grow the company out of the mess they were in, and Tom was sure he needed to go. Plus, Tom always felt Patton could care less whether Tom was there or not. As if every year, he had to be grudgingly convinced Tom was a keeper and not a blocker. That he Got Shit Done.

And then Dutch of course. Surely any change of control would have to expose him, wouldn't it? Dutch's influence on Tom's daily state of mind had metastasized into a tumor that was pressing on a nerve. The thought of him, the mere image of his personage in Tom's mind, was like a searing white bolt of pain. He knew the hatred wasn't healthy, born as it was in particular, at work, between the lines, where emotions get left at the door. Where all should be calm and cool. Professional. But Dutch fucked right through all of that. He was a force like no other Tom had encountered. The thought of him not only conjured up the damned range of dismissive facial expressions, the persistent verbal abuse, the irrationality. It extended to the other things Tom had noticed: the way Dutch lit up around attractive women, particularly younger ones, the way he winked and nodded at his boys, the fans he still had, the executives on his team he'd worked with forever, when they were all young, before Dutch's inexplicable ascension. The way he established an inner club that way, and not so subtly let you know you weren't in it. Tom could get lost in his loathing of Dutch. It was like binging on potato chips, reaching into the bag for another handful even as you consciously begin to hate yourself for your inability to resist. Dutch had to go or Tom knew he would have to go.

Perry Chin was the last bad guy of any consequence, Tom decided. EVP of HR the last three years. New to the company then. A cost-cutter HR guy, not a talent-builder HR guy. He was great at turning the screws on health insurance costs, taking something away every year that you got for free and making you earn it back with health assessments and cholesterol screenings and gym memberships. He was up to speed on all the latest outsourcing tactics, like having phone banks in India schedule appointments for interviews to fill open jobs, so admins in America could be fired. Patton loved him. Tom always thought the chief HR person in a company should be a champion for people, not a cost-cutting practitioner. He thought they should be warm personally, not unemotional and unapologetic about decisions that had a real impact on people. Perry Chin was a perfect complement to any CEO, the owner of a relentless, rational drive to reduce the resources part of human resources, year over year, with whatever evil creativity that took. And Tom simply could not read what Perry thought of him. Where was he getting his feedback? From the other bad guys, or the good guys, or a healthy mix of both?

The good guy list had to start with Mike Moran. He had recently turned 60, had been a C-suite guy for all of his fifties, but was not going to get the top job here, nor likely anywhere else. While he looked and talked like a CEO out of central casting, and he'd had an accomplished career, there was something missing. Or rather, there were two things that were not missing - humanity and humility - from his personal make-up, and in Tom's experience, it was the absence of those qualities, not their presence, that stamped an executive as CEO material. Tom liked Mike, had worked in his organization before this last restructuring, and felt confident that Mike thought well of him. He seemed to appreciate Tom's best skills – careful analysis, solid decision-making, getting shit done. He saw Tom's value in the reorg, and even though it was never expressed to him, Tom believed Mike had been the one that said from the start that Tom had to stay, had to be brought into the fold on the restructuring, had to have a role when it was done. Tom just wasn't sure he should be thankful for that. Was it just a prolonging of the inevitable, an extension of the torture? Surely, Mike Moran could not know that Tom might actually have preferred a package. At age 54? Why would he possibly want a package at that age? It surely wouldn't be enough. Mike Moran, good guy indeed, well-intentioned always.

Tom had to believe Stover was a good guy too. He still couldn't quite put his finger on why. He'd certainly said he had Tom's back when it was just the two of them in a room. He'd admitted his mutual loathing of Dutch, and therefore was certainly more ally than enemy, but there was still something disquieting about Stover. It was that whiff of CEO madness, that occasional irrational level of expectations, that gave Tom pause. Stover still dreamed of the CEO job, still coveted the bling, still wanted the shiny toy. And if those guys got the toy, uh-oh, things could change in a hurry. Those things said behind closed doors could be expunged from history, disavowed. But Stover was not going to get that CEO chance here, Tom was pretty certain of that. So, given his support of Tom, he made the good guy list, since there was really nothing he'd done to deserve bad-guy status, and there was no middle ground.

Tom was close to the end. While there were a host of peer-types and some other senior level people on the org chart, the people whose own fates could directly impact Tom's were just about covered. Thinking longer term and a little out of the box, he would throw one more name up for consideration, the CFO, a ridiculously smart woman ironically named Brenda Wise. She was a dark horse CEO candidate, seemingly groomed for the job since birth: private high school, Ivy League undergrad, a CPA, an MBA, stints in international, human resources, and now the CFO. Her CV read like a passport stamped with all the best travel spots in the world, identifying her as someone special, someone worthy of being asked to visit all those places. Tom had happened to choose Brenda's hometown when he moved his family to come to the company, and as it so happened, Tom's younger child and Brenda's oldest attended high school together, and the two girls wound up co-chairs of the school's improvisational troupe. Watching 17 year old high school girls do improv can be an excruciating experience. Without a script, their truths slip out too fast to contain, and what they know, or think they know already about life is terrifying to discover. Tom and Brenda shared that for a year, and it had created a little anchor for their relationship. They had sat in a smallish semicircle of chairs with the other parents and winced and shot glances at each other and commiserated good-naturedly afterwards. Tom liked Brenda. Even though she was drenched in that CEO potential, there was something different about how she wore it. She had been charitable to Tom in his role, perhaps owing to their shared experience, their shared apprehension of raising daughters in a world that still was a hard place for young women who speak freely and honestly. Tom chuckled at the continued dominance of male pronouns in their language. Yes, Brenda was a good guy, only because calling her a good girl sounded sexist and calling her a good woman sounded condescending, and probably also sexist.

Tom had worked for female bosses along the way, good and bad, just like male bosses. In fact, one of those female bosses had been a very significant influence on his life and career for which he'd been forever grateful. But in 32 years in Corporate America, at six stops, he had never worked for a company with a female CEO, few and far between as they were. He wondered if it was possible that the whole thing would be different, the whole experience of corporate life, shit, the whole way capitalism worked, if it was more commonly women who were in charge. Women who understood there was more to life than competition and making the quarterly earnings number. Women, who like Jim Morrison sang in Riders on the Storm, were the ones upon whom the world depends. The men? All most of them gave a shit about was winning, dominating, crushing. Of course the male CEOs preferred a scorecard marked with dollar signs and return on investment. Tom looked at his list of scribbled names. Dick-head men in the "bad guy" column. Reasonable men and a woman in the "good guy" list. Was the entire world as simple as that? It was a casual thought, and Tom could see it race down a philosophical track that he just didn't have time for right now. He didn't have time to dig for that meaning, not when his world was out of balance, when change was thick on the wind. He smirked at the thought that the fucking Armistice guys were literally 100% guys, and come to think of it, every other hedge fund runner or big name activist he could think of was a guy too. He had to keep his own guy thing going, his survival skills, his cool, his cynicism. He had to be sharp and alert and ready to fight. He was in a shit storm, and now more shit was in the forecast.

November 10, 2015

The publishing of the white paper cast a pall over the entire headquarters building. It was like a vacuum cleaner hose was pushed through a window, and all the energy was sucked out. Energy that was created by thousands of people rubbing up against each other, trying to get their jobs done, working for a cause. Buildings don't have their own energy, it's the people in them that do, and the white paper just obliterated all those individual energy fields like a smart bomb. There was now a collective clarity that the future was completely uncertain. Now everyone knew, not just the insiders, not just the cynics. The company was going to change, one way or another.

After the energy was gone, an eerie calm set in. Patton had said nothing about the paper internally, or about the new shareholder's stake. He had not held a senior leadership meeting where he would certainly be asked those questions. Stover had not addressed it with his broader team, and all he'd really said to his direct reports was, "Well, I'm sure we've all been here before, right? Let's stay focused." Tom talked about it to his direct reports just once, right after it broke. He told them the truth – that there was nothing Tom could tell them that would be anything more than just his opinion, and that this was not a time for them to be presented with opinions – they should form their own. Tom gave them the advice he knew he had to, the same advice Stover had given Tom and his peers –

stay focused on your work, do a great job, take care of your people, things will sort themselves out. It seemed that indeed, this was the desired message across the company. As that foggy calm settled in, people had gone right back to doing what they do, coming to work and trying to execute what they understood their jobs to be. The only thing missing was the energy. And even though Tom's messaging was consistent with others, and he knew it was the right messaging, there was something disquieting about the way people could just carry on doing what they always do. Because there was a fucking storm, and people were going to lose jobs, and shit could come completely apart any day, and with all that, how could these people keep showing up at meetings, acting like it still meant something? Yes, they did it without the normal energy, but they still did it. WHY? What was the point? Survival? Of course it was survival. That was all it was, and Tom knew that, heck he coached to it and lived it. Why was it bothering him to see others doing it? This was their way, just like after the reorg. The same behavior that drove Tom to distraction during his Stamp Out Stupidity Campaign. The relentless need to stick to routine, to be comforted by routine. It was the way of most people who know instinctively that when it comes to work, they are not in control of their own destiny. The big bosses determine everything. The big bosses were in a fight for their lives. Time to keep heads down, bask in routine, and wait to see what happens. Wait to see if a new set of big bosses will be in charge, or if they'd be stuck with the old.

November 26, 2015

It was a mild Thanksgiving day, so warm that by mid-morning Tom could go outside with the thick newspaper that had come this day rather than Sunday so that the wheels of Capitalism could begin turning at warp speed as soon as the Thanksgiving meals of 110 million households were finished and the Black Friday shopping madness could begin. It used to be that the big retailers waited until early on Friday morning to force customers to stand in line for their best deals. Now the ads were screaming about midnight openings and one or two even boasted about violating the sacred Thanksgiving celebration itself. The message was clear – if you want to save the most money in our stores, you must abandon your families or your sanity or both. Tom could imagine how hard Jeff Bezos must be laughing, offering to treat customers with respect by delivering the best prices on things directly to people's doors and just waiting for Capitalism to catch up and wipe out all the dumbasses that ginned up these ads. Shit, even on a day that was a gift from nature, on what was always his favorite holiday, Tom could not evade the stench of greed and stupidity.

Sometimes Tom wondered why he didn't enjoy his own home the way he enjoyed his in-law's cottage at the beach. It was a lovely home, his home, and this past summer Michelle had expanded the scope of a deck project to include a new lower patio as well, upon which she set a foursome of

Adirondack chairs that Frontgate had artificially aged to look like the ones at his in-laws' that had weathered naturally over time. If they were on vacation at the beach, and Tom was up before the house, as he always was, he'd be sitting in one of those Adirondacks enjoying the feeling of being outside, the eerie calm of the morning, the shorebirds performing their inscrutable chores. Why couldn't he do the same here? Was the beach house a paradise that only existed in the future, and his own home a prison of the present? His house here in the suburbs backed up to a large undeveloped tract, and his backyard was ringed with pines that kept it private even in the late fall. It was certainly a sanctuary in that regard, just like the beach house, and it was his, available to him throughout the year, just steps from his bedroom.

So Tom had looked out the window this day, had felt the out-of-season warmth in the air when he fetched the paper from the driveway, and decided he would go out there and sit in one of those faux-weathered Frontgate Adirondack chairs and try to relax. The sorting of the editorial content from the ads had pricked a hole in his hoped-for serenity, so Tom dug into the sports page and tried to lose himself in the meaningless march of another group of young men through his consciousness, putting up their statistics, becoming part of history, earning a shit load of money. Money. Always money. The word his mind could never escape. Within seconds, Tom realized why this was not just like the beach. While the pine boughs were slowly shaking their needles in a gentle unfelt breeze, and the sun was starting to tickle them from behind the house as it rose, and the air was warm and sweet-smelling of pine sap, there was something missing. Silence. Instead, the dull roar/white noise of the highway beyond the trees destroyed the illusion that this was a sanctuary. Just like the looming pain of another Monday in corporate hell intruded upon every weekend, every holiday, taking what should otherwise be an opportunity to enjoy life to the fullest and injecting it with a heavy dose of dread. Tom could taste what the morning would feel like without that highway noise, and without that Monday dread. And he wanted so badly to taste it soon.

December 4, 2015

Sometimes it's a good thing if your boss trusts you enough to share things that might be shocking revelations to others, and sometimes it just means you're able to see your own future all too clearly as a result. Mark Stover had been very open since bringing Tom back into the integrated organization, that he had no idea how to work productively with Dutch Bagley. In Mark's own words, the man "was a buffoon, a blowhard, so over his head in his role it's painful to watch", opinions that validated Tom's own angry view of Dutch. Nonetheless, hearing the person who is supposed to be the buffer between you and a leader you can't stand to be around admit that he's no shield at all, but a commiserating peer is a little sobering. Tom had carried the verbatims of their various conversations on the subject around with him as a reminder that there was both hope and danger in Stover, and to proceed accordingly. Which for Tom was to support him both publicly and privately, but to be hyper alert to who might have Stover's back if he broke and went toe to toe with Dutch. Did Patton support him? Moran? When the board approved his pay package did they see him as part of a long-term succession plan? Or could Dutch simply torch Stover at will? Not that it would ever go down like that. No. Tom always wanted to see endings with spectacular drama, envisioned his end as such all the time…but he was almost always disappointed.

And so it was with Stover. His boss, his buffer, his closed door confidant, had abruptly resigned yesterday, and today he was gone from the building forever. While Tom's peers speculated about whether the boss was really leaving on his own accord or was being pushed out, Tom faded out of the conversation because he clearly knew the answer. Like a ganglord in a turf war who knows his muscle just got taken out, he also knew that soon, very soon, someone could come looking for him. And he knew who that someone was.

Since there was no successor named immediately, there were a few people wondering if Tom would get the role, or wishing he would, but while he appreciated their kind interest, he knew there wasn't a chance in hell. On the surface, Tom looked to be a natural candidate, he understood that, but as long as Dutch had him in his crosshairs, he wasn't going anywhere but away. How ironic. A man Tom believed emblematic of the Peter Principle in full fury was still there, capable of ending it for Tom in a heartbeat – a man already beyond the level of his own incompetence could be telling Tom he was at the level of his. If this is the way it all ends, Tom thought, how appropriately absurd.

December 11, 2015

Two weeks before Christmas, the white paper silence was broken, and with it, the company's water was broken as well. Reuters released a story that Patton had worked out a deal to sell a 22% stake in the company to Armistice, and the board was going to expand by three seats, all of them going to candidates chosen by Armistice. The stock was up another 6% in pre-market trading, and by 7:30 am there was an email scheduling a directors and up meeting in the auditorium at 9:00. As people filtered into work there was more buzz in the building than there'd been in a long time. Tom could feel the pulse pounding ever louder as more folks arrived for the day. As usual, he'd been in since the crack of dawn, and he'd been busy. It was time to get serious about Armistice. Just exactly who the fuck were these guys?

It turns out Armistice was really just one guy, although fuck, Tom thought, the one guy was basically Batman. In fact, the New York Post called him just that fifteen years ago, the first time anyone heard of Billy Baron. They called him Billy Batman because of an incident that took place outside a nightclub in Manhattan. Baron was a young hedge fund manager at the time, not even out of his twenties, but already running his own shop. As he recalled it in an interview a year later, for a 'ones to watch' story in Forbes, he had stepped out of the club to get some fresh air when he saw a man trying to get a woman to get into a car, holding her roughly by one arm. Baron approached the man and had barely begun to get a word out of his mouth before the man turned to him and took a swing. What then ensued is that Billy Baron employed 16 years of martial arts training that started when he was a pre-teen for the first time in a real-world violent encounter. By the time it was over, two other men had emerged from the car and felt the fury of Billy Batman's black-belt-certified hands and feet. According to an eye witness, Baron "kicked the first guy in the chest, knocked him into the side of the car, then the two other guys get out, and this guy goes just psycho on their asses, like serious Ninja shit. One guy, he tries to get out of the back seat and the dude kicks the door into his face, hard. And the guy that's coming from around the car, he's a big fucking dude, but this guy does that karate chop shit and just opens up his face, man. And the girl, she bolted, and then the cops were there and it was over. Over in like seconds man."

Tom wondered how the hell he'd missed the story, or why he hadn't heard of the guy at all, but then again, fifteen years ago he was with another company fighting for its life and he had a family to raise, and so for the most part, it was head down, plow ahead. And then there was the fact that after the Forbes article, Billy Baron hadn't given an interview since. He'd gone completely secretive, holing up in a modest office in New Jersey with about a dozen employees, and focusing on building his hedge fund business. Tom could find only a few references to Armistice in connection with other special situations in the market. Their required statement of holdings at the end of the previous quarter revealed a fairly tight portfolio, including a couple of companies in similar industries to Tom's. They had not previously, to this point, released a white paper or acted in a hostile manner in acquiring their stakes, but with some further digging, Tom could see that firms in which they'd invested had soon after made draconian cuts in headcount, usually very soon after Armistices' involvement. That was as far as he got before he needed to leave for the auditorium.

Though the headquarters building employed over 3,000 people, the auditorium held only 300, or about twice what was needed these days to host a directors and up only meeting, so the partition walls at the back were employed to force everyone forward into cozy rows, shoulder to shoulder, comrades in arms, sweaty competitors, guarded, wary, chatty, buzzing. Tom found his way near the front; it was expected of him as a senior vice president to be in one of the first two rows. He found an aisle seat, as close to an exit as possible. At the front of the amphitheater-style room were four embarrassingly dated chairs that may once have seemed modern, back when they were on the set of the Mike Douglas Show. Milling around, waiting to take those seats, were Caleb Patton, Dutch Bagley, Mike Moran, and Brenda Wise. The CEO, the Head of the Americas, the Vice-Chairman, and the CFO, respectively. There they were, two of the bad guys and two of the good guys, still together, still on top of this simmering mess. They were smiling and joking, or so it seemed. They definitely seemed looser than they had in months. Good Dutch appeared to be present. To Tom, it looked like he was flirting with the communications manager who was trying to get a volume check in her headset while graciously listening to Dutch pedaling his charm. Tom could feel the saliva in the back of his mouth warm slightly, and he could feel his brow furrow reflexively. God, he hated that man.

At exactly one minute to nine, the four leaders took their seats, their lapel microphones in place, and Patton touched his right finger to his right ear, his not-so-subtle signal that it was time to start, right on time, and it was time for the room to listen, while he spoke.

"Good morning. I have to say, this morning feels a little different in the building. I know you've all read the news, and you've seen the stock in pre-market trading – what is it now, Brenda?"

"$19.50".

"$19.50? Not bad, not bad, right? I will tell you, right about now I am in full gloat. You saw a lot of press come out a few weeks ago that was not very complimentary about this company. About this company's leadership, our future, our strategy. Well this morning, I'm pleased to announce a major vote of confidence in our plan, in you as a team, in our company and all of our associates. Armistice is taking a significant stake in this company because they know what we know, that there is a lot of unlocked potential here. And you can see by the reaction in the market, that other investors agree."

The taste of this bullshit was so vile, Tom felt like he might actually throw up. Full gloat?? All that shitty press that came out was basically quoting the fucking Armistice white paper! You figure out how to give them more than 20% of the company, three board seats, and suddenly, it's a vote of confidence in your plan? You had no fucking plan! You had the remnants of seven failed consulting projects leaning up against each other like a makeshift shelter in a hurricane. The fucking stock is up because other investors figure it won't be long before Armistice looks to take the whole thing private.

And they're voting for the Armistice plan that was in the white paper, the one with all the cutting and dicing and chopping and slicing, dressed up as transforming, streamlining, optimizing, and repositioning. Patton continued.

"With this investment from Armistice, we get continuity. The four of us sitting here are still running this company. I've had several long meetings with Billy Baron, the principal shareholder in Armistice, over the last several weeks, including many well before the white paper was published, and I'll share more about that in a minute. I told him what I've told you. I'm done cutting this company down. I want to grow again. I don't want to milk the company for profit. Armistice has patience, and more importantly, they have some experience with other companies similar to ours that they've invested in. They're going to help us in a lot of ways. We're still a public company, but with a far greater concentration of shares with one investor. I will continue to be the CEO of the company, and I'm pleased that Mike and Dutch and Brenda are all continuing in their current roles.

Tom was processing fast. Several options that were once possible seemed to have narrowed. There was possibly still a chance that another stab at the jugular vein of company leadership would force him out, a spurt of blood he could sit his ass on top of and ride right out, with a decent severance package. But that might be as good as it gets. And the chance seemed slim. Since the same group was still sitting right there in front of him, what would really change about the need to keep Tom in place that drove his role in the reorg? Dutch would still hate him but grudgingly tolerate his staying because Moran knew his value. Patton would continue to accept, if not completely respect him. He'd have to stay and preside over further cutting of his team, continue to be made to do more with less, and as a prize, get introduced to a new set of assholes, probably tipping the balance of power above way over to the bad guy side. Tom looked around the auditorium. How were other people enjoying their manure breakfast? There were faces looking forward, heads up instead of staring down at laps or phones or some scuff mark on a shoe. There were smiles. There seemed to be relief. Most people didn't like to see a ton of change all at once. The company was not being sold. It wasn't being merged. There apparently was no housecleaning at the top. For good or evil, this was still the team. And the stock! The stock was up! Didn't they know why? Hadn't anyone but him read about Armistice? Whoosh, whoosh, here comes the blade again, and some of your forward facing heads and slightly upturned chins are going to make it a swift and easy swipe for the executioner's sword that will once again be unsheathed. Fuck, Tom thought, with a heavy heart, as Patton droned on about the current plan and why having Armistice aboard would only make it easier to execute that plan. Fuckfuckfuckfuckfuck. The truth was supposed to be liberating, but for Tom, in corporate life anyway, the ability to see the truth was oppressive.

"I think you'll find Billy Baron to be a pretty fascinating guy, and I do expect that many of you will have a chance to meet him." Tom snapped out of his reverie of misery as Patton began to talk about the new sheriff in town. "Billy and I spoke at length about his process when his firm takes a stake like this in a company, and one of the things he likes to do is meet with small groups from around the company, to get a full cross-section of perspectives. I think we're all going to learn to think a little differently with

Armistice and Billy on board. He has some refreshingly original views on what it takes to be successful in any business."

Tom's mind raced over the hundreds of words he'd read about Billy Baron's investment choices in his morning research and he struggled to find what was so original about "unlocking value" in maturing, more traditional businesses, which was just his buzz word for lopping off heads. Since the dawn of time, men with power have tried to get other men to work as hard as they must for as little as they can. Slavery, indentured servitude, forced labor, threats of starvation, subsistence wages. To some degree, all somehow still existed somewhere in the world, even today. But here in America, here in her corporate heart, it had fancier names. Here we pay wages, provide benefits, and obey laws. But it still comes down to people, and how few of them you could possibly employ, at the lowest possible cost, and still execute the primary business of the organization. So what was Billy Baron's big contribution to the world? Describing the oldest power play on the planet in a nifty catch phrase, 'unlocking value'? Fucking spare me, Tom thought. And then he laughed inside at the unfortunate pun. No, don't spare me! Fire me, lay me off, downsize me, rationalize me out, package me, make me a casualty!

"Let me say a few words about the white paper Armistice published a few weeks ago. This is opening up the kimono a little bit on how deals like we've announced this morning sometimes work. I'm sure many of you read that paper and the suggestions" (small cough) "for the leadership of this company." Patton paused and let a tiny grin crease his face, trying his best to look mischievous. "And I'm sure many of you recognized most of those suggestions as currently in our plans, and perhaps thought, like I did, pardon my expression, but 'no shit, Sherlock'. Well, there was a reason their white paper looks a lot like our plan – we've been talking to them for months about a partnership. They released the white paper because negotiations were stalled on board seats and such. Was I completely happy about it? Not at the time. But this morning, I'm pleased to say that we have the deal we wanted all along, and a great new partner. At this time, I'd like to open it up for questions. I've never known this to be a shy group, but as we have in the past, we're going to give you five minutes to write down a question on the index cards we handed out when you came in, and if you would pass them to the end of your row as you finish, the communications team will start to collect them and see if there are some common themes we can answer for you".

Tom didn't know if it was his age, his experience, an unfortunate natural gift, or the insidious infection of CEO-madness in his brain, but he had the ability to see everything all too clearly, to understand the base, deepest meaning instantly, to smell corporate bullshit before it's even had a chance to leave the asshole it's coming out of. The idea that Patton had sold Armistice on his vision for the company, only to have them put it into more scathing terms and use it as a negotiating lever was absurd. Armistice had publicly whacked him with a two-by-four, and Patton had spent the last three weeks furiously fighting for his life as CEO, trying to avoid the next blow, which would undoubtedly have been a threat to set up a proxy battle with other large shareholders to force Patton out. There were lots of details undisclosed in the press release, and Patton had not addressed them either. First and foremost among them – while still CEO, was Patton still chairman of the board of directors? Would the board stay at the expanded level, or would some of the old guard be forced out, the complicit ones, the thumb-twiddlers collecting their shares and flying in first class to rubber stamp Patton's endless missteps and his hundred and thirty million dollars of compensation over the course of his largely unsuccessful tenure? Now that he'd saved his skin, would Patton quickly do whatever it took to make Billy Baron happy? More cuts? How would you like yours served? With a cold cup of comfort, or straight-up mean?

Tom looked around at his coworkers, many of them jotting down a question on the index cards that had made their way down the row. People would ask the questions Tom already knew the answers to. Patton was half right when he said this wasn't a shy group. When given an opportunity to be anonymous, they weren't shy. Before the index cards, people only asked softball questions at these meetings. Then they complained in anonymous surveys that the company culture didn't always support open and honest communication. So now, they got to ask questions anonymously. Like medicine, it always seems to be about treating the symptoms rather than the causes. It's harder to get to the cause, to the meaning, so treat the outcome instead.

Tom, sitting at the end of the aisle, gradually became the recipient of a small stack of cards with questions on them, most of them folded in half, as if anonymity still had to be cloaked in some degree of modesty. Tom knew most of the people in the row to his right, and he knew they'd be cautious knowing a senior vice president was at the end of the row collecting the cards. They would be subconsciously playing their own game of Good Guy, Bad Guy, and wondering if Tom was one of the senior leaders totally in the know and on board with the plan, or a more subversive leader, one who's speaking his mind behind closed doors on behalf of the team.

Tom used to think he was reliably seen as the latter, courageous enough to ask senior management the tough questions, as long as they were asked with respect, thoughtfulness, and an offer to be part of the solution. He was going to be that guy here, as he had been in his prior companies. But then things went sour with Dutch and Patton remained an imperturbable rock, and Tom felt less and less like speaking his mind served any useful purpose. He began to realize he needed another avenue for courageous honesty. He needed to have it with himself. The Stamp Out Stupidity Campaign had been his last attempt at bringing his full self to work, using honesty as an object lesson and treating the truth as the only thing that mattered. When it failed, when the madness continued, when the distrust of Patton and Dutch became an ulcer, Tom had withdrawn into his shell. Inside, out of sight to others who could only see a well-coiffed head of silver hair and a fast-paced purposeful walk, the shell was not a sanctuary but a chaotic swirl of disgust, fear, anger, repugnance, and resignation. But Tom popped his head back out, carried on as if everything was no worse than ever, and stayed in the gravitational pull of his universe. More wary and quieter in ways he hoped were not perceptible to the people who looked to him for leadership. As the cards accumulated in his hands, he did not glance down at them. He made eye contact with people who looked his way instead, and tried what he hoped looked like a reassuring smile. Something that signaled he was no spy for Patton, no bullshit seller, just one of the team. Tom still wanted very much for people to see him as a 'good guy'. Now it was clear to him that calling bullshit, screaming that the emperor is naked, sounding the shipwreck alarm, would not be seen as a 'good guy' play. These people did not want that truth this morning. The stock was up. The devil they knew still seemed to be in charge. He'd already said he was done cutting the company down. We're all going to grow again. Tom was now officially neutral, or neutered, he wasn't sure which. His natural urge to equate honesty with good kept returning a bad answer. Keeping silent didn't seem as bad as it used to. It almost seemed compassionate. It was Tom's curse to see things too clearly, not the rest of these people. It was not his responsibility to shatter their illusions, even if he granted them the self-awareness that they knew they were injecting themselves with hope to make those illusions real. It was his burden to see the full truth, to cast aside hope, to shoulder the load of leading into the teeth of a wind that would not relent. Tom passed the cards he had to the communications associate without adding one of his own questions. Time would give the answers he needed soon enough. Now was not the time.

December 25, 2015

Another morning alone in the dark, awake so long before the house it was as if he lived another life each day before joining the one the rest of the world was living. When the kids were much younger, these hours on Christmas day were filled with the anticipation of joy, their joy, waking to the wonder of boxes of all shapes and sizes for them to open. Everything they asked for from mom and dad was wrapped, and then there was a bonus unwrapped one, from Santa. Left as a thank you for the milk and cookies that Tom had enjoyed when he woke up, even earlier than anxious children. It was one of the only days of the year when these early hours didn't contain an ounce of dread. It was truly a counting of blessings time. Tom had given up on Judaism for his own reasons, but secretly, one of them was to be a part of this.. As a child, his best friends in his first neighborhood, the nice one before the family business collapsed, were all Christian. Tom watched and listened to the build-up of excitement they felt each year as Christmas day approached. Their living rooms were filled with light, and the tree, strung with all sorts of interesting objects, gradually collected those wonderful piles of colorfully wrapped boxes as December grew older. Tom tried to defend Hannukah. It wasn't just one night, but eight! But there was no beautiful tree, just a strangely shaped spinning top and a candle holder. And it didn't fall on the same day every year. It was just weird, and Tom didn't like that feeling of being left out. His father sensed it one year and took a stab at giving Tom that Christmas morning feeling. After Tom went to bed one night during Hannukah, his dad had unboxed this massive set of army men, complete with model helicopters, tanks, and medic tents, and set the whole thing up on the floor of the den to look like a full scale division assault. Tom could still remember the little catch of wonder in his chest when he woke up that morning and walked into the den, but nothing could change the fact that Tom was different, simply because of the religion his parents practiced. And in the next town he lived in, the one with all the dickheads, the difference became an excuse, a cause, a path to bullying. It didn't take Tom long to consider his logical options. His great grandparents had changed the family name from Kupinsky to Cooper at Ellis Island. His name was generic American, he could be related to Gary Cooper, the sheriff in High Noon. While Tom's father had cousins who really looked stereotypically Jewish to Tom, with short round bodies, thick lips and prominent noses, Tom's father was good-looking in a completely non-ethnic way, and as Tom came out of his awkward adolescence finally, he felt like he had inherited those generic, unidentifiable looks. He looked in the mirror and saw someone nobody should object to. If he could move on, get out of that town, get to college and never come back, no one would ever assume he was Jewish. No one would use his religion as the foundation for their understanding of him, and certainly not to persecute him, as the bullies had. It was a thirteen year-old's strategy, but damn if it didn't turn into a life decision. He would officially be nothing, if asked. He would say he was 'born Jewish', if asked. Because truth mattered to Tom, even in escape. He would say he was 'raised Jewish", if asked. All true. But Tom knew he had the power to make a part of himself disappear in plain sight, and therefore the power to change his circumstances. To refuse to be defined by them. He never allowed himself to think of it as cowardice, just a natural, logical choice. An almost Darwinian choice.

And if Tom ended up with a Christian wife, his own children would not have to hide, to change, to adapt. They would have every advantage from the start. They would celebrate Christmas from the start, would be part of the joy, would make Tom happy with their happiness. That was Tom's conscious thinking about dating when he got to school, to avoid falling for a Jewish girl. As it happened, he met and married a pastor's kid. His golden key! Another life decision cemented before life had even begun. In Tom's desperate need to be the one to define to the world who he was, he willed into life a new family story, one that would begin with him, and the wife he chose, and the way his children would be seen and treated by the world. He told himself he was doing what good parents do, making his children's path easier than his own.

But like everything else in his life lately, Tom's Christmas morning musings had driven right off the road into angst. Even though Tom had long ago reconciled his choices, he took no pride in having purposefully sought to make his children a part of something he envied growing up. He quickly realized they, like he had, would develop their own belief systems and may not always embrace this privilege their father had consciously tried to grant them, the privilege of being in the majority. Conversations about what grandma and grandpa believed in that was different than mommy and her family would of course become part of their story. That daddy was something called an agnostic and that's why he didn't go to church would of course become part of their story. Being confirmed in their mother's faith would be another part of their story. What they did with all of that would be up to them. And as Tom realized they would, his children had already shown him the ways they would escape the generational pull of their parents, the things they would keep, the things they'd discard, the things they'd change. In the end it was at least somewhat comforting to know that if he'd taught them anything, it was that they were free to become what they will become. That everyone was born with that power, has the right to exercise that power, should fight to retain that power. He hoped they'd judge him by that belief and the outcome, and not by the decisions he made for himself.

And if Tom had some misgivings over the decision to abandon his born faith and identity, what other decisions should he also reconsider more carefully? Did he marry the right woman, choose the right career, accept the right opportunities? Who could possibly second guess everything, and who would want to? Of course he married the right woman, here they were, 31 years later, still making a go of it. And then he stopped. That next big question, about the right career, and everything that flowed from it? Well, that was it, wasn't it? That was the unlanced boil on Tom's ass, and boils don't know one day from another. Merry Christmas, boil on my ass, Tom thought, to give himself that deep grimace-laced chuckle that resonated in his head when he needed it to crowd everything else right out of there. Merry Christmas to Tom Cooper, cool, calm, collected, contented Tom Cooper. Centered, senior, and wise Tom Cooper.

January 11, 2016

The calendar can be a relentless reminder of the repeatable nature of life; the national holidays in the same place, the personal milestones marked out and etched in memory, birth dates and anniversaries, the due dates for your rent or mortgage and other bills, they all keep coming around; and then you add the rituals of whatever business you're in, and soon you see the bars of your existence. For nearly twenty years now, Tom took the days between Christmas and New Year's off,, as most of his industry did, a temporary truce for all to observe their responsibilities to holiness and family. Or at least, family. And then on the first Tuesday in January not falling on the first or second, the industry's big annual trade show would start. There was no avoiding it, sitting there on the calendar in perpetuity as if it had earned this spot between New Year's Day and MLK Day, and for Tom, it always felt like getting into his car on a frigid morning and not waiting for it to warm up before dropping the pedal to the floor and roaring out of the driveway. Eight to ten contiguous days off used to be more than enough to center Tom, remind him of his blessings, even encourage him to think about how to be better at everything in the year ahead. In the early days going to the big show was even something he looked forward to, though that level of emotional commitment had long ago waxed. This time, the experience had been as unbearable as Tom thought it would be.

Nothing quite like gathering with your competitors and suppliers and industry media, and wearing the badge of the industry participant that just dropped a big ownership bombshell before the holidays, after struggling very publicly to meet its financial targets. And Tom had to studiously avoid Terry Simmons, even though his company had a large presence, because he was just done with him, had decided nothing good could come of a chance or intentional meeting with him. Tom had dropped f-bombs on him, nearly cracked his phone handle hanging up on him. And Terry had followed through on the threat to have his CEO contact Patton, and a meeting had been scheduled with Stover, but now Stover was gone, Patton had way bigger things going on, and they could all just fuck themselves.

Tom took dinners with people he liked, drank too much at the cocktail hour with people he didn't, did his usual professional job of deflecting rumors and speculation, and somehow managed to get through it. He was back at his desk on Monday morning, in need of some serious inbox trimming and table-setting for the day and week ahead. In the midst of Tom's process of quickly doing away with the intrusions of bolded new entries in his workstream, shuffling between delete button and terse responses to bullshit and nothing, a new message came in, subject line and sender designed to stop him in his tracks. It was from Patton, time-stamped to find out who opened emails at work at 7:00 am, when the subject line was 'urgent, response required'. It wasn't directly from Patton, of course, but from Christina, his admin, also known as Conan the Admin. Tom dutifully opened it. One of his strategies for staying employed had always been to study what his CEOs valued, deep down in their evil little hearts, and Tom knew that

Patton was obsessed with how much time people committed to the company. He never walked the building….except on the morning of snowstorms, when he made the rounds to see whose offices were dark at 8 am, and again at 9 am and again at 10. Tom had always been a morning person, so it was easy to make a habit of parking in a spot near the door that Patton used, so he'd see for himself the hours Tom kept. So he'd have to say, "well, there's no question he puts in the time". Tom lived close and had a four-wheel drive vehicle. He made it in when it snowed too, just as early as a clear day. That's how he knew Patton made his multiple rounds. And that's why he liked to be the first person on senior staff to respond to Conan the Admin's strategically timed email requests.

      The email was to Tom and five other senior vice presidents from around the company. Billy Baron was ready to start his listening tour, and Tom had the honor of an invitation to a dinner that very evening, here at headquarters, with five of his peers and Batman himself. By now Tom had finished reading everything he could find about Armistice and Billy Baron, and he wasn't much further along in his evaluation of what was likely to happen next at the company. The companies that Armistice still had substantial holdings in had done nothing bold or visionary or strategically powerful in the last few years. But they had all reduced expense to sales ratios and returned the excess earnings, the out of balance earnings, back to the shareholders, of whom Armistice of course, was amongst the largest. Stock prices had risen modestly. There were no home runs Tom could identify, and yet, all in, this hedge fund started over 15 years ago now had made its founder a billionaire, at least in the estimation of the media. He was forty-one years old. Thirteen years younger than Tom. Where did these fuckers come from? That's what Tom was most curious about. Where did these guys get their nerve, their balls, their superior attitudes? When did they decide they were the proverbial smartest guys in the room?

Wasn't Tom the smartest kid in class all through grade school? Didn't his junior high guidance counselor tell his parents his Iowa test scores were off the charts? That was during the discussion about the sudden change in Tom's grades, the screaming matches with his father over C's when until then it was nothing but A's. Tom didn't talk about the spitballs, the wedgies, the punches, the book dumping, the tripping in the hallways. All the tricks the bullies liked to pull off to humiliate him. Fuck school. It continued like that through high school, middling grades, arguments at home . He was supposed to do so much better. He was supposed to be so much better. His parents were focused on the first, but Tom was trying to fix the second. He had to find a reason to want to do better. To need to do better. Eventually, escape became the reason. At the end of it all, as if to punctuate his father's argument, Tom crushed his SATs and got into a good school. And for Tom's final proof that he could have been one of those smartest guys in the room, there was the four hour marathon evaluation he took before his last company hired him. This was career-on-the-rise Tom. Apparently, the test showed that he was capable of understanding the most complex of business situations. That he should be expected to deploy superior reasoning skills. That he should work well with others because he had a calm, measured, personality. He was hired because the test was never wrong and the test said Tom Cooper was going places in his career. And here he was, after all of it, pretty close to what he should be, wasn't he? How could he complain about the career he'd had? How many people made it this far? How many people provided for their families the way Tom had?

But right there in front of him, ahead of him, on top of him, were the reminders that he was pretty much nothing compared to what he might have been. The ones who truly had "fuck-you" money. The CEO's like Patton, who banked over $100m running public companies. Aren't you supposed to fucking invent something the world needs or loves to make that kind of money? Aren't you supposed to cure cancer for that kind of money? And then there was the Billy Baron stratosphere. What was inside of guys like that? Forty-one? A billionaire? And never ran anything but money? Tom studied that thought for a moment. That was it, wasn't it? Instead of letting money run you, you win when you run money. At least, that's how you have to think about it if you want to be Billy Baron. When you want to deal only in the dead. The dead whose faces are on currency. Piles of paper with dead people's faces on them, that's what you run when you run money. Running money required no blood, no muscle, no heart. Running money required no buildings, no machinery, no people. Who were these guys that looked like Tom once looked on paper, that came to do this? All day, that's all that Tom wanted out of dinner with Billy Baron. To know who the fuck he thought he was, to invite himself into this company, to attach this company to the money he ran. And now that they were married, Tom's company and Billy's money, what kind of abusive husband might that money be? That money in the black-belt trained hands of Billy Batman Baron?

A few minutes before the calendar notice called for, Tom made his way to the small executive dining room that the company reserved for small gatherings like this. He noted there was likely a message about frugality in the fact the dinner was here, with corporate catering in control, rather than at one of the many fine restaurants in the area. Three of the others were already standing awkwardly in the room. The dinner table had been shortened to its smallest size, and set with a white tablecloth, china, silver, and glasses. A table along the wall had a bucket of ice with a few Bud Lights stuck in it, and another with two open bottles of wine. A second table held two platters, one of cheese cubes and crackers, the other vegetable crudité and ranch dip. Corporate food for sure, guaranteed to go untouched, and in Tom's imagination, re-packed into containers and trotted out at another function in the building later in the week. Tom recognized one of the IT SVP's, very new to the company; the head of finance for international business, and one of his friends from the product team. Soon the others arrived as well, a field sales guy Tom worked with occasionally, and the head of a small subsidiary Patton had acquired three years ago as part of one of the seven failed consulting projects, a young gun Tom had never met. The only woman in the group was Maria, Tom's friend, who headed design and branding for the company. Tom gravitated to her side after saying hello or introducing himself to the others. Maria was young for her position, a couple years into the company. She seemed nervous. Tom had noticed she had a trait many women in corporate America did, in that she spoke in a way that almost every sentence sounded like a question that needed to be answered. As if every position she took was not official until someone, usually a man, nodded or grunted in approval. The trait got worse when she was with very senior leadership.

"Well this will be a first for me," she said to Tom.

"How so?"

"I'm pretty sure I never met a billionaire before."

"I have, but definitely not one nicknamed Batman." Maria laughed. That story was all over the building now of course, as well as the urban legend that if he heard you call him that he'd fire you on the spot. Tom touched her elbow and pointed to the bar table.

"Beer? Wine? Might as well, right?"

"I don't know…" Maria hesitated. Tom pointed at the food table.

"You could have some carrots and broccoli. They never get stuck in your teeth or fly out of your mouth by accident, right?"

"I'll have a white wine," Maria smiled. Tom was happy to lead the way for everyone to feel comfortable grabbing a beer or a glass of wine. They were grown-ups, weren't they? It was here, wasn't it?

And now here they were, standing awkwardly again, but with drinks in their hands, waiting for Billy. Someone made a nervous joke about the five-minute rule for meetings. It was now ten past the hour and no sign of him. And then the doorway darkened, not with Billy's presence, but because an enormous bald man, one of the largest human beings Tom had ever seen, had edged through the opening, eyes darting around the small room, before nodding with a slight smile and fairly gracefully backing right out again. And then Billy Baron came in. Tom was furthest from him, furiously chewing a cheese cube he'd just popped in his mouth, sizing him up, this mysterious billionaire, as he swept into the room, and quickly worked his way around to introduce himself before gesturing with a wave for all of them to sit. The cocktail hour was over. That was probably why he was ten minutes late, to give them a courtesy look at cocktails and snacks, but let them know he had no use for those things himself. Let the peasants have ten minutes with the cheese and the celery and the crackers. Give them cheap wine and tepid beer. Then bend the knee and let's get down to the business at hand.

Billy was a little taller than average, nearly six foot, athletic, with close-cropped black hair just beginning to show some silver. He was suited up, with no tie, and the perfect break in the pant leg and the way the jacket exhaled just a quarter inch of starched sleeve at each wrist told Tom it was custom all the way. When Billy shook his hand and said hello, Tom looked directly at his face, as he did with everybody, looking to lock eyes, at least momentarily, but Billy's eyes were staring at something two inches over Tom's head, apparently, or his ocular muscles didn't allow them to look down. Or he had eyes like a fly and he really was looking Tom directly in the eye. He smiled and said hello, but with eyes focused elsewhere it was like greeting a robot. Indeed, the hand was strong but the grip was weak, and strangely cold. Tom noted everything. He was like a robot too, sometimes.

Billy had brought another dinner guest, an older man, older than Tom. One of his principal investors. He'd followed Billy around the room and introduced himself as Bob Hapley. When they'd all settled at the table, Billy welcomed them.

"How's everybody's day been?" A chorus of murmured superlatives. "I want to thank you for joining me for dinner on such short notice. I know you all met Bob. Bob, do you want them tell them about yourself?"

"I own things." Bob looked around the table and smiled and shrugged. "What, you wanted something more expansive than that?" Everyone chuckled.

"Bob is one of the principal investors and a board member of Armistice, and one of the smartest business people I know." Salads and bread appeared. Billy made a sweeping hand gesture at the table. "Why don't you go around the table and introduce yourselves?" And as soon as he said it, he got to work with his salad. Tom was sure the group was specifically small enough that Billy knew exactly who all of them were and what they did, and so was not surprised to hear him add, "and tell me what's on your mind, what you're concerned about", so he could flesh out the profiles with small samples of self-expression. Tom was seated one down from Billy, to his right, and Billy turned to the person on his left to start, giving Tom four introductory speeches, and potential follow-up questions, to formulate his remarks. And to study Billy. Intently.

As his colleagues took their turns, Tom observed the give and take, and could quickly see that Billy was a man of great intelligence, with a disarming enough nature that the enormous ego he knew must be lurking beneath that calm surface did not have a bombastic voice. He responded to people's comments with some probing questions, but in many cases with a zen-like metaphor. He didn't smile often, and when he did it was fleeting. If Tom could sum up the overall impression, it was one of inscrutable self-amusement. Like Billy was playing with them. His new little mice. How would Tom describe what he did for the company when it came his turn? Titles had become so vague and illusory after so many reorganizations. Tom had pieces of this and pieces of that.

How would Billy want Tom to describe it? In his head he flashed to Jack Nicholson in A Few Good Men screaming about being wanted. That's what Tom could tell Billy. *I'm the guy you want on the wall. I fight the company's suppliers every minute of every day for every penny of profit that exists in a dollar. I'm the guy who gets shit done. I train good people. I make bad people go away before you have to fire them. I'm an expert cutter and reorganizer and dirty-deed-doer. I'm your guy because I'm right up in your brain with you, I know exactly what you want from me. I can do it mean and I can do it kind, I can do it thoughtful and I can do it blind.* Tom stopped writing songs in his head and watched and listened to his peers as intently as he did Billy. They were all smart enough to pull off sounding passionate about what they do and confident about what they, and the company, could accomplish. They were smart enough to be honest about obstacles and challenges, but pull it off without sounding like they were whining. They gave cautious performances in front of the new master. Tom decided he would skip any long explanation of what he did on the assumption that Billy and the Man Who Owns Things had read an org chart. He had decided he would look for a truth he could speak to and keep things esoteric when it came his turn. He would give the name, rank, and serial number – Tom Cooper, senior vice president, sourcing, supplier relations, and sales operations, that would say two things – A, he had lived a long time and acquired a lot of skills, and B, his company had been shrinking and combining jobs.

When the IT guy to Tom's right finished a thinly disguised pitch for more capital so he could fix a few of the company's problems faster, it was Tom's turn, and Billy had turned his head slowly in Tom's direction, smooth and serpentine, and for the briefest of moments their eyes met, as Billy said, "Tom, I've been looking forward to hearing from you". It was just the sort of distracting thing Tom would do to throw someone off, give them an idea there was already much you knew about them, or you had spent some time thinking about them. Put them off whatever speech they were preparing to start with and make them react to something. Tom had already listened to how Billy invited the next person to speak three times and this was indeed the first time he made an allusion to having some knowledge of the person. In Tom's mind the test here was to see if there was any hesitation in Tom, any swift calculus about the obvious meaning, that Billy had invited Tom to this first dinner of his listening tour for a reason. Would Tom be trying to figure out the reason before choosing a response? Tom felt Billy would not want to see hesitation. Tom should be ready to speak whatever was on his mind by now, without fumbling over which words should come out based on what he'd just heard.

"Well, thank you Billy. I imagine then you know that I'm the SVP for supplier relations, sourcing, and sales operations, for the Americas. The first two parts, for the Americas, the third part, for the entire company. Here's what keeps me up at night: our resources are stretched thin after so many small reductions, and the big reorg we did back in September, and there hasn't been enough time for the company to figure out how to take stuff off the plate so the people we have left can focus and get some things done."

"Aren't you the company?" Billy was not looking directly at Tom as he said this, but Tom was speaking, and thus felt he should answer for the group.

"We are the company. And we have common failings as a company, one of which is we can't seem to ever reconcile that fewer people to get the work done means we have to be leaders about how we get the work done. We have to help with processes and meeting schedules and reporting lines. We're not good at that. We just say, 'everything's still got to get done, so figure it out.'"

"I disagree." Billy paused there. Another recognizable trick. Tom had made several points, which one did he disagree with? Tom knew how to parry – silence. Less argumentative. Puts the speaker on notice that more information is expected before a proper response can be given. Billy did indeed continue. "I think people work best when you give them a specific goal but very little direction about how to achieve it. Direction from the top is great for allocating resources in a disciplined way against the right strategies, but how to get the work done with those resources should be on the people who really understand the work."

Tom absorbed the idea and couldn't believe what a perfect segue it was to his next point, as if Billy had wanted to move him along to precisely what he was about to say. A worthy sparring partner to be sure, Tom thought.

"That I can't argue with, but it does lead me to the other half of our responsibilities as a leadership team." Tom continued to take the moral high ground of the collective "we". When he'd reached the level of company officer he'd sworn to himself forever the accountability to the team, the full team, to not ever say, "I was just following orders." He'd always held himself accountable to speak up.

"The other thing we're not good at, and you correctly identified this in your white paper, is the first part of what you just said – direction from the top needs to be disciplined about supporting the right strategies. If we can't get the first one right, it is hard for the rest of the team to figure out what to let go of." Tom had taken a little gamble to see if he could get a rise out of Billy. Let him know he'd read the white paper, and done his homework as well. Bring his own words into the discussion so the attribution couldn't be disputed. Tom felt a little giddy, mentally and verbally sparring with a billionaire half a generation his junior. He continued.

"We've thrown a lot at the team over the last two years in particular. But if you really want to put it in perspective, I've been here eight years, and I've been involved in a different consulting project all eight of those years. Every one of them did something to the organization, moved pieces around, took people out of their natural jobs, blurred reporting lines. And they almost always involved doing more with less. New people come in to senior level jobs and they don't have that context of just how many people used to do the work, or how it might have been organized when it was working better. They just see that things aren't working, and then they bring their own ideas about how to fix them. I'm sure I was guilty of that when I first came, and if you want to hang me, guilty of it every year since." Tom thought about his Stamp Out Stupidity Campaign failure and decided it was off message. This was not the time to claim martyrdom. This was still a confessing of royal sins. He smiled and paused a bit and looked right at Billy when he said "hang me" to let Billy know he wasn't really being defensive, just colloquially self-deprecating.

"Coming back to that direct answer about what's keeping me up at night, and it's what I hope your involvement brings - better clarity and vision and prioritization, so a lean team of really good people can execute and deliver on whatever the strategy is. We don't have it now, and that's what keeps me awake." Now Tom was staking a position and stating his own expectations for his new lord and master. He was firing the salvo that the current team was already lean enough. That it wasn't their fault the company was undervalued and floundering. That Tom himself, and the rest of the senior leadership team, had to be the ones held accountable. What a great opportunity this actually was, Tom thought, as he took a breath to reflect on what it was he had actually just rambled on about. Maybe Dutch had managed to put a red X in a box next to Tom's name, as a loser, a logical "next out". If so, he'd just had a chance to state his own case, to sound rational and smart and accepting of responsibility. He still had to consider the slim chance that things could actually work with Billy Baron's involvement. Maybe Billy had already seen right through Dutch and he was trying to validate that first impression by checking in with the people Dutch thinks suck. But Tom also wanted to say what truly was on his mind, so that if Billy did want him to stick around, Tom would know it would be with an open book on what he stood for.

"And what do you think that strategy should be?" Tom had wondered earlier if Billy would go there with each of them this evening, but had considered it too trite a topic, particularly considering Billy himself, or his firm collectively, had authored the white paper that laid out their vision pretty specifically. What did he really think people would tell him? Something completely contrary? But here it was, the fat toad of a question, a ticking bomb floating in the air waiting for a response, the ticking getting louder and more insistent at each passing millisecond before Tom could craft his reply. A reply that might determine whether his career at the company would continue or not in the coming weeks and months. Which outcome did Tom really want? Hadn't he been practically begging for a package he could live with to just get the fuck out of here? Here was his chance. Fuck the idea from ten seconds ago that Billy could possibly save the place. Say something contrary and provocative and argumentative and see where Billy goes? See if there's a pool of anger he can throw a stone in to get a ripple? Cement his likely swift exit?

Well that wouldn't be entirely smart, would it? Wouldn't it be better to profess a love for the challenge, a commitment to the future, a desire to stay and win? And then hope that he still gets a gentle push out the door, with the more generous severance? And there was the matter of timing. Tom had those shares vesting at the end of the fiscal year, now just 11 weeks away. Tick-tick-tick-tick-tick-tick. How long had the question hung in the air? Tom needed to decide his whole future and speak now. He chose the middle lane and made it up as he went along.

"I don't know that I could lay out a traditional answer to that question, with four to five succinct bullet points of exactly what we need to do right now. But what I will say is that whatever that strategy is, it has to be rooted in what our customers need, and how we can uniquely serve those needs, because for way too long, our strategic discussions have been too internally focused on our needs, or more specifically, our shareholders' needs. How do we get our customers to buy more stuff, or expenses to shrink, or both? How do we get the stock price to go up? I'd like to see a strategy that gets it right for the customer first, and lets rewards like share appreciation follow."

There. He'd just pretty much thrown Patton under the bus, even if he did continue to use the royal we. He'd also just told their biggest shareholder that his needs shouldn't be their first priority. But how could Billy argue he was wrong? All Tom had done was make a fairly common argument in business strategy – that if you take care of the customer first, financial rewards will follow. Tom also knew he'd essentially dodged the question, and now was wondering whether Billy would take him to task for that and press further. What he got was a fleeting smirk, and then a release from the spotlight.

"Fair enough. This company has a very complex business and structure. I assume if there was a perfect strategy to take it forward, we wouldn't all be sitting here tonight, right?". And with that, Billy turned to the next person. Tom felt his brain shift back from full-on crisis mode to normal processing. Had Billy just decided that Tom was perfectly well placed? A senior executive smart enough to know what a strategy should be based on, but not brilliant enough or bold enough to craft the strategy himself? A reliable soldier who would take the direction of the new boss and execute to the best of his abilities? Or did he think Tom was a coward, unwilling to say what he really thought? What was Tom's overall score, now that his direct interaction with the new master was over? He knew Billy must have made an instant decision on him by now. Was Tom satisfied he'd shown him enough of who he was for that decision to be modestly favorable? Why the fuck did Tom really care? Did it matter at all what grade he would get?. Did he give a shit what Billy thought?. Isn't he the enemy? Fucking punk billionaire who's never run anything but money? He just wanted it all to be over and decided, one way or another. He wanted certainty. It was definitely not coming to him tonight. There's some certainty. It wasn't something he was going to get from Billy anyway. The true certainty. That had to come from Tom, didn't it? Didn't Tom alone have the power to grant himself certainty? And really, it's just the short-term certainty. That's all anyone could really ask anyway. What's going to happen to me tomorrow? What's going to happen to me eleven weeks from now? Tom knew the answer to the second question. That was one of the only certainties he had in his life. 9,000 more shares would vest. The restricted shares, the ones the company gave you for free in exchange for extending your sentence. The carrots they kept adding to the end of the stick every year. And this year was the one Tom had been waiting for - the grant from three years ago when the stock was really in the tank. The value of it that just grew nicely with the Armistice bump. What that payout would add to his life. More certainty. Another building block for retirement, for escape. Big enough to panic Tom at the idea he could somehow lose it. And he could. He had to be employed on that date in good standing. He couldn't get fired for cause between now and then. Stover was gone, his partial shield. Dutch was still lurking. Now here was this fucking billionaire parachuting in. So many ways Tom could envision having his eject button pushed. What if the Terry Simmons thing came back to bite him? Stover had found it amusing when Tom told him how he cursed him out and slammed the phone down. Wasn't Simmons' CEO going to call Patton? What if Billy had taken his mental note and was ready to put Tom on the immediate exit list? Fuckers. No one could take those 9,000 shares. Get there and let whatever happens after that happen. Tom was like a lone coyote guarding a big deer carcass, wondering how long he can preserve it for himself before the big bad wolves come to claim their share. The sound of Billy's voice, rather than the drone of the international finance guy to Tom's left, pricked the mad bubble of thought above Tom's head.

"I want to thank all of you for your candor, that was great". Tom looked around the table. The first course, a salad of mixed greens and slivered carrots and radishes, with some shaved parmesan, was being cleared. Tom noted that only he and Billy had finished their plates. The servers swiftly replaced the salad plates with dinner, starting with Billy. His plate was set down and Tom noted it was just a simple grilled breast of chicken and a large pile of spinach. When the next plate went down the same breast of chicken was covered with a sun-dried tomato coulis, there was a side of wild rice, and the portion of spinach was much smaller than Billy's. Someone had paid attention to this detail ahead of time. Was it Billy himself? The enormous bald man?

Billy was quite skilled at speaking and eating at the same time. Tom watched him carve off and eat two bites of chicken as soon as the last plate was set down, while the servers were refilling water glasses, and asking folks if they would like some wine. Billy had no wine glass in front of him, just a bottle of Fiji water and a glass. Another decision made in advance. Was everything a message? The trimmed down meal, no alcohol, Billy's athletic frame sharply draped in the custom clothes. The decisions made in advance. A man in control of everything in his life. The kind of man you had to listen to. And now Billy was ready to hold court.

"I heard some interesting things from you, some themes I want to come back to. But let me start by describing for you the essence of my business philosophy. I like to call it 'thinking commercially'. There has to be a business purpose to the things you do. Particularly if you're spending money on them, and in business, everything you do involves spending money. It's always being focused on the return on that money that defines what I mean by thinking commercially. But let me give you an example. You may know that my firm holds a rather large stake in Ayden-Linnett. They have a beautiful corporate headquarters building, larger than yours, and the campus includes a large pond that curls around the parking lot and runs up to the side of the building. They built it that way, the designers, so the glass of the building would reflect the pond for the majority of daylight hours. The building looked like it was made of liquid. Quite stunning. When we came in, we went through the company expenses in detail, and we found a line item for $3,500 a month that just said 'swans'. There were a pair of swans in the pond, and I was told they were leased, because their presence kept the Canada Geese away. Before the swans, they had a terrible problem with goose shit on the sidewalk from the parking lot to the front of the building. I asked them if it would cost less to just have the landscapers pick up the goose shit, and in fact it did, so we fired the swans. That's what I mean by thinking commercially." Tom couldn't stop himself from smiling. He hoped Billy would see it as an acknowledgement that he got the point, but the smile came from somewhere else entirely. Yes, he was smiling at the punchline, "so we fired the swans". But not in wise agreement of the point it represented, but in the grim humor of how perfectly it summed up everything Tom hated about the last 32 years of his life. Yes, let's fire the beautiful swans. Because we can. Because it makes sense. Because everyone will understand the lengths to which we will go in our pursuit of another dollar of profit, another penny of profit, another fraction of a percent of return on investment. Yes, we will even fire the swans. Tom thought that might make a nice name for a movie about this whole fucking mess, this whole fucking enterprise. "So We Fired the Swans". Billy was far from done.

"I heard a couple of you say you think the company lacks clarity of direction." Tom's skin goosed up a little. He'd been one of those to mention their ineffectiveness at providing better direction to the team. "I think clarity is fine up to a point, but people have to be comfortable with ambiguity too. The world is changing rapidly. Successful companies test a lot of different things to understand what works, and then invest in the ones that prove out. Sometimes that looks like a lack of clarity. But look at what Microsoft has done, repeatedly. They release imperfect product. They wait for their customers to tell them what's wrong with it, and then they work quickly to fix it. Their customers don't punish them for that, they reward them. If they waited until everything was perfect before releasing it, they would not be the company they are today. I would suggest that it's not a lack of clarity, per se, that has been at the root of your challenges, but instead, an inability to work well in an environment without clarity." Something familiar in that phrasing made Tom arch his head slightly to one side, like a dog that thought he heard you say something exciting, like "walk", but maybe misheard. "To operate with certainty without the need for clarity." That was the definition of a *Visionary* that was part of the ratings game for the big reorg. It sounded stupid then and it sounded stupid now. It might be a fine skill to expect of a cadre of senior executives, but once you had a big business up and running, one that took thousands of people to maintain, you couldn't expect all of them to do their jobs in a fog of uncertainty. Why didn't god-damned smart people like this asshole understand that most people want more out of life than their jobs and careers? That they're happy to come to work with a clear purpose and understanding of what's expected, and a reasonable chance to get it done, five days a week? That they don't all need to be god-damned visionaries? Billy was continuing.

"You're in a fairly traditional industry, but you have to look at what's happening in the world outside your industry. You have to look at how great companies are being built. The entire team is committed, they don't have a concept of time, other than that everything is urgent. They are constantly probing and pushing themselves to break new ground. Companies like that are attracting the best talent. I'd suggest the path to success here is going to come from taking the same attitude that start-up companies have and applying it to this traditional business. I'd be willing to bet that when we leave this dining room tonight, the lights will be low throughout the building and there will barely be a soul working". Tom began to smell one of the largest piles of bullshit he'd ever been served up as rationale for another headcount reduction. It would start with the assumption that what was wrong with the company was not the people, but the culture. The culture was not imbued with the urgency and fire of the best companies out there, the new companies, the ones filled with dreamers whose idea of work/life balance was to work now, and have a life later. They were the companies where everyone was young and hungry, where the ties were gone, replaced with ping-pong paddles. So how would they change the culture? How would they find that elusive elixir that convinced an entire body of people to commit themselves above all else in their lives to company success? Well, you can't change a culture without changing the people, can you? And there it would be...the rationale. A new set of bold words to test everyone against. Who needs workers that want to be given strong direction, enough training to be successful, and enough resources to do their jobs well? Those kinds of workers suck. They don't stay late. They don't live and breathe the company. They're what's wrong here. Yeah, this would be the worst one yet. The worst rationale. The hardest sell. The largest pill to swallow. A fucking horse lozenge. Tom was done listening to Billy Fucking Baron. He wasn't sure how he finished his thought, what words he used. Tom just saw Billy's fork dive into his pile of spinach, the cessation of his statement realized by a visual cue, not the absence of spoken words. The volume came back up with the sound of forks scraping plates around the table, seemingly everyone taking a pause to get some food down, including Billy. It wasn't quite an awkward silence, but not actually having heard how Billy finished his thought, Tom wasn't sure what the logical next conversation topic should be, and he didn't want to be the one to break the quiet with words out of step with what was said last. Since no one else was speaking either, it would appear whatever Billy finished with had ended the portion of the night where they talk about how to fix the company.

Bob Hapley, Billy's investor, broke the peace.

"I, for one, am really excited to see what Billy and team can make of this company's assets."

He said this while pausing above his chicken, fork in left hand, knife in right. Tom thought he looked like a caricature of a fat cat businessman poised to carve up yet another plump roast of a business. An old, bloated, American business that needed to be trimmed down to a modern company. Tom could see small spots of chicken clinging to the knife blade. They were the people who would disappear during the carving. He saw a small pile of skin on the plate that Bob Hapley had already carved away. An entire division sliced off? Or just the fat? Hapley was grinning as he looked around the table.

"You people are going to find that Armistice investing in your company is the best thing to ever happen to your careers, trust me."

Tom nearly gagged at the last two words. They were the final curse. They preceded a lie nearly every time Tom had heard them in his long working career. Trust me. Trust Billy. Trust Patton. Trust Dutch. No fucking way. No, Tom said to himself. Nope. No. Trust no longer existed in the world. Christ, Tom couldn't even trust himself any more.

January 12, 2016

Meet the new boss, meet the other new boss. Robert Jarrett was announced as the new Mark Stover, Tom's fifth direct boss in eight years, a move he'd expected and prepared himself for. When Tom was hired, his responsibilities were created out of pieces other executives were giving up, in yet another flavor-of-the-day organizational redesign. Robert was one of those executives contributing to Tom's portfolio. They say ethics are what you do when you know no one is watching. The corporate corollary involves teamwork and respect, revealed by what you do when you transition your responsibilities to someone else in the organization, particularly someone new. To Tom, Robert revealed himself clearly eight years ago as someone who really didn't give a shit about teamwork and respect. He seemed more concerned with finding out whether a new hire was a rival brought in to cut in line for the next plumb job. In the intervening years, Tom saw him often enough in different roles and worked with him in an off-again, on-again way as their assignment paths turned and twisted to see some changes, some maturation. Robert was a hot personality type to Tom's cool. He flashed to anger quickly and easily, but just as swiftly and ably returned to a professional demeanor. He channeled it so others would call it passion - wise of him - working to make that be the definer of his reputation rather than being just a hothead. Tom could respect that. He could see right through it too. Robert was calculating, like Tom was. He was smart. And he was a bully. Deep down, Tom knew that. That's what those first few months revealed, so long ago now. Robert was also a long-standing member of Dutch's good old boy network. And he was Tom's new boss, the point of the stick, the proxy for Dutch and Patton and now, Billy Baron. So Tom would need to deal with whatever issues he might have personally and make sure he got along just fine with Robert. He knew that he would be just as indispensable to Robert as he'd been to Stover. And he knew that Robert was smart enough to recognize that pretty quickly. At least for the short term. In the long term, well, there was no long term anymore, was there?

Tom had had a chance to sleep on his dinner with Billy Baron and had awakened this morning certain that he wanted no part of whatever the inscrutable billionaire had in mind for the company. It was only a matter of how and when he would find his way out. He had to be smart about it. No doubt about that. No getting fired. He had to get to the vesting date. To April 1. Even in the short span of weeks since Tom began furiously working the numbers, when the white paper was published and the stock started churning, his personal situation had changed. His mother's dementia was advancing faster than the doctor thought it would. Tom's father had slipped into deeper depression and was not a good caregiver. Tom wanted to be there for them, to be a safety net if his mother needed extended care, or his father in-home help. He couldn't be there for them personally, not with the distance and the time, so it had to be the money. Tom had one kid out of school, but over Christmas break his daughter talked about stretching her stay out to get a masters. People needed him. The real people in his life.

So that date, that end of fiscal year date, when not only the modest bonuses would be valid, but much more importantly, those stock grants would vest, had to be the North Star he steered to. April Fools Day. The last fiscal year Tom hoped to ever fight for, the last quarterly and annual report date, would of course fall on April Fools Day. After 32 years, the farce would end on the day the jesters are honored and nothing is to be believed. But only if Tom could co-exist with a closet bully for two and a half months, and stay out of Dutch's crosshairs, and survive any Billy Baron surprises, and just keep his cool head, and keep Getting Shit Done. He could do that, couldn't he? He could do all of that, because he was Tom Fucking Cooper and he was tough-minded and resilient and he had seen it all and survived it all and it was only two and a half more months. And it mattered too much. As much as he hated to admit it, the money mattered. It was just enough to tip the balance in Tom's confidence to survive what would come next. Get to April 1, and Tom could take a whole year off if he wanted to, to try to discover a purpose he could get excited about beyond providing for those around him. Fall short, and Tom would feel compelled to chase one more job right away, one more chance to get to his number, the number he'd decided he needed to reach, to make him feel the entire span of his adult life had meant something. That he'd secured the health and well-being of himself, his wife, and the generations before and after. All those terrible things he had to do, had to count. And if he had to do them for 10 more weeks, so be it.

From Tom Cooper's private journal. July 2000. Age 38.
Employer 4.

The location was Las Vegas, an impossibly shiny sink down whose drain millions of dollars are poured every day. The occasion? Ostensibly one of those 'business entertainment' evenings where buyers and sellers get together and spend the seller's expense account on food and booze and slip in a business topic or two. On the evening in question, that definition was stretched thinner than a pro athlete on Father's Day. In attendance, a couple VP's from the vendor, and a couple more on our side, and me, present this evening simply because my personnel file is now officially stamped "high potential". This trip was designed to create some exposure and learning for me. The evening out was just a perk of the life I'm being groomed to join.

Let me describe what a five-star restaurant experience means these days. It means there are actual Renoirs, not reproductions, on the walls of the elegant dining room. It means the solicitous wait-staff is articulate and incredibly well-informed as to the vagaries of the menu. It means they unfold your napkin for you and place it on your lap. It means they provide a tiny upholstered footstool for the ladies to place their handbags beside their chairs. It means they serve you a gratis appetizer (in this case thin breadsticks wrapped in Prosciutto) while you enjoy a glass of wine, or a Bombay gin martini, as I did. All of these amenities of course come with prices so exorbitant they are not printed on the menu.

I began with an appetizer of escargot, six tiny mollusks swimming in a pool of garlic butter for likely the cost of a hundred flu vaccinations in Somalia. A months' wages in a Chinese shoe factory probably paid for my entrée, two impossibly tender medallions of veal loin accompanied by three tiny cannelloni stuffed with wild mushrooms. It was truly wonderful eating, and I washed it down with another Bombay gin martini. I don't know the cost of those martinis, but it would be safe to estimate that one of Sally Strothers' children could eat for two months for the cost of just one. The olives were terrifically tasty, by the way.

I have been trained over the years to accept this occasional taste of the highlife on someone else's tab as an essential part of doing business in America. We all work hard, we're away from home, we need to eat. I ordered top shelf liquor with my eyes wide open. But somewhere between my boss whispering that the tab for five people, before the tip, was over $800, and noting that the tickets to the show we went to see after dinner were $100 each, I began to feel a little uneasy. The fellow next to me didn't even finish his appetizer or his dinner, and here we were, 5 people blowing through over $1,300 of other people's money.

It's not like our host had a lot of it to spare. His company has been shuttering factories and laying off workers for years now, as they've moved production overseas. In our company, operating performance has declined for three years running, and our frontline managers are working long hours with less help than they've ever had in the past. Yet here we were, on expense account, having a grand old time.

I suppose we all do what we have to do in life, to put food on the table, to take care of our loved ones. I chose not to be a social activist or liberal politician. I chose a career in business. Corporate business, to be precise. And I've slogged through some tough personal times, sometimes putting in 80 hours in a week, been literally down on my hands and knees, putting socks back on a hook or folding jeans. I've felt so stressed by the pressures of my career that I've vomited in my driveway taking the trash to the curb at night. And though my company is struggling for sure, at the moment I'm doing well personally. Is it so wrong of me to accept an invitation to a fancy restaurant and a show?

In the grand scheme of things, while I still have a shred of Ted Kennedy left in my body (I think he ordered the martinis), yes, it is wrong. It shows a disdain and disregard for shareholders and frontline employees alike. Not so much because $1,300 saved here and there would have saved those factories from moving overseas, but because sacrifices have been asked of others and should be taken from all. There is lots of talk in corporate America of the need to retain good executives. Taking away the perks of expense account entertainment, whether it's meals, shows, or skybox seats at a ballgame, puts you at risk of losing good people to other companies that aren't so fanatical about controlling costs. Should I, whose job takes me away from my family 100 nights a year, be asked to stay in a tough section of town in a broken down motel and eat all my meals at McDonalds? Would I begin to feel REALLY depressed about my job if they did set those guidelines? Yes I would.

But there has to be a reasonability test. In Las Vegas, we failed it.

January 19. 2016

Nothing like a dreary Tuesday in January to have a toe to toe battle with yet another supplier. Tom's people had raised what they considered to be a serious breach of exclusive distribution arrangements committed by one of their fastest growing vendors. The set of facts that Tom had reviewed had convinced him that the supplier had so miserably failed to control where their product was sold, that it was now his problem, or more accurately his company's problem. Tom's own problems were much deeper than a fight over channels, but this breach his supplier had created was such an egregious mistake that it brought forth real, professional, business-driven anger. His inner-CEO was so incensed that Tom let him have the run of his brain, just to see where he'd take it if he just let the little sucker have the wheel.

Technically, what Tom did to respond to the situation before the weekend, was to breach his own contract with the firm in retaliation and drop the price on their products in the marketplace. Legal letters vetted by chief counsels were exchanged on Monday and the ensuing escalation of hostilities demanded that a 'top to top' take place between the management teams, more easily arranged because this particular supplier happened to be local. Steve Light was the President and he came in with his national sales manager, an empty suit who'd joined the company so recently he was barely versed in the background. He would serve merely as a witness to humiliation. Tom had his newly appointed boss sit in as well. He'd brought Robert into the loop, and he was in agreement with Tom's assessment of the potential damage of the suppliers' initial action. But at that point, he didn't want any protracted negotiation, or heaven forbid, a court case or an arbitration hearing. What he wanted, with a company on the ropes and a quarterly number of their own to hit that at the time was an illusion at best, was money. Cold hard cash. Principled strategic stands aside, Tom needed to get in the ring and punch his way to as much currency as he could get his hands on. And he did so. Magnificently. Like a late career Brando calling on every trick he ever learned to give us Colonel Kurtz in Apocalypse Now, Tom Cooper went to work.

First, he hit Steve with *righteous indignation.*

"Steve, I'm glad you could come on such short notice. This has escalated much too fast, and I'm sure we can resolve it today, we've got all the right people in the room, I'm sure." Tom used two set-ups in this short intro. He snarkily put Steve on the defensive about the timing of his team's response to this situation, now that Tom had thrown a significant fistful of shit into the fan, and he confidently assigned Steve decision-making powers on behalf of his company, in front of Tom's boss, so that any wavering in coming to an agreement, would expose him as weak and ineffectual. Then Tom set up his case, like the prosecuting attorney he may have been destined to be, one of many unknowable and uncorrectable possible career mistakes.

"Steve, this started three weeks ago when we saw your product in the market, available from Pyramid, to be specific, at pretty damn sharp prices. The same product that you allow us to sell only in the specific channels designated in your convoluted distribution contract, and at wholesales that don't allow us a heck of a lot of margin. And now my customers can find the same product, at or below my price, from Pyramid? It's unacceptable! My team called yours immediately, called out the issue, which your pumpkins were completely unaware of, and their response was, we'll get back to you. A week goes by, and my guys finally tell me what's going on, and I make my first call, to Craig." Tom nodded to the new national sales manager, one of those he'd just disparaged as a pumpkin, purposely misspeaking his name, then not acknowledging the mumbled correction to "Greg", before barreling on.

"Craig says he's trying to track down how this happened, he doesn't know how Pyramid got the goods, but can we give him some time? I told him he could have all the time he wanted to investigate, but while he did, I was going to make your product available to the same customers at the same price Pyramid was for as long as Pyramid was advertising they had the product. He told me that was a violation of our agreement, and you guys could stop shipping us. He begged me not to take this action right now, because you guys were preparing for an important board meeting, and it would be embarrassing for you." Tom then dropped down into a deadly calm tone, another pitch lower, more menace and carefully controlled outrage.

"So, you were concerned about appearances, and I was concerned about the very existence of my company. Pyramid is the most disruptive force this industry has ever seen. They don't give a fuck about your convoluted distribution policies and contracts. They don't just want to compete with us, they want to take all of our business. Do you understand that?

They want, no, they expect, that we will be gone in ten years, if they execute their plan right. So while you were agonizing over your deck for the board, I was fighting for my company's survival." Tom paused and waited, staring hard into Steve Light's eyes. Steve assumed it was then his turn to talk. This was a planned move, for Tom to catch his breath, then have the opportunity to further disrupt Steve by interrupting him. Steve cleared his throat and began to say something, but Tom waved his hand at him dismissively and continued.

"I know you're going to tell me that you don't know how Pyramid got these goods, and you'll track it down, and you'll close the leak, but in the meantime, I'm going to compete with them on a level playing field. I may technically be in breach of our contract by doing so, but you've put the entire future of my company at risk. We didn't create this mess, you did. And now you're threatening to stop shipping us, which you tell me about on the official letterhead of your fucking chief counsel." After his blow-up of Terry Simmons, Tom had developed a new appreciation for the proper use of an f-bomb in the workplace. A new weapon in his arsenal. Now Tom was ready for Steve to jump in.

"Well, I don't know that we created this mess, as you call it, but we certainly do understand why you have concerns, and as we've said, we're working diligently, account by account, looking at shipping records, looking for who might be moving goods sideways to Pyramid, and we'll close the leak, but it's going to take us some time. But, as you yourself said, your action is in violation of our contract, and by its terms, I can stop shipping you. I really have to stop shipping you."

"You really don't seem to grasp the magnitude of this for us. This has major long-term implications. And you did create this mess. You overproduced. You had to move excess inventory. Either you sold it to people who never had that kind of demand and just ignored the obvious, or you stuffed your wholesale channel with it to hit a sales goal, and they slid it to Pyramid at a lesser discount to keep the pile moving, or you sold it direct to Pyramid. It doesn't really matter. What it signals is the end of your model. You can't assign arbitrary channels any longer. Pyramid is changing the game – they have changed the game. You just don't seem to know it yet." Tom was leaning heavily on the one thing every business person respected – the fight for survival when you truly believe your life as a company is threatened. At that point, what the fuck good is any contract? Just a bunch of words meaning nothing in the real world. Steve wasn't done digging in.

"Be that as it may, your continued violation of our contract is creating a massive problem for us with our other customers, and I have to exercise my rights under the contract and withhold shipments. You know neither of us wants us to do that. You're a very big customer, this would be meaningful to us as well. That's why we offered you a discount on purchases for the next 60 days, which is when we expect to have Pyramid cleaned up." And there it was, the door to the vault was now open. Tom had just a few more punches of righteous indignation and survivalist rhetoric to deliver.

"Exactly. You know you did something wrong because you offered me a short-term discount to remedy it. 2% on purchases for sixty days. So, I back down, take your goods out of the channel, watch Pyramid make me look like an idiot, and soothe my wounds with a 2% discount. I sell my soul to the devil for a handful of shekels." Tom knew he was mixing up metaphors but he'd found that saying oddball things helped throw off an opponent. A little short-circuit malfunction as they tried to follow what he was saying while trying to maneuver around some odd piece of language or phrase without losing the overall meaning. "I honestly don't think there's any amount of money we should be talking about here, we should be talking about tearing up the distribution contract and moving on with our lives in a new world order. Are you ready to discuss that?"

There it was, the *meeting agenda surprise*. Of course, Steve was not ready to negotiate the destruction of a carefully constructed and legally vetted set of distribution agreements on the spot. But now he had to find a way back to what he was smart enough to know was the real purpose of the meeting – to find the price at which Tom would back down, and his firm would not have to follow through on the stop-shipment threat.

Steve chuckled a little and tried a disarming smile and head shake. "No, I'm not ready today to discuss tearing up our current contract."

Tom was ready to move in for the kill shot of any negotiation, the *presumption of control*, when the hammer comes down. But first, he couldn't resist throwing in a little *verbal evisceration*. Pitch was so important here. The goal was to deliver stinging barbs in a calm, deadly, almost cavalier tone, to piss the other side off a little, to add to the impression Tom was going to be an unreasonable prick on this one, so don't fuck around. Tom got as conversational, almost charming, as he could.

"Okay then, let's go back a little further, for Robert's sake, and recap where we are. Steve, you were in here not two weeks ago, a week after my team first threw the penalty flag on Pyramid, but before they told me. It was our normal quarterly meeting, and you knew what was brewing then, you had to. Unless of course, your team is in the habit of keeping you completely in the dark. But on that day, you brought Greg in," (right name that time, staring right at Greg to let him know that of course he knew his name) "for his big introduction, and you sat there and talked about the future, and you didn't say a word about this nasty little problem with Pyramid. You know me well enough to know my feelings about your distribution strategy, and it was blowing up, and if I didn't seem to know about it at the time, you, apparently, certainly weren't going to bring it up. Unless of course I'm correct that your company can have dog shit all over its shoe and you can't smell it, and you really didn't know. So, I'll give you that. You were ignorant at the time. But then when I did get involved and asked for a response, you know what your team said? 'We're really busy with a board meeting and can't get back to you till next week. Steve's too busy writing a deck.' At that point, perhaps I was a little angry. My belief from your reaction was that you really didn't give a shit any more about where your stuff was sold, so I did what I had to do to compete. Unlike you, I gave fair warning. With no acceptable response I acted. And then Steve, only then, did you pick up the phone and call me. And did you apologize for not being up front about the situation? To the best of my recollection, and I have a pretty good memory, no. Did you make fixing it your number one priority? Let's see, I believe the first words were something along the lines of, 'Tom, you've created a really tough situation for us and I need you to take our goods down from your site, and honor our contractual commitments'. We had a very cordial conversation, which didn't last very long, and within a couple hours I had your breach notice. All in, just an impeccable display of partnership with one of your biggest customers." Tom paused, and Robert's silence let Steve know that there was no point in trying to counter, there was no audience to play to, Tom was obviously the designated attack dog on this one, and he was fucking good at it.

So, the denouement began, the *presumption of control*. Even though Tom was the one legally in the wrong at that moment, he had to get paid to come back to legally in the right. He had to act like it pained him so much not to push this thing to the limit and get the lawyers in the room, that the only thing that could cure him was more cash. This meant guiding Steve to the right answer. "Look, no one wants this to reach another level, but honestly, what you've offered me while you work through your distribution issues is not nearly in line with the risk you've created for us. I shouldn't even be happy with 10 times what you offered". This was Tom's way of saying, 'Empty your pockets and give me the most you possibly can.' It wasn't, 'Would you?' it was, 'You will'.

Steve, beaten bloody at that point, said, "I just don't have that kind of money to give you," setting Tom up for the close, the death blow.

"Then you need to give me everything you do have." And what that turned out to be was a 6% discount for 90 days, as opposed to 2% for 60. Both sides could quickly calculate that $2.5m additional dollars were sliding over to Tom's company's side of the table.

The performance felt like a capstone. It took all of twenty minutes. Robert told him it was a pleasure to watch him work. He got an email from Brenda Wise, the CFO, thanking him for the extra contribution to the quarter, and a, "Heard you did a great job," congratulation. But after the momentary flush of pride in his masterly performance, Tom felt nothing but sadness. Steve was just a couple months from the end of a long career and Tom had made him look bad at his company and exacted a meaningful transfer of profit for both of them. But Tom's regret also extended to taking cash to stand down from a position he knew was right. He had executed to the very best of his ability what his company needed him to execute in a very expedient way. Being right about the strategic implications earned him a condescending pat on the head, but the hearty pat on the back was for going out and maximizing the cash haul. Tom could only shake his head and wonder how companies run by leaders who supposedly rose to their positions because they were strategic thinkers, returned time and time again to mortgaging the future to hit short term financial goals. Seemed like the story of his career. Sacrifice. Sacrifice your family life for career success. Sacrifice your heart for cold-hearted analysis. Sacrifice your future to pay the bills today. Sacrifice your principles and beliefs to serve the shareholders. Sacrifice.

January 19, 2016

The next night Tom was home with Michelle, finishing dinner at the cocktail table with cable news on. It had become their practice with the kids away at school. Any pretense that the dinner table was a place of robust family discussion each evening was thrown away in favor of being 'entertained' while eating. The talking heads were rattling on about the behavior of Donald Trump, who was inexplicably a leading candidate for the Republican Presidential nomination. Tom didn't need to listen. He knew all too well who Trump was. He was Dutch Bagley. He was a grown-up bully, and a really obvious and mean one at that. God he hated him, Tom realized. Apparently, so did Michelle.

"I can't believe the Republicans would actually nominate that friggin' idiot." She said to Tom and the television at once.

"I know." Tom was of a similar mind. It felt like the beginning of the end for the American empire in some B-movie plot.

The talking heads were discussing the possibility of Trump skipping the next scheduled debate because he was feuding with Megyn Kelly, who was going to be one of the moderators. They then played a clip of Trump from the previous summer telling another anchor that Kelly had 'blood coming out of her eyes and her whatever', followed by more clips and tweets of Trump trashing women for their looks, their weight, their age. Michelle was riled up.

"What kind of person thinks they can talk about women that way?" she demanded to know.

Tom considered the question for only a moment, because he was already revulsing inside as the montage of Trump quotes brought him spiraling right back to high school.

"The worst kind," he answered. Tom wanted to stop thinking about Trump, so he changed the subject to work. He hadn't told Michelle about his meeting with Steve Light the day before. "So I didn't mention it last night, but I got a big thumbs up from my new boss yesterday and a congratulatory note from the CFO." Tom sounded a little sarcastic, so Michelle replied skeptically.

"For what, or do I not want to know?"

"I brutally raked a supplier over the coals and renegotiated an existing offer to get the company an extra $2.5m for the quarter. Robert actually told me it was a pleasure to watch me work."

"Well that's good, isn't it? Didn't you want to prove to Robert he needs you?"

"I suppose so. But I was a total dick to the president of the vendor. I even mis-named his VP of sales on purpose. I mean I was bad." Tom thought again about Steve Light. He had not developed a ton of respect for his business skills, but he'd always been professional and gentlemanly. And he was several years older than Tom, about to retire. What kind of person professionally humiliates a decent guy who's retiring in a couple of months?

"Haven't you always told me you have to be a dick sometimes in your business?"

Something about the phrase 'always told me' activated a vein in Tom's brain that immediately started pounding on the inside of his skull. It was the truth knocking from within. Not just a dick because of the way the business world works. Not just sometimes. Inside that brain he was a dick all the time to the world at large. He mistrusted others, he assumed bad intent, he had his guard up, he had his bullshit sensor on, he looked for threats in every face. Every time he told himself he didn't have to be that way, something or someone confirmed for him he did. He couldn't escape it. Tom opened his mouth, and the thing that needed to get out, the thing doing that pounding, suddenly came rushing forth.

"I never told you this, but in junior high and high school I was bullied pretty severely." Tom turned to look directly at Michelle, met her eyes, locked in. "I wasn't the only one, but I was the one that they never let up on. They spit on me. Held me down and dripped big loogies over my face and I wanted to scream but I couldn't because I didn't want them to drop into my mouth. They tripped me in the halls, dumped my books. Kicked my books down the hall after they dumped them. They tortured me in gym. Tried to hang me up by my underwear all the time. I can't tell you how many different kids thought it was okay to just fire a punch into my arm when they walked by me. By ninth grade I was the shortest kid in my class and still hadn't gone through puberty so I was an easy target, I guess. They called me Jew Boy or Pillsbury Jew Boy. In junior high I tried to fight back - even got suspended for a week for fighting. But in high school it wasn't only the kids in my class, but older kids too." Tom noticed Michelle's eyes getting moist, and his own voice felt alien and hoarse, but he continued calmly. "I really tried to understand why everyone hated me. Maybe I talked too much in class. Maybe it was because I did theater. I looked for every possible reason I could control. I stopped going to synagogue after my bar mitzvah. I shut myself down in class. I stopped doing plays in high school. I started to think I just must be a hateable person. I tried to erase my entire identity." Michelle had let a few tears loose onto her cheeks, but then wiped them away. "When I met you I was so afraid of screwing it up for any reason. Even after the bullying stopped, when I finally went through puberty and started lifting weights and I tried to be a normal kid, all the girls avoided me. There was too much peer pressure. I was that kid everyone used to mess with. Who could be seen with me after that? So, you know the rest really. You know what I told you about high school. That I just didn't fit in. Just didn't like it. Small town bullshit. Typical story. You said the same thing. It seemed like enough to say." Tom stopped. He wasn't sure where to go next. He knew why it came out. It had been boiling. First it was Dutch coming back into his daily life and now Robert was his fucking boss. It was Tom being a bully himself to Steve Light. It was Trump on TV. How long since he'd stopped talking? Michelle was just staring at him. Now that the tears were gone from her cheek, she actually looked a little angry.

"This went on for years?" To Tom she sounded both incredulous on the facts, and perhaps more so that he'd managed to keep it from her for decades.

"Yes." Tom said simply.

"I'm sorry. I mean, first of all, I am sorry that you went through that. Of course, I am. But also, I'm sorry, but I'm having a hard time that this is something you've never bothered to tell me about. I've told you everything about my life before I met you. Now I feel like there's this huge piece of your life I'm just finding out about and I wonder what else I don't know."

Jeezus, Tom thought to himself, how could he not get a little sympathy here? What the hell else does she think she doesn't know about his life? She met him when he was barely 18!

"Hon, what else could I possibly be hiding from you? You've known me my whole adult life. Obviously, this wasn't something I wanted to talk about. Obviously."

"So why now, all of a sudden like this?"

Tom didn't want to use a trite psychological term like 'triggered', even if it apparently fit.. "I'm trying to explain something to myself, I guess. I'm trying to understand why I've been a dick so often. I'm trying to explain it to you." He looked directly into her eyes. Didn't she see that there was real pain there? He wasn't trying to make her see it, it was just there, wasn't it? Michelle did not reply, but she did shift her body to open it toward him and held out her arms.

"Come here." She said.

Tom obeyed, diving into her embrace head first, putting his face into the softness above her breast and below her shoulder. She hugged him and rocked him a little bit, like a baby. He felt in some ways it was perfunctory and automatic - that instinct a mother has to quiet a crying baby by picking it up and holding it this way. In his heart he wanted a fiercer, tighter hug. One that acknowledged he was her grown-up lover and life-long companion and he was in pain. But as she continued to rock him, he acknowledged that his expectations were too high. It was him that had allowed distance to creep between them as the years went by, and then, as if to prove his moody silences may have been hiding dark secrets, he'd just revealed one to her. Tom accepted the hug for what it was, a comforting. He pulled himself out, leaving the embrace with a quick peck on the lips.

"Please don't say anything to the kids about what I told you. I'll find a way to tell them both about it someday." Tom got up then and picked up their dinner plates from the coffee table.

"Thank you." Michelle said. Tom plodded into the kitchen, rinsed the dishes off and put them in the dishwasher. He felt a swirling of different thoughts and emotions about what he'd just revealed, some of the words and phrases that he hadn't had to use in decades. Michelle's response. His response to her hug. His chest began to feel light and tingly. Anxiety. Uncertainty. If he let the feeling get away from him, it would soon turn to nausea. He forced his thoughts away, to work, to what was on his proverbial work plate the next day, just as the dinner plates settled into their grooves in the rack. He had to stay sharp. Work was a bitch and that was not going to change. Just thinking about it stiffened every muscle in Tom's body, and that's the response that choked off the anxiety, forced it out of his chest with the next breath. On the whole it had been a good night. It was good to get that out. Time will prove that.

January 21, 2016

It didn't take long for Billy Baron to make his next move. An internal memo from Patton marked URGENT & CONFIDENTIAL arrived at the usual pre-dawn release time for Patton memos. It was addressed to the senior leadership team.

Please keep the following information confidential until 3:00 pm today. At that time, we will be releasing the press briefing below:

Stansfield Corporation today is pleased to announce our intention to purchase 100% of the outstanding shares of Broadview Companies, with the intention of merging the two firms to offer customers a more dynamic platform for engagement with both of our companies. While the companies make different product lines, the overlap in the customer base provides an opportunity to craft a cohesive set of solutions for these customers that will be unique in the industry. Broadview Companies is currently 32% controlled by Armistice Holdings, which recently secured a 22% stake in Stansfield. The obvious synergies in purchasing power, administrative support, and marketing weight makes this a great deal for all shareholders of

Stansfield Corporation stock. The management of Broadview has accepted the terms of our tender offer and since there is little product overlap, we anticipate no antitrust concerns from the SEC, and expect this deal to close within 90 days.

Tom was quite familiar with Broadview, even knew a couple people who worked there. He'd noticed they were on the list of Armistice holdings, but hadn't considered the possibility they would push to merge the firm with Stansfield. Now that he was reading the words, it made perfect sense to him, and he briefly noted that his normal self would have picked that up. Just another reminder he was off his game, or that the game was just not one he wanted to play anymore. The 90 days to close would take Tom past April 1. In his mind, it was clear then. When the deal closed, it would be the end for him. He would not be a part of it. But in the meantime, Tom knew, there were a whole host of potentially distasteful days to come. Big companies that merge don't just show up on the day the deal closes, introduce themselves, and begin the process of integrating. Oh no. While there were laws governing the kind of information they could share while the SEC did its due diligence on the deal, there was plenty they could talk about and prepare for. And since in this case, there was a very motivated matchmaker involved, Tom knew he would soon be engaged in pre-merger work, including those dreaded talent evaluations that would inevitably be the validation of which older, disposable workers each company would send home as soon as they had the chance. Of course, Tom himself could be identified as one of those workers, setting up his tight rope walk. Any action after the merger would be governed by a severance plan that would apply to all those being let go, something standardized. If Tom sensed he was being targeted for a post-merger job elimination, he should stay still, keep his balance, and wait. And vest those shares. Before the merger, Tom would continue to be just another 'at will' employee, capable of being fired for cause with nothing to show for it but unpaid vacation time. That could not happen. That would be stupid if his sense was right. He would stay still and quiet on that rope. He would let April 1 pass peacefully, and then wait another few weeks for the denouement of the merger close. But if Tom got dragged right into the muck of pre-merger work, if he flat out got told he wasn't going anywhere, he'd have no choice but to move forward on that rope. He'd have to regain enough balance to move. He would have to play the game, act excited about the potential for success with the combination, and willingly contribute to the internal preparations. At least until after April 1. Then, if he'd had enough, so be it. He'd hop off the rope or get pushed off it, or set it on fire in front of him, but after April 1, there'd be a safety net down there, and he really wouldn't care what caused him to fall.

Tom had no patience when it came to his future. He had to increase his understanding of his own situation. He had to go through LinkedIn and see who had jobs like his at Broadview. He had to see how old they were, how long in their jobs, how accomplished in their careers, where they went to school, whether they had the MBA Tom never bothered with. He had to see which way things might go in a post-merger world. He had to get a jump on how to walk that rope. If they had a superstar that could do Tom's job, he would have a better idea that inching positively toward April 1 would be his move. Tom wondered who else in the building was doing the same. He worked with a lot of smart people. Surely some of them had Tom's same sense of self-preservation. Damn. The company still had a year to close out, money to find, real work to do, and yet another massive distraction had arrived.

Tom exhaled through his mouth, making the exasperated motor boat sound of lips flapping in the breeze. He hit delete on the email from Patton before his admin stumbled across it. Even as he did so, he knew it didn't matter. Even though the note went to just the 30 or so people on the senior leadership team, the entire building would know the news well before the 3 pm press release. It wouldn't come from Tom. There was no reason to tip off his direct reports early. Let them stay focused on their work and hope the grapevine doesn't find them too soon and start the parade to Tom's office for his thoughts and some reassurance. That was what Tom needed to work on. The response to his own people that was as honest as possible without revealing that Tom had decided he would soon be leaving them to fend for themselves. He had to find the positives in the merger that he could actually appreciate with his cold business logic, before returning to the dark area of his brain where the images of the walking dead lived. The walking dead that would be walked out of the building when it all finally went down.

January 25, 2016

Clearly, this merger with Broadview was firmly on the radar when Armistice dropped the white paper and bought its first chunk of stock. Otherwise, how could Tom be looking up at the big screen in the auditorium at a directors and up meeting and seeing such a comprehensive plan for the integration work to come? People had to be working on this stuff for weeks. Armistice people. The anonymous drones that worked with Billy Baron in New Jersey. The first slide was an org chart, titled "INTEGRATION TEAM". The top box on the chart, the overall lead, was already filled. It was Mike Moran, the Vice-Chairman. Reporting to Mike would be 14 dedicated leaders of identified workstreams. These people would come out of their jobs and work solely on integrating the two companies over a 12 to 18 month period. Tom's nerve endings started to tingle. Mike Moran was at the podium now, taking command of the meeting.

"Eleven of the fourteen leaders have already been identified, and we will be announcing those appointments over the course of this week and next." The boxes for those 11 workstream leaders changed from gray shading to blue on the big screen. "The other three will be identified by the end of next week and announced the week after that."

Tom processed that statement quickly as he stared at the three unfilled boxes. One of them might just as well have his name on it. It was a workstream he'd be perfect to lead, and he realized now that he'd missed a third potential way out, a different tightrope to walk. He'd been through two mergers already in his career at other companies. He was a big help on this last restructuring. He was a problem solver. He Got Shit Done. Tom could sell himself right into that box. It would be a smart exit. Hell, it would be the smartest exit.

For senior people just below C-suite, turning fifty began the process of disappearance, like the slowly fading grin of Alice's Cheshire cat. Executives in their fifties are like out of favor Politburo members in the old Soviet Union – one day they're in power, the next day they're gone. If you're in one of those senior slots and you've tapped out on your career trajectory, you become a serious liability for talent-hungry companies. It's okay to progress through your fifties and even into your sixties once you reach a c-level job, but if you fall just short, you become a blocker. Somewhere just behind you was an up and coming executive in their forties who still had a shot at a c-level assignment. Those leaders were gold. They needed one more jump and bump before getting that plum job....and usually someone in their fifties was in their way. Sometimes, in the right circumstances, there was an opportunity to avoid an uncomfortable "mutual parting of the ways".

Once upon a time, these were called sunset assignments. Some special project for the CEO, a temporary fix-it role in an unpopular foreign outpost, or perhaps a major acquisition that would require a dedicated transition team. It was often a very respectful way to ease an older executive out of the way while getting great value while you still had them.

Tom started to think this could work. Wasn't he just a perfect set-up? He was central casting! 54 years old. Hair gone mostly grey. A solid, Gets Shit Done guy, but topped out here. Just had a chance to get his boss's job but got passed over for a younger guy. Lots of experience to tap. The integration job would take Tom past 55, with ten years of service. Rule of 65. Trigger some nice benefits. He could accept the thanks for taking on the assignment and respectfully part ways. He would have a nice cushion then. Beyond the minimum he had calculated for a post April 1 departure. He might even get to his number then, the first one he claimed as his, when he got here 8 long years ago, the number that would allow Michelle and him to live out their retirement dreams, in their own beach house, on their own terms, with plenty of room for grandkids and plenty left over to travel.

As Mike Moran continued to linger on the organizational chart of the integration, describing each of the workstreams, Tom began to work with the assumption that he would definitely be the one who would fill one of those remaining three gray boxes and as it settled in, he wondered how he thought it would have been acceptable to leave in any of the dumb ways he imagined he might. How was he really going to be comfortable with just getting past April 1? How had he convinced himself that after that he could go out falling, failing, tumbling, screaming, or punching and he would not care? How could he have decided that, knowing that a year from now he'd still be just turning 55? Knowing for sure he'd have to go back to work. And not as a golf course starter either. No. He had to have a smarter exit than the one that just a week ago, a day ago, he'd been plotting.

A smart exit would be much more fitting. For Tom, it had to be this! He would report to Moran, who was also perfectly cast as the super-senior-but-never-the-CEO-and-never-will-be guy who always gets tapped for the big sunset gig, the head of it all. And best of all, Moran was not Dutch. Tom could stomach a very specific assignment for 18 months max, if it was Moran he reported to. He was one of the Good Guys.

If Stover was still here, this would go easier. He would have positioned Tom correctly. With Moran. With Patton. Steered it around Dutch. That fucking box would be full by now, with Tom's name. Now it was Robert who would be his first hurdle, and yet Tom couldn't let that stop him. He didn't get where he was by waiting around for things to be handed to him. He had seen too many peers roll out of big jobs and then begin tumbling back down the corporate ladder at one smaller, desperate loser company after another. Gone from an SVP job at a good company, they get picked up as a VP at a fair one. Then it's down to a director at a poor one, and then eventually back to a manager level, perhaps at a good company again, but one which just wants to fill a need and can get superior knowledge and experience at a bargain. Tom's LinkedIn connection list was peppered with people who had reached out at one time or another down that chute looking for his help in securing a job, even if it was one well beneath the person's qualifications. And then there were many who had given up on finding another corporate gig and preferred to list themselves as President of their own consulting firm, using the royal we to describe what they do for clients, even though it's a team of one, and there have been no clients yet. Tom always told himself he wouldn't let that happen to him, but as recently as the day before, hours before, he was going to risk it.

Mike Moran had moved off the organizational slide to a metrics of success slide, where Tom's eyes barely registered anything but the bolded acronym EBITDA. The river water was rushing in Tom's head, taking his stream of consciousness with it. It was crazy wasn't it? The money at this level? Even at a company doing as shitty as Tom's was in the eyes of its shareholders. Getting out of here at 54 with nothing but one more vesting date, compared to stretching to two more years at his current earnings and getting a nice sunset severance package at 56? Quite possibly a life changing difference. Tom didn't need his charts and his calculator to know that. But for days now he'd been content to walk away from those years, certain he would not survive them. In his current capacity. But things were moving fast. Over the course of the last month this had looked to Tom to be the classic buy and slash operation, dressed up as a strategic repositioning. But now there was a merger. And mergers meant integrations. And integrations need teams, and leaders. Always be flexible, Tom reminded himself. He sat up straighter in his chair. He glanced around the room. Robert held the key to the empty box with Tom's name on it. The key to his number. The Golden Ticket. Where was Robert? Why was the box still unfilled? Who else could possibly do a better job than Tom?

Or couldn't anybody? What made Tom think the integration role would be any more pleasant than the hell he'd already imagined for the near future? Moran said 12-18 months. Could Tom really handle another year in the saddle? One last thrust? Stretch his career, hold onto all these terrible skills, slice and dice his way through a merged list of names that would form the final team? Make all the right choices? Send all the losers home? He could, couldn't he? Then he'd graciously decline the opportunity to cycle back into his old operating role. Receive another six months in severance. Sit around until his noncompete wears off. Maybe teach some college courses. Write some blogs about the industry. Fish about for that next thing, financially secure. It was indeed, the smart exit. As opposed to the dumb exit, the one he'd become semi-obsessed with. Just walking away. No plan. Too early to retire. But just walking away all the same. Walking away because he'd become a hollowed-out husk of a man burnt to a crisp on the outside. Yes, that was quite likely the dumb exit, now that there was a smart alternative.

Tom could not let this pass, could not be shy about going after it, even though it would mean lying through his teeth to a man he respected. He would have to not only get Robert's blessing, but also Mike Moran's. To achieve what had suddenly become his number one goal, Tom still had to be perceived as caring about the company as if it were one of his own children. Pulling that off day to day was tough enough… confessing it out loud when you didn't really believe it, to people like Robert and Moran, who are trained bullshit-sniffers, was another level altogether. If he could make it happen another Academy Award nomination awaited him. Maybe even a lifetime achievement Oscar.

January 29, 2016

It took until Friday to get a half hour on Robert's calendar, three days of silence about the last three gray boxes on the integration org chart, three days when someone else could be pitching themselves successfully for the role. At least the time gave Tom a chance to hone his story, to decide how much truth to put into his desire to be part of a transition team, how much willingness to signal about turning the role into a sunset assignment as opposed to a stepping stone. If Tom was indeed walking a tightrope until April 1, it was an outdoor tightrope, one that could bounce and sway with the wind. He knew he had to be careful with Robert. Tom could avoid talking to Dutch, but talking to Robert was the same as whispering in Dutch's ear.

Robert and Tom had already spoken about their own working relationship, the day Robert was announced. Robert had said all the right things about valuing Tom's experience and needing his steady hand on the team, with so many new people and younger executives in expanded roles. Tom had said all the right things, congratulating Robert on his promotion, promising to respect his decisions and assuring Robert that he, Tom, would be a supportive leader on his team. And then they had gotten right into the details of the business, what the hits and misses were, what Tom was doing about each, how he was going to help close the gap on earnings before the end of the quarter. This conversation about the integration would be their first time alone since the meeting with Steve Light that yielded the company the extra cash for the quarter. That success should be the proof that Tom's head was still in the game, that he was still putting company first. Tom stood chatting with Robert's admin for a couple of minutes before his appointed time, and when Robert's door opened, another of Robert's direct reports, Jason Cruz, one of those younger executives in expanded roles, walked out.

Tom's brain processed two images simultaneously, the org chart slide for the integration team, with the three boxes yet to go blue, and the resume of Jason Cruz, which included eight years of consulting before joining the company in a strategy role six years ago, and a steady progression of promotions into operating roles since. His mouth said "Hey Jason" while his brain quickly assigned the tag 'competitor for the blue box I failed to consider'. And as Robert took a quick look at his email inbox at his desk, Tom felt a small rush of panic as he realized that an integration role could also be a good fit for an up-and-comer to show their strategic-thinking skills and cross-functional leadership capabilities. He was glad he'd decided to put his own positive spin on his interest in the role, in the prep work for this conversation.

"Come on in Tom, have a seat." Robert said it without looking away from his screen, or he would have seen Tom already seated at the conference table. "Karen just put 'one to one request' in my calendar, what can I do to help you today?" Robert used that phrase often, to show he believed in servant leadership. Tom hated the contrivance because it also set up the clear power dynamic that the boss could do things the subordinate couldn't do on their own.

Tom came right to the point.

"I wanted to talk to you about the merger, and more specifically, the integration team." Tom stared directly into Robert's eyes as he said the last words, looking for any reactive ripple. There was none, so he continued.

"I've given this a lot of thought, and I think I have a strong sense of what this merger can deliver if done well, and I'd like to be a part of making sure it's done well. The team lead for Supplier Strategy was still open on Tuesday, and given everything I've done in my career, I know there's no one better suited for that track than me." Tom had decided to take this route that implied he wanted to be part of the future, without trying to sell Robert on the phony idea that it would be a great professional development opportunity. He didn't want to sell Robert on his fit for the role either – that would hopefully be obvious. He really just wanted to know as soon as possible if Robert would support Tom's desire for the assignment.

"I don't disagree. But I can't afford to lose you from the team. The merger's going to happen, and the shit is going to start flying as soon as it does. The integration is going to take the year to year and a half they say it is, but in the meantime, we've still got a business to run, and if you were on the integration team, I'd be hard-pressed to do that." This was significant. Not only had Robert just shot down Tom's sunset role idea less than a minute into the conversation, he'd simultaneously indicated with some certainty that Tom was expected to be part of the team after the merger, still part of the day to day, still a senior vice president, still fucking here. Tom had to press ahead with his preplanned options for a negative response on the integration role, and worry about the implications of missing out on a post-merger exit package later.

"I've given that some thought, and I'll tell you, Hamilton's ready to step up another level – maybe not to everything I have currently, but let's face it, I only have what I have because the company felt I could handle it without fucking it up too much, but it's not a job anyone can do in a combined company. Too big by far. We have to re-org anyway." Tom searched Robert's expression for any semblance of agreement or acknowledgement that Tom had made a cogent point. Nothing. The classic Robert death stare, and then a quick glance down to break their locked eyes, before looking back up and staring straight into Tom's eyes again.

"I know Hamilton's ready, but I have a plan for that. And I do have a plan for the integration role as well. I did consider the idea of having you do it. You're absolutely right that you'd be a great fit. But given where we are, and getting the sense that there's not a ton of talent in supplier management at Broadview, I need you doing what you're doing, more than anything else." Tom realized it took a lot for Robert to concede that Tom was critical to the team beyond the immediate future, and it indicated that at least for now, Robert was probably a trustworthy buffer between Tom and Dutch. But this was not the answer he was looking for, not a shut down, no chance for further discussion, I've got someone else in mind answer. The quick finality gave Tom pause about his final counter, but he decided to go ahead and play the card. He was going to get as close to pure honesty as he could without jeopardizing his employment before April 1. He was going to bank on some degree of empathy, some degree of compassion for a fellow human being buried somewhere underneath Robert's calibrating stare.

"I guess I appreciate that, but I have to tell you, I'm not sure how long I've got left." Robert let a momentary look of deep concern cross his face. Tom sensed an unintended reaction to his words. "Not in a terminal illness sense, Robert, but in a mental health sense. In a happiness sense. I'm getting to the end of my rope. I've been through too many mergers and reorgs and downsizings. I'm tired of it. At this point in my career I just want to feel like I'm contributing to making something better. I have no more agendas, I'm not looking for a promotion, I don't have room to grow. I don't have another box to check on my way to the top. I can stay in an operating role, but I'm not happy now, and I don't foresee getting happier in the middle of another merger. I thought the integration role would help me do those things – make a good company out of two shitty ones, help set some people up for success that I care about, and at the end, figure out if I still had the energy to do this. I thought it would be the best way for me to support you as well. Put someone less experienced in the integration role, and you'll be paying as much attention to that as you will to the day to day. You won't sleep." Tom wondered if Robert would buy any of that altruistic shit, or even his personal concern for Robert's quality of life. But he did want him to buy the unhappiness. Tom was just so damn good at masking whatever his true feelings were that Robert would have to take him at his word on this one. He wanted him to believe the truth that was inherent in his story – that no one can keep doing this and keep both their sanity and their soul, and deciding which one to sacrifice has consequences.

Robert just stared back at Tom. Tom watched his eyes for a tell, some sign that he'd gotten through, but those black eyes just continued to stare ahead. Then Robert let out a slow breath and leaned back in his chair, still staring right at Tom, but not through him, as he was wont to do.

"I'm really not sure how to respond. It sounds like you just told me you really don't want to be here. I mean, I know where you came from before here. And I know what's gone on here. how long has it been? 8 years, 9?"

"Just past 8. 'And counting', I guess".

"I'm sympathetic, Tom, I really am. There's a lot that hasn't been fun the last several years. But I gotta know if you're up to the job you have, because it's a big job, and even if we define it differently after the merger, it will still be a big job." Tom felt just a smidgen of authenticity in Robert's voice. He was several years younger than Tom, but close enough to know what another few years in this nut-cruncher might do to his own mental state. Tom could see he did not intend to ever, ever, let himself utter the words Tom had just uttered, but all the same, he'd visited the place they came from. Tom was not speaking gibberish. Robert continued after a brief pause and Tom's lack of response.

"So the bottom line here is that I'm not going to take you out of your current role and assign you to the integration team. If I gave everyone who's unhappy right now in their current role the choice of whatever new job they wanted, I'd have a line down the hallway. If you tell me you need a little time off ahead of the merger kick-off, I'll be flexible with you. But I need your head in the game for sure, as long as you're here."

And there it was. The Dare. I dare you to quit. I dare you to walk. I dare you to threaten your own financial security for the rest of your life. If you don't take the dare, you're still mine. You still belong to the company. You're still an asset.

But don't ever lose sight of the fact that you're fungible. And fungible people can't make successful threats. Tom was not going to take the dare before April 1st. Tom did his best Robert death stare impression right back at him, trying to show him what a lack of compassion and understanding looks like. Trying to be his human mirror. He gently shook his head from side to side in grim acceptance of his fate, but also in a way that signaled that he believed Robert had just made a big, big mistake, and he wanted Robert to know he felt that way.

"Alright then." Tom rose from his chair, still staring back at Robert, forcing Robert to stand too. Tom knew he had to say what he said next. "I respect your decision, and you'll have my support and best effort. As long as I'm still here." He was intentionally throwing Robert's phrase back at him with just a hint of inflection that the "as long" part might not be that long. That summed it up didn't it, at this level? As long as you could walk in the door in the morning and walk back out in the evening, nothing less than the best would be tolerated during the hours in between, and nothing less would be given. Through bitterness, unhappiness, even red-hot hatred, professionalism would shine through. Tom turned around and walked out the door without another word.

From Tom Cooper's private journal. October 2008. Age 47.
Employer 6.

Early morning, dead of winter. I walked into my favorite room in our new house, the office at the front facing the street, facing east. A vaulted ceiling allows tall windows that let in the emerging light of the day. Our neighborhood sits in a clearing at the top of what just thirty years ago was a pristine, heavily forested hill. A hundred years before that the hill was a farm, completely bare of trees. I know because the stone wall marking the property boundary from long ago runs through the woods that stretch out behind the house. Settlers back then cleared all the land for agriculture, to feed a growing population. After it all grew back, a developer cleared the trees, and he built some enormous homes, and he built some that were simply large and comfortable, and people with the wealth to afford them settled this little plot of land again. Unlike the first settlers, who undoubtedly knew their neighbors, I don't know the other people sharing this settlement. We did not take down these trees together. We each forged our own path here in various ways, linked mainly by our common ability to earn enough money to afford these homes. The space between us is generous enough that we don't have to do much but cordially wave to each other as we back out of our driveways.

The house directly across from us, over which my sun rises every morning, is one of the enormous ones. Mine is one of the 'simply large'. I haven't met the occupants yet, though my wife has. They have a son in high school with my kids, around the same age, but they haven't met them yet either. I don't think anyone here is particularly antisocial, either in my house or across the street. I think this is just how people act who can afford to live in neighborhoods and homes like these, and I'll have no problem getting used to it.

As I stood in my office and looked out those tall windows on this particular morning, I felt agitated and uneasy. I stretched myself to afford this place, and now the economy is collapsing all around us. I have a job that can pay the bills, but my cushion should I lose it has been greatly reduced by the nose-dive in the stock market. I wondered if everything I've done in my life to this point, to get to where I now stood, in a big home in an exclusive neighborhood at the top of a hill in a fine town, was the right way to live. Have I really done right by my marriage and for my children by working 60 hour weeks, and more at home, to get ahead of others, to get the promotion to the big money jobs? To get this house? Is this really a healthy way to live, ensconced in a big box, barely knowing my neighbors, no time to get involved in the community? Have I had a good life to this point? I know I've done well, but have I lived well?

I turned around and faced the other side of the room. A built-in bookshelf runs the length of the interior wall, lined not just with books, but also tons of photos. There are pictures of the great-grandparents and grandparents, now deceased, on both sides of the family. People who could not imagine living as we're living today. Pictures of our families now, and friends, and all of us smiling of course. That's what people do in photos, try to show the world how happy they are. And they are genuinely happy, because they're in the company of the people they care the most about. But no one is happy all the time, and not every smile is real. I searched for my face in all the pictures. I saw my smile. Was it true happiness in that moment? How much else was on my mind right then, and how much of it did it command?

February 9, 2016

Earlier in his career, Tom had a job where he was required to translate back and forth between consultant speak and real life. His employer at the time was just as addicted to the brand name brain power of the McKinseys, Accentures, Bains, and Boston Consultings of the world as his current bosses. Tom's title was "Director of Strategy", but what he mostly did was hold hands with the consultants and try to make sure they didn't fuck things up so grandly they'd be back in another year; a different big name in the industry called in to fix what the other guys broke. He sat in on stakeholder interviews, took his own notes, and then helped the consultants make sense of what the practitioners said so they could reach the right conclusions. Not that Tom had all the big ideas and right answers, but he did know pretty instinctually and usually accurately what wouldn't work, or what wouldn't be accepted by the rank and file and therefore undermined. He became fluent in consultant speak over the course of that assignment, and had since reaped the benefit of being able to see bullshit coming a mile away, and in the eight years at this stop, he'd certainly seen a bucket full of both consultants and the stuff they generally peddle.

So when he heard the phrase, "Center of Excellence", three years ago, further defined by the malodorous definers, "Promote Collaboration", "Share Best Practices", and

"Amplify Learning", he could see a disaster coming. A new job and team was to be created, headed by at least a senior vice president, that would "advise, support, guide, and provide governance" to the business unit teams that they would be assigned to support. In other words, the outside consultants had recommended the company create an internal consultancy, and the company actually implemented it. Tom was petrified they might think he'd be good in the role, based on his resume and experience. Roles like that were career death sentences, in Tom's mind. It was clear to Tom that the role would have no teeth, would at best simply be an analytical support team, and at worst, a clusterfuck of misaligned goals and metrics, fuzzy reporting lines, and political infighting. A no-win, piece of shit job.

But Tom did not get that job. The company found an outside candidate willing to swallow all of the bullshit, say thank you, and ask for more. His name was Hirschfeld, Walter Hirschfeld, an old family name oddly old-fashioned in the century of Jasons, Justins, Joshuas, Jordans, and a million other J-names. Hirschfeld let everyone know he was actually the fifth consecutive Walter Hirschfeld in his family tree, but all of them had different middle names, so there was no Roman numeral V at the end of his.

Hirschfeld was a gregarious enough sort, tried hard to get along with everyone, tried to play the role he was assigned, employed a massive vocabulary of strategic terminology on a daily basis, proposed and advocated for a wide variety of initiatives that sounded good on the surface but were generally fraught with landmines and complexity, and generally made himself a nuisance, in Tom's mind, to the people he was brought in to support, including Tom. He was about Tom's age, but seemed to believe he still had a shot to become the CEO someday, and Tom was sure he felt his hiring from the outside was a signal that the company was short on strategic thinkers, or else they would have promoted someone inside to a job like this, with its high visibility and consultant's imprimatur. Tom had by then begun to lose the remaining patience he had for the games and politics of corporate life. The company was not getting enough shit done, and that being Tom's specialty, it irked him when people spent too much time worrying about the nonsense and the bullshit. Hirschfeld seemed quite focused on managing up and pleasing the COO and the CEO and proving that the Center of Excellence concept would work. And Tom had a lot on his plate, and really didn't need any help at that stage of his career, so while he treated Hirschfeld with courteous, professional respect, even when they disagreed, he did not go out of his way to make him feel welcome at the company, and certainly didn't try to get to know him personally. Hirschfeld was commuting every week, away from his wife and a child still in high school, as he had for the two years at his previous stop. That's a tough life. Tom could have been nicer. He knew it, but he just couldn't summon the patience to do it. He was trying to survive. Dodging Dutch. Making his goals. Helping to deliver quarterly earnings. Serving the shareholders.

And sure enough, as Tom had predicted, the Center of Excellence was gone just over a year after its grand inception and Hirschfeld's hiring, dying like a star dies, collapsing into itself until all that remains is a black hole. Hirschfeld went into an operating role, and in the September reorg he became one of Tom's peers, reporting to Stover, and now Robert.. Tom had begun to tolerate him, had gotten to know him just a little bit. He learned that Hirschfeld had a creative side – he was a guitarist, and had found his way into a local bar band. That was pretty unusual for a corporate executive in a multi-billion-dollar company with CEO aspirations. With his own deep connection to music, Tom found this news unexpected, and it made him begin to see Hirschfeld in a different light. But still, they were not close, nowhere near close enough to have predicted what he was about to learn.

Tom had just come out of a meeting that was intense enough that he had not once looked at his phone in the last 30 minutes. As he checked it coming out the door, one of those admin phrases that always made the hair stand up on his neck was flashing on his screen – "PLEASE FLEX! 15 minute meeting, Robert's office." Starting now. Tom always got a little jolt of excitement when he received a message like that. It always led to an announcement of some sort that would bring change, and Tom was a change junkie. Part of the fun was guessing on the way to the meeting – couldn't be Robert leaving or getting promoted – he just got the job. Did Billy Baron pull the clothes off the emperor and fire Dutch Bagley? Was one of Tom's peers leaving? Jen Brentz had been hired to replace one of the departed hotshots, and the other job was filled from within, so all the seats were full now. This one was hard to peg. He was apparently the last one to get there, apologizing while at the same time taking note that he wasn't last, that Hirschfeld was also missing. Robert didn't waste time.

"I'm very sorry to have to tell you some very sad news. Walter Hirschfeld has passed away. Apparently it happened Monday. As you remember, he wasn't at staff on Monday, and when I couldn't reach him Tuesday, and he didn't come in, we began to get concerned. And then his wife called us last night and informed us that Walter had passed."

Tom's mind raced, and as he imagined it would for anyone, naturally went to the memory banks, looking for the last time he saw Hirschfeld alive, and while he couldn't recall if it were Friday afternoon or Monday morning, he clearly remembered the encounter. They were approaching each other in the hallway that ran through the cafeteria, two professionals working for the same boss, each on their own agenda and schedule, save for team meetings. They usually said a friendly hello and kept going, respectful of the treadmill pace and that one of them, statistically, was already late to a meeting. Tom remembered thinking as they passed, that Hirschfeld had not seemed his upbeat, positive self lately. A little more serious. He had come on to the team under Stover, and Tom suspected he might be struggling a little bit with Robert. Maybe also angry that he did not get the job – after all, he'd been brought in to a big role, and while the company decided to pivot and eliminate the job, they'd kept him, and he'd done nothing in his role to diminish his reputation and standing. In Tom's mind's eye, this last passing in the hall played forward and back in high definition. Hirschfeld's voice and eyes were lowered, he gave a tepid 'hey' and a weak nod, from a face devoid of light. It immediately led Tom down the dark trail to wondering if Hirschfeld had taken his own life, just as Robert's voice was continuing,

"We don't know the cause of death. I don't really have any other details right now. I hope to speak to Doreen, his wife, and I'll let you know more when I know more." This was stunning. Tom's heart was pounding. He quite possibly had seen a person in need, and did nothing more but grimace a hello back and keep moving.

A second meeting two days later confirmed the worst. Once again, the team was pulled together, this time a larger group. All of Hirschfeld's direct reports in addition to Robert's whole team, plus Donna from HR, and a person Tom, who once again was the last one to the room, had never seen before. She turned out to be an outside specialist in suicide counseling. A couple people were crying. Robert didn't need to say what was obvious from the introductions, but he shared quickly and simply that Walter Hirschfeld had left work early on Monday, and never made it home. His body was found, and suicide was determined to be the cause of death. No other details available. None necessary.

Tom felt waves of guilt, but defiantly dismissed them, as he always had, then regret, for not getting to know Hirschfeld better, and then, most powerfully, curiosity, a gnawing hunger to understand how whatever he was dealing with could have been so powerful to end what seemed to be a pretty damn okay life over it. It had to be a pretty damn okay life didn't it? Because it was Tom's life, too. They were so alike on paper you couldn't distinguish between them. If only Tom had reached out, he might have found they were alike deeper down too. Now he could only assume they weren't. Or they were. Tom had never imagined he could take his own life, even though he thought about it at the heart of those years he was bullied, a young teen on the wrong side of puberty. He thought about it in the way Tom Sawyer thought about it in his favorite childhood book. The whole town would turn out to mourn, and how sorry they all would be that he was gone. How guilty the bullies would feel knowing that they drove him to disappear, to die, probably by his own hand. But that was a long time ago, and it was not a thought that Tom had ever considered again. But he certainly understood unhappiness. Yes, he certainly understood that.

The next several days were a blur. Little pieces of the story filtered into hallway conversations, but Tom was convinced no one really knew anything. For sure, enough people could recall seeing him on Monday morning in the office, but Tom still couldn't confirm in his mind whether that last moment between them occurred that day, or before the weekend. He just didn't want to imagine it as Monday morning, and play it back with a different ending, one where Tom reaches out and grabs Hirschfeld's sleeve and asks him if everything's okay. Where he tells him he's noticed he's not been himself lately and was concerned about him. Even if that second part would be a lie unless, by concerned, he meant speculating why. So he stopped believing it was possible he saw him within hours of his leaving the office, and eventually, this world. Even if Tom had grabbed his sleeve on Monday, would it have really made a difference? They were just co-workers, cordial, but not friends. What could he have possibly said in that deep moment of need that Hirschfeld would have responded to?

Tom spoke to a few of Hirschfeld's direct reports. They all had seen what Tom had, but for longer. He just stopped being the same man they all thought they knew for the first couple years he was here, sometime over the last six months, depending on which one Tom talked to. Some of Tom's deep guilt eased.....everyone close to Hirschfeld saw what he had. No one else reached out and touched him on the sleeve. No one else told him they were worried about him. No one in this setting, in this corporate ball that was still a high school dance in so many ways, really got to know their co-workers well enough to predict a suicide risk. If someone's looking down, they all assume some aspect of work has got them tied up in knots, in which case, sympathy, as if for one who has a cold, is all that's required. And if it's something deeper, something at home, they're too polite and professional to ask.

February 16, 2016

A week after Hirschfeld's suicide, Tom was sitting with his team in a row of faux Louis XIV chairs in a downtown hotel. It seemed like an odd place to hold what the family had described in their invitation as a celebration of his life. But now that Tom had settled into his seat in the large function room he began to understand why it made sense to hold it here, particularly as Hirschfeld's brother-in-law, who apparently was serving as a master of ceremonies, welcomed those in attendance by introducing each in groups. Members of the immediate family of course. Hirschfeld's college friends. Members of the band Hirschfeld had been playing with in the area, and of course, the very large contingent from work. That's why the memorial was here. It was very convenient to the home office where Hirschfeld spent the last years of his working life.

Tom hadn't given much thought to the guest list for his own funeral, but he hoped to hell it didn't look like this. Close friends and family, whoever's left, sure, but an entire platoon from his work life?. The entire senior executive team was here, sitting together, including Patton and Dutch. Tom had a flashing vision of that row as the defendant's table in court. He suddenly had an overwhelming desire for this to become a trial, and to be called as a witness.

As it began, in his mind, Tom saw it as such. First Hirschfeld's wife, remarkably composed and calm given the circumstances, welcomed them all. Tom had only met her once, a few months ago, at a holiday party. She thanked everyone for coming and giving their support to her and the children. She addressed the cause of, or rather the motive for death, right up front.

"I know everyone wants to understand why Walter has left us, and I just want to assure you that there is no big story here. There was no divorce pending, no financial trouble, no gambling problem. I don't know that any of us will truly know why..." Tom noted that the phrase 'no difficulties at work', did not make her list.

And then, for the next hour, one person after another came forward – brother, brother-in-law, mother-in-law, college friend with funny stories, college friend with a touching tribute, musician friends. No one from the company rose to speak. The longer it went on, Tom couldn't help but feel that it was obvious what the family and friends believed had happened. And perhaps the real reason this memorial was held here. It could only be work. After all, didn't they just finish telling all assembled what a great dad, husband, friend, and bandmate Hirschfeld was? How he had everything going for him? It felt like the case for the prosecution had been made, with no cross-examination. It felt like the family had set the company up, invited them here to make them realize they were at fault. They had to be. The man they knew had to have been really crushed by something to take his own life. And they had examined all of the relationships they had with him, and not found that stone. Oh yes, they had a purpose holding this here, Tom was now sure of it.

Tom stared at the senior executives in their row, watched for some sign of uneasiness, queasiness, distress, sorrow. If it was there, he couldn't find it. They sat stone-faced, staring straight ahead. The women in leadership did not have tissues in their hands. The men did not dab surreptitiously at tears. These were all hard cases, to be sure. As Tom himself was. Of course they were all human, but still, they were different. They came to work every day with their hard candy shells and cold-eyed logic and CEO's relentlessness and battled. They all claimed the enemy was outside the four walls, the competition. Ostensibly, this was true, but they had other enemies – complacency, mediocrity, small-thinking, and since the outside enemy wasn't sitting right next to them every day, all that aggression had to go somewhere, and that was right there at home, inside their own four walls. Tom was a witness, but complicit too.

On or about Hirschfeld's last day on earth, Tom might have been in a position to make a difference, but he was not. His uselessness was born in the way he'd responded to Hirschfeld when he joined the company. An annoying fly to be brushed away from his face. Politely of course. How would he answer why? Why did Tom pay forward the welcome he felt he'd received at the company to a new coworker? Wasn't he smart enough to see the perpetually corrosive effects of that kind of behavior?

Tom thought about Jen Brentz, the most recent similarly leveled outside hire to come in and work directly with him. He went out of his way to be a resource to her, consciously, as if foreshadowing there would be something he needed to atone for. Isn't that what the guilty did? Showed their awareness of their incriminating behavior? Jen was now a friend, after only a few months at the company. Were these just different times, or was he nicer to Jen because he himself needed another ally? With the CEO seated at his desk in the corner of Tom's brain, he was never sure if his motives were his or simply the logic required of him. And yet, he knew that a lot of his own daily hatred for the company was the sink or swim culture. It was something he could at least do something about, personally. He could show it in the way he welcomed Jen onto the team as a coworker. And he tried to ignore the other part of his brain where a smart-alecky nag suggested that it didn't hurt that Jen was attractive and smart and not annoying in the least. Thank god this wasn't a trial. He might have to plead the fifth.

The last person finished their reminiscence, and there was a moment of awkwardness. Half of the room had not really had its say, but the other half had said, 'Everything about Hirschfeld's life over here was wonderful.' Unsaid, hanging in the air, couldn't everyone feel it??

'How about the big group over there? Anyone want to tell us how that was going for Walter?'

And no one did.

So, with nothing left to say, the four musicians left in Hirschfeld's bar band came forward, to pick up instruments placed there ahead of time, to pay a final tribute to Walter Hirschfeld the fifth, but not the V, the rock guitarist they knew, the husband, father, and friend, the senior vice-president at the 117th largest corporation in the land. The combination that apparently no one really knew well enough.

The lead singer introduced the first song as one that was really special to Walter, one that they always finished with, when gigging at local clubs, to showcase his playing. The musicians began to play the first chords, as the singer finished introducing the song. But Tom didn't need to hear him say "Simple Man, by Lynyrd Skynyrd", because at those first chords, every hair on his body, crawling along his shins, up and down his arms, across the top of his back and up his neck, was standing at attention like barren trees on the Siberian Steppe. An icy wind blew through the trees, cooling the little pimples of sweat that had simultaneously burst open, cooling Tom's skin, and as the song progressed into the lyrics that were embedded in his very being, he wasn't sure he could keep his composure. It was as if he were Tom Sawyer, not Tom Cooper, sneaking into his own funeral, and being reminded why he should want to be alive. This was a voice, screaming in his ear – 'Get out! Get out while you still can!' He wanted to get up and go straight over to Patton, to the CEO, sitting next to Dutch Bagley, and tell the two of them this was it. He was done. But he didn't. He sat there frozen, a step beyond cooled.

"Simple Man" is a beautiful song, stretching as long as a musician wants to spend on the breaks, but at least six minutes in most cases. Those six minutes on this occasion were long enough for Tom to replay his own life a half a dozen times, as well as imagine all the different ways this phase of that life could come to a close. Tom could no longer imagine any scenario in which he could stay with the company – hell, stay employed at all. This was it, the final message. What's that they called it in MMA? The death blow? He needed to tap out. How fitting. 32 years in the cage, the octagon. It was going to end, he was going to get out, that was clear now. Maybe not the path or the destination, but the intent was certain, the ambiguity gone. There was some momentary elation in that realization, as if his spirits were being picked up by the chords and words that had meant so much to him and carried him up out of the depths of hell. It had to end. It would end. For him. For Tom. Not the way it ended for Hirschfeld. But in some way he would make his own. Walter's death now meant something he didn't likely intend. A gift to a man who gave him none. Who found him more than a little annoying for the longest time. Who did nothing to stop this. It would end now. That, Tom knew with certainty.

From Tom Cooper's private journal. August 2011. Age 50. Employer 6.

Maybe it's because I never found solace in religion. I know it sounds stupid and simplistic for a college graduate to say this, but I look for that direction and comfort in song lyrics. Always have. I know I'm not completely alone in this, otherwise, why would music with lyrics be so popular? So here I am, turning 50, a senior executive for the 114th biggest company in the country, married, two kids in college, and I'm seeking a new direction in life, and to find it, I'm listening to the words of wisdom in a song written over 40 years ago by a hard-rocking, hard-living band of southern musicians. Nuts, right?

Here's what Lynyrd Skynyrd had to say, in "Simple Man":

Take your time, don't live too fast
Troubles will come and they will pass,
You'll find a woman, you'll find love,
And don't forget there is someone up above.
Forget your lust for the rich man's gold,
All that you need is in your soul,
Don't you worry, you'll find yourself,
Follow your heart and nothing else,
Be a simple kind of man,
Be something you love and understand.

I loved this when I first heard it as a teenager, and while I've both ignored and followed the advice, I constantly find myself coming back to it and examining my life against its message. I found the woman and the love at 18, married her at 23, and never looked back. But the lust for the rich man's gold has been a complicated relationship with my heart and soul. When the pursuit started to take on a life of its own, I tried to rationalize that the quicker I could accumulate a pile of money, the sooner I could have that simple man's life. But how much was that, exactly? A lot more than a young fool might wish. Life is long when measured against what it costs to get through a day with shelter, food, and good health. Life is short when each day hurtles by in the pursuit of the means to those ends. There was a time I tried to be content with the balance, slowed it down, stayed a long time in a job that fit my life when the kids were young. I worked crazy hard for a comfortable living and I was home for everything that mattered in my family's life. But it didn't turn out to be enough. I could see dreams taking shape in the eyes of those closest to me – college educations, a retirement home at the beach, and in my own eyes as well. I could not let go of that lust for the rich man's gold. My simple kind of man likes to play golf, eat well, and someday wants to travel to all the places he's never seen but always wanted to.

But as the song warned, I've taken on stresses and pressures I've come to believe I never wanted. In many ways, I've become something I don't love and understand. I'm so close to the finish line...but still quite short. Hundreds of thousands of dollars in college tuition costs are looming, the retirement home is only half saved-up-for, and the one I have is owned mostly by the bank. But my soul feels busted, and my heart is not in my work. I still long to be a simple kind of man.

And yet....the world is a really scary place right now....everything still feels so tenuous, the economic shock still raw. .Is this really a time to let a song lyric tell me to take a risk and follow my heart? To chuck my corporate career just as it's reached its peak earning years to do something – anything – but what I do now? And I don't even have a clue what that is. As another Skynyrd title said, I'm Searching. And I hope to be singing yet one more of their lyrics:

They call me the breeze, I keep blowing down the road.

February 16, 2016

Tom drove back to the office from the memorial with no music on, no radio on at all for the 35 minute drive. He was absorbed with the implications of a decision he had no intention of reversing, at home, in the office, for the future. There was an underlying serenity of the decision being made, really, truly, finally. No more hedging, no more maybe, no more fear-driven transmogrification of panic about his financial future into genuine hope for the company's future. No more scheming for a sunset assignment. The only hope was to get out, to jump, to find out what's left inside of him and what to do with it later, but for right now to just go. So that was good, that was a base, that serenity. But Michelle had fears too, and just because Tom was ready to toss his aside, he had to consider hers too, didn't he? They'd been in this together since they were teenagers. He'd dragged her and the kids around the country and made them close to rootless. The trade-off was always going to be the secure financial future. Was Tom forgetting that? Michelle would want to know, she'd ask that. She'd always trusted him with the money, but she'd fought him for it over the years. She wanted to live in the here and now – remodel a kitchen, take a vacation, go to a show. Tom's instinct was to squirrel away first, to prepare for the worst. They compromised along the way, but damn, Tom better not fuck up the retirement. After all that perceived penury, did he in the end not save enough? Will he be ripping movie tickets in half when he's 70? Do they even do that anymore? It didn't matter. The decision was final. It was done.

At the office, Tom loaded a backpack full of what he considered his most important paper documents. Technically, it was company information he should not be leaving with. Tom considered 'technically' a close cousin of 'technicality'. Technically, he had most of the information in those papers in his head, and he knew what he could share with people and what he couldn't. The papers would help him recall facts, spin them into things he could say without breaking either the law or his own confidentiality agreements. And they would help him earn some money. There was a whole cottage industry of arranged phone calls between investment companies of various stripes and senior-level industry experts like Tom. These firms would pay Tom for his time on these calls, to dispense his wisdom and knowledge. He was taking the helpful papers now, before he announced any intention of leaving the company, just in case he was walked straight to his car, or his bag was checked on his way out the door. Tom never stopped scrapping for every penny he could, never wanted to forget what it felt like to be threatened by a lack of financial resources. He stooped to pick up dirty pennies in parking lots to this day, to remind himself of that. He tossed them in his cup holder and used them to scratch the lottery tickets he bought every time he stopped for gas.. The documents and decks he collected and stuffed in the backpack were like the pennies, they were a reminder of the safety net, but they also play their role in the gamble. That was the existential choice of all lives, wasn't it? Live for today or live for tomorrow? Tom had decided that living for today meant leaving his job.

There were things he still needed to do in the leaving that would help with living for tomorrow.

Once all the paper he cared to keep was secure, Tom looked at the clock and it was still only four. He opened up his email. He would clear out the dreck, trim it down, move the gears of his organization with yeses and nos. He could do it mindlessly while he prepared for the conversations to come. With Michelle tonight. Robert tomorrow. Tom started by deleting the obvious spam that managed to leak into his inbox. Then he opened up the first note that would require some reading and a response. And he knew it again, immediately, that it was finally over. The email was meaningful to someone on his team, but it was nothing to Tom. The word 'meaningless' didn't begin to do justice to what Tom thought of everything that was in that email inbox at that moment. It was part of the finality of his decision, and it felt good to feel the serenity of that almost literally warm up his veins once again.

"Fuck it", Tom said out loud, and closed his laptop. Michelle shouldn't be surprised to see him home early on a day like today. In the greater honesty he was trying to build with her, he'd shared how Hirschfeld's suicide affected him. Although, until Simple Man started playing he had no idea himself how much. He grabbed his backpack and headed for the door.

"Well, there was kind of a crazy moment, which I'll tell you about in a minute, but on the whole, it was not intentionally sad, you know, more of a celebration of his life, with lots of sharing of memories." Tom was home, coat off, standing at the island in the kitchen across from Michelle, the granite top between them an unintentional wall, though Tom knew there was still some metaphorical truth to it as well, after all these years. Too often he'd been quiet, moody, uncommunicative. Finally sharing his childhood bullying experience had helped. Tom had a pathway to explain what was happening to him now, even if he was still trying to grasp it all himself. He at least knew where it was rooted.

"How many people were there?"

"I'd say about 150 – but more than 100 of those were from the company. The whole executive team was there."

"So what was this momentous moment?"

"Well, do you remember about five years ago, I showed you that piece I wrote about Lynyrd Skynyrd's Simple Man, and how I needed a new direction in life?"

Michelle hesitated a moment. "Sort of, I think?" Tom wished it had stuck more firmly in her mind, but it was his life, not hers, his journal, not hers. The journal was only a half-secret between them. He didn't share everything he wrote about. But when he did share something, she didn't seem, in Tom's mind, to appreciate the depth to which the thing he wrote about consumed him.

"I told you Walter was in a local band. So at the end of all the memorials, his bandmates come up and play his favorite song as a dedication." Tom paused for effect, and because all the hairs on his skin were standing up again, all over his body, like a mini-forest sprung to life in fast-motion photography. "Simple Man. 'Forget your lust for the rich man's gold, all that you need is in your soul'...." Tom stopped. Michelle was staring at him, with just a barely perceptible hint of awareness. "It's the song that made me realize five years ago that I was not a person I loved or understood. That I'd lost track of the simple truths of life and happiness. And I'm sitting there today and discovering it was Hirschfeld's song too. And his way out of the same damn place I live, so to speak, was to kill himself. It was like...I warned myself, and somehow five years later, I hadn't done a thing about it, so someone saw fit to strike the guy next to me with lightning."

Michelle was staring at Tom in something less than astonishment but more than surprise.

"That is a little freaky." She said.

"It was more than a little freaky, it was the final straw." Tom breathed in deeply and looked directly at Michelle. "I'm going to leave the company."

"Okay." Michelle's response had an invitation to go on in its inflection.

"I intend to tell Robert tomorrow that my last day will be April 29. That's a month past the year end. I'll qualify for short and long-term bonus plans by finishing the year, and vest my last big slug of shares. That'll be very helpful. Giving him nearly three months helps him figure out his org after I leave, given he's got Hirschfeld's opening too." Tom was intentionally nonchalant despite the magnitude of what had occurred and the decision he'd made and now begun to communicate. The first goal of this conversation with Michelle was to make sure she understood that he had done all of the necessary homework on the financial end and that she should not worry. For that, he needed to be confident and factual. Then he would attempt to accomplish the second goal, to make her understand how deeply he had changed and how getting out of his environment was long overdue and necessary.

Michelle had the furrowed brow of apprehension. Tom placed his hands on the granite countertop that was part of a

$200,000 remodel a few short years ago. There were still tuition bills. They were only 54. Didn't Tom still have to work? What would he do, if not this? Tom imagined he was hearing those questions from Michelle, but they were in his own head. She still seemed to be deciding what to say.

"I know you've said you're unhappy. I just don't know how seriously to take you sometimes. As many times as you've talked about being unhappy, you've also pointed out how important each extra year you stay is to our financial future."

"Yeah!" Tom exclaimed, "Think about that! I wrote that Simple Man piece in my journal five years ago. And I've stayed for each of those five extra years that are so important." Tom was about to jump into how those five years had taken their mental and emotional toll, but he gathered himself and stayed focus on goal number one. "You have to trust that I've run the numbers. The restricted shares are key. The bonuses too. Believe it or not, as shitty as we've been doing, we built a lay-up plan this year for employee morale, so a decent bonus looks likely. I could take a whole year off, and we could easily live off those payouts without touching savings. And that will give me the time I need to figure out what I want to do next."

Tom remembered the times he'd had to make a similar persuasive argument about leaving one job for another. Once he'd decided it was the right choice, that it had to be done, he knew he would win any argument over the objections Michelle would raise about uprooting the kids and their own connections and friendships. It was an unequal part of their relationship, based solely on who was earning the money, and it shamed Tom that he felt privileged to exercise those decision rights, even as he built and delivered those persuasive arguments as preamble. That sense of shame created added pressure to make every decision look right in hindsight. Financially, he'd never failed to deliver. This time would be no different.

"I know you're trying to give Robert this extra time to get organized, but what if they just tell you to leave right now, if you don't want to be there any more? Then you would be gone before the end of the year. Isn't that a risk?" On the car-ride Tom had developed a plan for that, but he had no intention of revealing it.

"There'd be no reason for them to do that, and Robert's already told me how valuable I am to him right now. And that was before he lost Hirschfeld. I'm not going to some competitor, I'm just leaving on my own, for a mental health break. There's no reason to kick me out of the building." With the words 'mental health', Tom felt ready to move on to his second goal. He needed to feel Michelle truly did understand that his mental health had deteriorated. Hell, when it all goes down tomorrow, and she hears about his conversation with Robert, she'll wonder anyway. He continued. More serious. Quieter voice. Tenderness. Pleading heart.

"Hon, after today, I need to have the certainty. I need to tell Robert tomorrow. It can't wait. Every day that goes by I wonder if something even nuttier is going to happen and I'll just lose it. Spit out a bunch of venom at Patton or Dutch or Billy Baron. Get myself fired for insubordination. I'm serious. I need the peace of mind now." As he waited for a response from Michelle, it suddenly struck Tom that in owning the role of primary wage earner he had also hoarded the stress that had come with it. He needed someone to share it with.

"I'm just worried with everything you've told me about Dutch, that when he finds out, he'll make you leave before the end of the year, just out of spite."

"Hon, I have been telling you for a long time that I'm not happy doing what I do. I don't like the way it makes me feel, I don't like the way it makes me behave. I don't like the things I'm asked to do and the things I choose to do because I know they're necessary. Hearing that song start to play today was like being hit with a two-by-four. I'm not saying I'm Hirschfeld, but you could certainly look at my life and his and on the surface think we're quite alike. Obviously, he was depressed or deeply troubled by something, and I don't know if it was the job or not, but I do know the only deep unhappiness I have is related to my job. I hate my fucking job and I don't want to be eaten up with hate anymore. Not even for a day, let alone waiting till after the first of the year to announce." Tom realized he'd started by saying there were things he didn't like about his job but ended by saying he hated everything. It was hate, wasn't it? Wasn't that the point of this whole conversation? He hated everything about being Tom Cooper, SVP. He had no intention of killing Tom Cooper, but he was announcing his intention to kill what came after the comma. Michelle's brow had unfurrowed.

"I'm still worried, but I know you have to do it your way."

Tom desperately wanted her to just break down and fold him into her arms and tell him everything will be alright as soon as he is done with this part of his life, and the sooner the better. He'd opened up about the bullying from long ago. Hadn't he connected it to the present day well enough? All he had ever wanted as a kid was to be accepted. Corporate

America welcomed him with open arms and he became one of the cool kids. One of the powerful. One of the bullies. How did he let himself do that? That was never the plan. He was going to be the CEO, and a good one, too. Glinda of the North good.

"You do understand though?" Tom probed. "What I most want you to worry about is me. Not our finances." Now, finally, Michelle's face seemed to soften.

"Oh hon, I always worry about you first." She came around from her side of the island and put her arms out to place her hands on his shoulders. She looked into his eyes and shook him a little. "I do want you to be happier than you've been. I just hope you aren't misjudging Robert's reaction. I hope you're right that you need to do it this way." She kissed him once and then pulled her face back and squeezed his shoulders and shook him again, shaking her head and smiling a little. "You always have been a little nuts, but I've never been sorry to be a part of your life. I'll be here for you no matter what happens." Tom let a smile visit his face. In his mind, he evaluated whether he had accomplished his second goal. Did she truly understand where his head was? Perhaps after tomorrow, she'd know without having to discuss it further. But for now, it was enough to have her heart firmly in his corner.

February 17, 2016

Tom stared into his own eyes from about three feet away, in the men's room mirror. In five minutes, he would walk into Robert's office and make his play. Did he look distressed enough? It wasn't enough to just look stressed, or tired, or old. Anyone Tom's age could pull that off on any given day. He had to look empty, fearful, used up, fed up, manic, troubled, all of it, in turns and at once. Tom had not shared with Michelle exactly how he planned to give Robert his resignation this morning. He'd worked it out on his silent ride back to the office. He needed to give Robert a scare. He had to set himself up as both fragile and valuable, like a Faberge egg. He had to take back the rest of his life, and he had to do it starting today. He couldn't be too calm, too calculating, too in control. He couldn't sound like any other asshole scheming to get what he wants in this world by any means necessary. And he was confident, wasn't he? Or was he borderline out of his mind? Actually, being borderline out of his mind was an important part of the story. That was exactly what Tom was trying to achieve. If he believed it was true, it would be easier for Robert to believe it. And Tom would need to define that borderline meant he was still on the side where a productive man stood, as long as he could clear his mind about the acceptance of his resignation and his demands. So, did his eyes say it? Did they say how deeply troubled he was, some level beyond exhausted, but still with a glimmer of light that said that things were still generally under control? Was he or was he not in danger of running off the rails? Fucking Christ, Tom thought, and he grimaced at himself. It was 6:45 in the fucking morning and he was staring into his own eyes to psych himself up to go in and pull a Sarah Bernhardt, as his grandmother used to say, in order to end his career after 32 years. Of course, he was out of his fucking mind. And what was the trigger, the death blow, the nail in the coffin, the final straw, the big bang? A song??

Yes, damnit, a song. Tom had shed his religion not only because it felt like an unnecessary burden, an unnecessary identifying mark in the land where all are supposed to be equal. He shed it because it also provided no solace, no escape from the pain of adolescence, loneliness, and bullying. But music did. The right songs did. Tom's canon of musical favorites was his bible. We all look for comfort outside of ourselves. We may not believe, but we all still pray, and Tom heard the words of his favorite psalm, and they spoke to him. They said, 'get out now, by any means necessary'. They said, 'save yourself'.

But, wait a minute. That was proof he was out of his mind, wasn't it? Tom noticed he'd been leaning in closer, looking deeper into his own eyes as his mind sped up, so he straightened and took a step back and dissolved his face and shook his shoulders and looked again at himself as if he were his younger self, about ten years ago, before the move here. You are out of your mind, he said inside his head. Why are you standing here at 6:45 in the fucking morning getting ready to execute this fucking power trip, snap judgement, romanticized move to end your career at least five years prematurely? What's happened to your perseverance? What's happened to your quiet courage, your calm, your cool, your laid back? What's happened to the rock and roll SVP? Rock and roll indeed. Tom heard the guitar strings again, the opening notes, Simple Man, the memorial, Hirschfeld dead, wedgies in the gym locker room, Dutch-fucking-Bagley, spitballs on the bus, Billy Baron and his trained money, the bruises on his arms he hid from his parents. The expectations of others who kept telling him he had what it took, knew what to do. The CEOs that climbed up into his head and royally fucked it up. Nope. He was out. Done. Decision made.

Tom smiled, to crack the dimple in his left cheek, which activated the twinkle in his eye that said, 'All is well, absurd as always, but well.' It was the dimple that his mother commented on every time she saw him over the last year, like she'd discovered it for the first time, just the same as it was when she first saw it as she held him in her arms and looked down at his helpless little face and body and knew that this was what her whole life would be about. That dimple that told her that would be okay, that would be just fine by her. Tom couldn't let her sacrifice mean nothing, her whole life of caring and advice be nothing. His whole life of fighting to be something beyond nothing; to understand life; to maneuver in a world of people who seemed to know what they were doing. It all had to mean something. His own willingness to flail his body into the buffeting wind every day to take care of his family, of Michelle and the kids. It had to mean something. Everything about the last six months, shit, the last six years probably; told him that. He was never going to find out what it's all meant standing still. Persevering longer. No. The time to jump was now. You are sane, the smiling Tom Cooper told himself, you are very sane indeed.

Tom knew Robert arrived most mornings around 6:30, and kept meetings clear before 8:00, except for emergencies. His admin didn't come in until 7:30, so Tom was simply going to walk in and close the door once Robert had at least had a chance to organize himself for his day. Tom allotted him 20 minutes for that, but now he was ready to take the stage. The moment itself was important to him. Though Robert had been perfectly fine to him over the month they'd worked together as boss and employee, Tom still felt there was some retribution he owed, some sense that this plan of his would be a nettle for Robert, hurt his hand as he grasped it, disturb his professional life when he least needed it. And that he would deserve that.

"Knock knock," Tom spoke at the open door to Robert's profile engrossed in his monitor.

"Tom." Robert looked surprised and a little annoyed, but quickly smiled. "What can I do to help you today?" Fuuuuck you with that already, but today, you actually can.

"I need ten minutes of your time, if that's alright. I'm just going to close the door". Tom was making it clear he wasn't going to take no for an answer at 6:50 in the morning in a mostly empty office building, even if Robert told him he had a 7:00 am meeting, because he truly didn't need even ten minutes. He was assuming some Q and A time but not much.

"Sure, of course." One day after the memorial following the suicide of their co-worker, how could he say anything but? Tom sat down at the conference table and Robert came over and sat down, swung his left leg over his right knee, and folded his arms across his chest. Tom sat up straight in his chair and rested his arms on the table, so he could still be within three feet of Robert and look him right in the eye, right into his death stare. Whenever Tom spoke from the heart, he could feel the emotion creep into his voice, and he would often have to fight back a little tremor. But even as he mastered fighting it back, he also realized the power of letting just a little bit of it back in. It gave power and authenticity to his words, and that could be useful at the right times. Like now.

"Robert, I've decided to leave the company, effective the end of April, April 29, to be exact." Robert's facial expression barely flickered. "I told you when we talked about the integration role that I was getting to the end of my rope. This thing with Hirschfeld..." Tom paused. He let the feeling of guilt for being as nearly unwelcoming an asshole to Hirschfeld as Robert had once been to him wash over him, to work up the tremor. "It was the final nail for me." Tom subconsciously registered the full trope as including "in the coffin" and realized it was a shitty choice of words, but actually might work in his favor, to remind Robert that Hirschfeld, another direct report just like Tom, killed himself 8 days ago. "I've been thinking about finding another direction in life for a long time now, but I've let the financial implications of walking away keep me from doing anything about it. But this thing with Hirschfeld..." Tom paused again, conscious he had repeated himself and also conscious he had paused the last time he used the phrase, but he wanted what he said next to come out as something difficult for him to say to Robert, to show how vulnerable he was. "It's more than just that he was my age and doing basically very similar work, and was married with nearly grown kids. Just like me. No, it was that I saw him, Robert, the day he killed himself I think, and if not, then definitely the Friday before. He did not look like himself. Really down. I just said 'hey' and raised my eyebrows and kept walking." Tom had let his voice lower to something just above a hoarse whisper. "I could have stopped him and asked if everything was alright. I could have. But that's not who I've become as a person, and I blame work. Not you, not the company specifically, but work itself, or at least work at this level. And I don't like that person I've become, so for my own mental well-being, I've got to leave." Tom could have rambled longer, he had rehearsed a lot more words than that, but at the end, his business communication training kicked in and he stopped once he'd communicated the essence of his meaning. He continued to stare at Robert, forcing him to speak.

"That's a really big decision. We've all been impacted by Walter's suicide. Do you have any vacation time? Do you want to take a week off to think about this?".

"No. To the second question. I don't need a week off to think about it, my mind is most definitely made up. Yes to the first question. In fact, I have 21 days of accrued vacation time. I plan to use two of them a week every week, until my last day. I'll probably take every Thursday and Friday, but I'll be flexible to when you need me. I feel an obligation to the company, and to the people who work for me, to stay long enough to bring the year home, and to get the early work done on the merger, the people stuff, I'm sure. But there's only so long I can stay, and so much I can take." Tom had been absolutely flat, slow, deadpan. He kept staring at Robert, knowing by refusing to blink that his eyes would moisten and reinforce the emotionality of this moment.

"Are you sure you just don't need time to process what happened? You heard the grief counselor – even if we really didn't know Walter well, or didn't feel we knew him well, obviously, in hindsight, it still takes time to process your feelings when a co-worker takes their life. You haven't said you're going to go to another job, what are you going to do with yourself?"

"I'm not going to another job. That's not what this is about. It's not completely about Walter either. When the camel's back finally breaks, you don't blame the last straw. The help I need dealing with Walter and what happened is the certainty of knowing I'm going to get out of this part of my life. And part of the reason I want to do it this way is to help my parents. They live down-state, about an hour and a half. My mother has dementia and my father's pretty depressed. This will give me a routine to get down there every Thursday and spend a couple days." Tom continued to look directly at Robert. He was really feeling the strain in his eyeballs.

Robert shifted in his chair. He looked away from Tom but not for long. Tom wondered if he'd really needed just that little bit of time to formulate his response.

"I'm going to have to go to Dutch, and he'll probably want to go to Patton, to sign off. I can't promise you how they're going to react. You know how much shit is going down right now, and you know how close we are to year-end."

"I know the timing sucks. That's why I'm telling you now, and not two months from now. This gives you time to plan for what comes after the merger. And no one will have more at stake than I do in bringing the year home strong. Three days a week, point me like a weapon and fire away."

"Let's talk about that now. You don't need me to tell you that - what is it, ten weeks?" Tom nodded. "Yeah, telling those guys that you're going to basically work part-time for the next two and a half months and then leave the company......it's not going to be a great response."

Tom put some steeliness in his voice and gave his own response.

"First of all, I have the vacation time, and I intend to take it. In fact, I'll be leaving a day on the table. Second of all, you just offered to let me take two of those weeks right now. Three days a week of me, with a merger coming at you like a freight train, closing the year, giving you some time to replace Walter...is better. It should work for everyone. If you think Dutch and Patton won't like it, don't tell them. Like I said, it's earned vacation time. And I'll be flexible to when you need me."

"I'm not going to keep anything from anyone. They'll have to know all the details." Robert exhaled and even seemed to slump a little in his chair as he leaned back into it and away from the table. Tom had not truly considered, in any empathetic way, how Hirschfeld's suicide had impacted Robert personally. What if one of his own direct reports had done what Hirschfeld did? Wouldn't that be just tearing Tom up inside? Tom was using the hole in Robert's staff as a leverage point for getting his own desires granted, but in a forward-looking way. He hadn't thought about the leverage coming from the pain of what had already happened. As he looked at Robert, he could feel just a tiny twinge of remorse for walking in here and using the recent death of a co-worker to his advantage.

But it was going to work, Tom was sure of that. He might kick the decision upstairs, but he had bought that Tom was serious, and he was already on record how much he needed Tom on the team right now. 10 more weeks of Tom, even at 3 days a week, was better than no Tom two weeks from now. That was the point Robert would make to Dutch, and Tom could imagine Dutch knotting up with conflicting emotions – hating that Robert felt he still needed Tom, hating that Tom was negotiating an exit that included ten weeks of part-time work, but happy Tom was leaving. Patton would probably be pissed that any goddamn person on his team would think they could just cry, "mental health" and work part-time for a couple months, establish their own sunset assignment, essentially. But then he would get pragmatic. He would tell Robert to squeeze every last drop of right-now work out of Tom. Control every one of his hours those three days he's here to the company's benefit. Use him up completely by the time he walks out the door. After all, they did just sit in the same memorial yesterday that Tom did. They were still human, weren't they? They could be pissed and hate Tom for this, but some part of them would have to understand, wouldn't they? Robert was not fighting him any more. Dutch and Patton would accede. This was going to work!! But he had to know for sure, didn't he? For all of those conversations to happen just as Tom unspooled them in his head earlier, in his planning, in his accounting for risk, it had to start with Robert believing there was no talking Tom off his plan. And it had to end with Robert saying it would be better for all concerned if Tom departed on his terms. Tom felt he needed to hear Robert say it.

"I understand. What's your recommendation going to be?" Tom would not let his gaze drop. He was starting to be aware of some stiffness in his neck, in addition to the wateriness in his eyes from the strain of keeping them wide open and trained on their target.

Robert dropped his foot to the floor and placed both his palms on the table and pulled his chair a little closer again.

"I'm going to lay it out for Dutch just like you just laid it out. You do know the first thing Dutch is going to say is good riddance?" Robert forced a little smile.

"I'm aware."

"But I'm going to tell him what I told you when I got this job. I need you here right now. If you don't want to be here two months from now then we're just going to have to figure it out. But right now, as you proved a few weeks ago, you're much needed." Tom felt the small jolt of winner's euphoria rising in his chest. Robert continued.

"Just so I'm clear. Next week, you plan to be off Thursday and Friday, and every week after that until April 29th? As soon as next week?" Robert was writing now, on the small pad he kept on the conference table.

"Yes. Do you need an official letter of resignation?"

Robert looked up from the pad and back into Tom's eyes.

"No." Deep end of the pool. As long as Tom could grab the ladder and hoist himself out, no one cared to hear why.

"Okay. Just let me know when you have something official so I can speak to my team." Tom rose and extended his right hand, locking onto Robert's eyes one last time. "Thank you for understanding." Robert accepted the handshake. In Tom's imagination, he was looking into his future as he looked at Tom. Kind of like the before and after photos of Clinton, Bush, and Obama, and how much 8 years aged them. Tom was only five years older than Robert, but here he was, standing in front of the younger man and telling him the candle does sometimes burn out far sooner than you might expect. Not only in words, but in the cautionary tale of his actions.

Tom spent the balance of his day in an uneasy state of uncertainty. He was certain he'd done the right thing, not certain he'd done it the right way. When he'd told Michelle he was going to leave, there was nothing about the pitiful sharing of his personal pain and his need to soothe his exit with three-day workweeks. He didn't want her to question his questionable methods. On the car ride home the day before there was this pounding need to craft an exit that had some drama to it, that convinced everyone involved Tom Cooper was a damaged man. Truth was, he wasn't sure he could last until April 1 without exploding into an even more dramatic supernova of an exit. He did need the certainty. He needed it to convince himself he couldn't rationalize his way out of this feeling. It was real. He needed to exit and he would exit.

And yet, there was a darker truth as well. Tom wanted his exit to leave a mark. To piss off those to whom he was giving notice. To tie it to the trial they all attended the day before. This was his sentence issued. Real or imagined, he wanted to know that they had failed Hirschfeld and Tom as well.

The hours of the day dragged on and the sky outside darkened. Tom was pensive in meetings. Between them, in his office, he played solitaire on his computer and listened to music. He checked his email frequently for anything urgent. He checked the company's stock price. He browsed his favorite news sites and even went down click-bait rat-holes to see what famous sixties and seventies television stars looked like today. And then finally, at 5:36 pm, as he was looking at Cindy Brady in her sixties and trying to tie the image to the memory of the little girl he grew up watching in the '60s, he got a pop-up notification marked 'CONFIDENTIAL', from Robert.

Tom opened the email as if jolted to do so by a skipped beat in his heart. It was short and to the point.

"Dutch and Patton signed off. Just share your intention to leave and when with your team for now. You'll get your days off as we discussed. They don't want you talking about that as part of some agreement. That's for you and me."

Tom felt first a tightening in his chest and then a bursting of excitement and anticipation that he could only liken to what it felt like the moment he realized he was about to finally lose his virginity and that was over 30 years ago. It worked! It worked! It worked! April 1 was now in the bag! The vested shares! His sanity! He was free! He was done! He was leaving! He was running! He was never going to work another full week in corporate America! Wait, what? The bursting elation in his body momentarily stalled. He was only 54. He had decades to live. He had no plan. Then just like a cranky engine that finds its gear again, the bursting chest feeling came back. Fuck it! He was free! It was over!

It was over. Tom's manic thinking pace slowed to nearly a stop, something it rarely did, something he rarely could control. It was over. The finality Tom had been begging for, the certainty he was missing earlier, at least for this phase of his life was finally, fatefully, delivered. Tears welled up in his eyes. He let them be blinked into two small trails down his cheeks, drops of happiness on his skin. He read Robert's email again, and he only had one thought. What song would he tee up as he pulled out of the parking lot? What would capture the essence of this day and cement everything about it in Tom's memory? What could say everything that needed to be said about a 32-year trip to hell and out?

Tom's car was parked very close to the building, having arrived early for his ambush of Robert. As he approached the big revolving exit door, Tom heard the internal security doors open and close behind him, and heavy footfalls clack across the lobby tiles. He did not look back over his shoulder, but something in the heaviness of the footfalls sounded familiar. Tom strode quickly across the circular entrance drive to the small employee lot across the street. He saw that Dutch's big SUV was still there, and Tom instantly knew who was walking behind him. Tom was pretty sure Dutch knew it was Tom from behind, but he hadn't called out to him. What would he say to Tom at this stage? Would he ever say anything to Tom before he left? Tom walked more swiftly, justifying that he was not running away from a potential conversation with Dutch, just hurrying because it was cold. Their cars were several spaces away from each other, so if Tom got to his car fast, in the darkness, there would be no reason for Dutch to believe Tom didn't have the courtesy to wait up and say thank you for approving his exit plan, as if he even expected Tom to do that. Probably, narcissist that he is. Tom opened the door to his Prius and tossed his backpack, so light without his laptop thrown in, onto the passenger seat, got in, and closed the door. The Prius was Michelle's idea. She thought they should send a message to their children that they were serious about the world they were leaving them, so they got matching hybrids.

As much as Tom wanted to get that car into reverse and get out of that parking lot, he had to set up his music first. Get the classic iPod out of his bag and hook it up to the car stereo. Spin the wheel to the song he wanted. As Tom was facing forward now, he confirmed it was indeed Dutch who'd just exited the revolving doors, earpiece in, and mouth moving, as he strode with his long wool overcoat open.

Tom started the car, allowed the headlights to reach full brightness, put the car in reverse to back out of his space, and pressed play. He cruised past the back of Dutch's black mega-mobile, a Tundra or Suburban or something else with an XL at the end of it, just as Dutch was opening his door.

"And now, the end is near, and so I face the final curtain." Frank Sinatra's unmistakable voice filled the small cabin of the Prius.

"My friend, I'll say it clear, I'll state my case, of which I'm certain." Tom turned the volume up higher and smiled ear to ear.

"I've lived a life that's full. I traveled each and every highway, and more, much more than this, I did it my way." The music began to build dramatically as Frank paused for the next verse. Tom thought about his journey, the broken companies, the mergers, the trips to China and Taiwan and Mexico and the metal-bending factories in Iowa and Arkansas and Mississippi. He thought about all the ridiculous dinners in Hong Kong, New York, Vegas, and many smaller, more forgettable cities. All of it different, but all of it motivated by the same thing: money. Tom's need for it, his bosses' demand for it. Money was the reason for every decision, every move made by every chess piece on the board. Every bad act, every noble hour of hard work, every numbing drink, all came down to the same thing, the battle for the buck. The war for survival.

"Regrets, I've had a few, but then again, too few to mention". Tom avoided regrets like the plague. He smiled even more broadly if that was possible, and the tears started to well up again. He'd thought this through a million times. The old canard about what doesn't kill you makes you stronger. The wedgies and the spitballs? Stronger. The punches rifled at his biceps? Stronger. The clueless bosses? Stronger. The bankruptcies and mergers? Stronger. You can't regret what's made you stronger, can you? Everything he was as he was walking away was shaped by this, and while he didn't love that shape, at least he knew it, and now he was doing something about it.

"I saw what I had to do and saw it through without exemption." The college educations, the retirement dreams, the safety net. He fought damn fucking hard for all of that, didn't he? He needed to do more, but he'd done a lot, hadn't he? Tom was really crying now, as he cruised to a stop at the long red light at the end of the corporate driveway.

"I planned each charted course, each careful step along the byway." That was today in a nutshell, wasn't it? A strategic plan well-executed. That's what made Tom a valuable employee. That was his calling card. Tom Cooper Gets Shit Done. More than that. Gets the right shit done. Always does what's expected. Honors thy mother and thy father by getting into a good school and getting a good education. Puts that to use doing a good job by doing whatever the boss wants. Figures out pretty quick who the real boss is, the CEO, and learns to think like him. Does what he wants. Does it well. Does what's expected. Tom did and did and did and did. For others, that's what he told himself. Not really for mom and dad, not really to show the whole stupid fucking town he grew up in, not for the CEO. Not for himself. For the real people who mattered, for Michelle and the kids. He'd done what they'd expected, hadn't he? Hadn't that been the old-fashioned deal he made with Michelle? Put your career on ice. Stay home with the kids, at least until kindergarten. He'd somehow managed to make that happen. So well that Michelle stayed home right through getting those kids off to college. She found her superstar career and he had two awesome kids to thank her for. Tom Cooper could fucking make things happen. And now finally, he'd done something important for himself. He'd terminated the ride. Tom erupted into song with the chorus line.

"And more, much more than this, I did it my way." Tom was walking away on his terms. He was walking away undefeated. No one had ever called Tom Cooper into their office and told him he was out of a job. He'd worked for some shitty companies, too. Companies who had to let a lot of people go. Never Tom. Tom was always clean-up on aisle six. Tom was a survivor.

There was the feeling of an ominous shadow to Tom's right, and he turned to see Dutch's car pull up to the light in the right turn lane next to his Prius. Tom could see up through his passenger window that Dutch was still talking on the phone, looking typically self-important. God, how he hated that fucking man.

"...but through it all, when there was doubt, I chewed it up and spit it out" Fuck Dutch and fuck all those kids in high school who tortured him and drove his true personality into a shell and made him feel like he had to be the one at fault if nobody liked him.

"I faced it all, and I stood tall, and did it my way." Tom thought about the hockey goalie he pummeled to finally end the bullying. He thought about how he always told himself he would have the last laugh, and it would be a laugh because he wouldn't let them turn him bad, turn him into the assholes they were. But the fuckers almost got him again, didn't they? The completely over the top pricks like Dutch and Terry Simmons in the corporate world filled Tom with hate and nearly stopped the laughter in its tracks. Nearly sucked all the joy out of life. Tom looked up again to his right at Dutch filling up the window frame. Hating him so much made him hate himself. That was the crux of it, wasn't it? He had to stop hating himself. What was it about Dutch he hated so much? Was it his fault he got promoted above his capacity? How had that happened anyway? Tom knew there were times he himself had skipped the line of normal progression because 'somebody up there liked him'. Tom knew how to present himself, how to drop the right buzzwords, how to project an aura of competence and confidence. He knew he was masking insecurities, he knew at times he was bluffing with bravado, but he did it to get ahead, to set up a promotion, to protect his future with mentors based on nothing more than good impressions. Did he hate Dutch because he was even better at that shit than Tom? Or did he just hate that Dutch was just one step away from where he himself stood? How many people out there hated Tom? Who had he wronged along the way? Who considered him a bully?

"…for what is a man? What has he got? If not himself, then he has naught. To say the things he truly feels, and not the words of one who kneels…" Tom was belting the words again, knowing the song was coming to a close, the tears running freely, and at that moment Dutch looked to his left and down, a motion Tom saw in his peripheral vision. In his face-forward view, the right-turn signal turned green.

"The record shows, I took the blows, and did it my way." Tom was facing forward, scream-singing, sobbing, and laughing so hard inside he thought he'd burst. Was this what it felt like when hate left your body? Dutch hesitated a moment before realizing his light had turned and his car lurched away from its parallel position with Tom's.

"Goodbye Dutch, you mother-fucking cock-sucking asshole shithead son-of-a-bitch's ass." Tom used a phrase he hadn't used since sixth grade, when he invented the string of epithets as a way to get every profanity he knew into one sentence. It filled him with the warmth of absurdity, chasing out the cold rivers of hate. Frank Sinatra had finished. Shuffle play chose the next song. The very familiar chords of Stairway to Heaven…"does anybody remember laughter?" Oh it couldn't be, could it? That ironic, really? Tom laughed out loud now. Remembering laughter felt really good.

From Tom Cooper's private journal. September 2005. Age 44. Employer 5.

A 54-year old man went home the other night and told his wife his thirty three-year career with the only company the two of them had ever worked for was effectively over. That career, with this company, had been delivered the certain death blow in the form of an annual performance appraisal that described his work this past year to be below standard. Accompanying the review was a "performance improvement plan", a "PIP", which outlined specific improvements that needed to be made in short order – 60 days – or else termination from the company may occur. Normally, the PIP was expected to return 50% of employees to standard performance, and 'exit' 50% who just could not manage the improvement. But these were different times. The company is preparing to merge. This man is in a job that is highly redundant. These two documents, created and delivered now, just a month before the deal is due to close, are therefore, effectively a death knell. It's perfectly obvious once we get a chance to put the two companies together, that the first people to get cut will be those on both sides perceived to be the lowest performers. These pieces of paper, backed up digitally of course, are the record that will end this career, not the actual PIP that was delivered. And the man was smart enough to know this.

This 54-year old man has never lost a job in his life. He's worked hard, succeeded in getting to the level he always dreamed of reaching, but this is a 'what have you done for me lately' job and world, and we are constantly 'raising the bar'. He had a poor year relative to others, at the wrong time, and now this proud, hard-working man had to go home with the stamp of failure for the first time in those 33 years of working life. If that sounds cold and hard-hearted, it's because it is. If it must have taken a tough-minded, passionless boss to deliver that kind of news, it would be because it did. And for the third time now in my career, I was that boss. I was wearing the ancient executioner's mask.

In yet another test to separate the future senior executives from the rest of the director pack, the ability to address poor performance quickly and in a forthright manner, to deliver tough messages, to hold others accountable, to feel free to fire people and hire better talent, is a measured attribute on our performance reviews. Just as I am judged on my ability to do something positive like 'actively support and encourage the growth and development of all team members', I am also rated on my ability to don the black hat and thin the herd. I try to work hard on all the things that are expected of me, so I have become adept at bringing professional closure to the employment of poor performers. It truly is a skill that requires quite a lot of acting.

Once a target is identified, you must act as if nothing has changed in your relationship. You continue to hold all of your employees to the same high standards, but in the case of the targeted employee, you begin to build a log of evidence. Written memos to file follow every one on one conversation, documenting the expectations you've delivered to the person, and their response to your appraisal of how well they're meeting them. You subtly withdraw from being an active partner with them in their business to see how well they sink or swim on their own – and even when they begin to sink as you suspected they would, you do nothing to save them. It's a subtle isolation, and in the interest of a good clean, legal separation later, it has to be done without the target realizing it. This is where more acting is required. You make a point to be the same normal, kind, caring person and manager you've always been, even if you see a floating bullseye on the employee's forehead every time you look at them. When it comes time for the hard conversation, it will be about performance, not about personal animosity.

The hard conversation itself is like the opening night of a play. I write my script, learn my lines, and just before I go on stage I get into character. My character needs to separate the human person he's come to know, like, and respect from the shell of a faceless employee who is not delivering good results and has not shown the ability to turn it around. I tell myself how much I dislike that shell, how that faceless employee puts MY livelihood at risk by dragging down the overall team's results. I prepare myself for the pitiful excuses and weak counter-claims the empty shell will likely respond with. I rehearse the lines I will use to pop those listless balloons. In short, I separate both of us from the human beings we are. The ruthless boss informs the lousy employee that unless substantial, sustained improvement occurs, the end of the line is near. It's the only way I've found it palatable to do this at all, and I thank goodness I've found the ability to compartmentalize the role. Maybe I'll get ahead on acting skills alone – I can play anything they want to assign me in all its gritty realism, in the hopes that one day it leads to that most coveted of all acting jobs in corporate life – senior executive. The audition continues.

March 15, 2016

Tom was enjoying one of his negotiated Thursdays off, six weeks from the end of the line. Michelle was visiting her mother. His daughter was back at school. His oldest friend in the world had come to visit. Seaver Adams. Not named for the Mets pitcher, though Tom Terrific of course became a boyhood idol, but for an old English word for fierce stronghold, and that's exactly how Tom had always thought of the boy who lived across the courtyard in the apartment complex, with his mom and three older brothers. A kid who loved life so much nothing could knock him down, not the occasional beating by a brother enraged over some mischief or another, nor the curse of teenage acne, the top of the pyramid kind, with doctor's visits and creams all over his body. He had plenty of friends, and he gladly added Tom to the list, though Tom was just emerging from his bullied phase, an outcast at school, and really, had no other friends at all. Tom was amazed by Seaver's self-confidence, his big laugh, the way pretty girls saw past the acne and wanted to date him. He and Seaver would sit around on summer mornings, slinging crazy ideas back and forth over cribbage, with a Woodstock era soundtrack. They talked about the fucked up world, the bad shit it did to people, what they would do about it as soon as they got out of their fucked up town. It was like the green room for life. Last two years of high school, anything possible but also everything in peril.

They got through it together, although Tom was never sure what he really brought to the party. Seaver was a lifeline for him, a jolt, a kick in the ass, a rock.

And Seaver was an inspiration. He followed his craziest dream. He followed his heart. He tried to make it as an actor in LA. He lived his real life aggressively and passionately, just as he dared to dream it. Not every dream came true, and like all lives, the path twisted in some pretty unexpected ways. But nearly 40 years on, he was a college theater professor. He was inspiring more young people with dreams, propping up the weak, giving confidence and voice to the meek. He had his spring break, and lived just 100 miles away, so the two old friends had set this morning aside to spend time together in the moment.

Tom was in rare form, spinning up his horror stories of the last nine months of a corporate life that was finally ebbing out of him. Ironically, Seaver was beginning to understand that world in his own career, teaching as he did in a state college network, with its tight budgets and bureaucrats. They had lived such different lives, mostly apart from each other the last four decades, and yet it was like they'd never stopped having a conversation. Whenever they got together, it just picked up where it left off, no matter how many weeks or months had gone by since the last time they spoke. This conversation had begun at nine, over coffee and three-month-old Christmas cookies. They were laughing uproariously nearly non-stop by noon. Then Tom's phone rang with an only vaguely familiar number. It was the cell of Jen Brentz, his partner in crime at work these last four months. She sounded awkward on greeting, and then just said that she was indeed, feeling awkward about the call, and why. She apologized for bothering Tom at home, but she needed him.

"I'm with Donna, in her office, with the door closed. I know Robert told you on Monday he wasn't replacing you, and now I guess I have to fit all of your people into my world, and I have to go down two directors at the same time. I don't even know where to start. And I wouldn't call you like this, but I have to give an answer to Robert by the end of the day, to show him what that looks like. I know this is terribly awkward, but I think you know, of my four now, which one I would send home. And I don't even know how I can possibly give everything she had to the other three. And then of course I really don't know your business well enough to know what you would do on your side." Jen was a seasoned pro, like Tom. She had her personal shorthand corporate speak in high gear. "My four", "your six". No names, just heads and head counts. No talk of firing or laying off people. Just 'sending them home'.

"You have to go down two directors?" Tom realized he practically shouted the question. Is this what Robert meant by widening spans of control, just eliminate higher level jobs and spread out the worker bees?

"He didn't tell you that?"

"Not specifically, no."

Tom was being a little disingenuous. Robert had given Tom the fairly staggering news that they weren't going to replace him on Monday. When the two hot-shots bolted for the door on the heels of the Labor Day reorg, the company conducted an emergency search for replacements. The list of interested candidates with the right skills was thin, and in the end, they made one big job and one smaller job, hired Jen for the bigger one, and promoted from within for the smaller one. When Tom gave Robert his resignation, they went back to the also-rans from that search, but ultimately, according to Robert, they decided to "do some moving of things around internally". No replacement for Tom, reorganization instead. Tom assumed it was departmental. Robert had asked him for thoughts on his people, had hinted he might use the opportunity to widen spans of control, and then dropped the bomb that the widening would start at the top, with Jen inheriting all of Tom's responsibilities on top of her own.

Of course, he should have suspected there was more to the story after speaking with Robert. The Tom of even a month ago would have known they were not all the way to the dark heart of this saga. He would have sniffed out the room-freshener-over-bullshit smell that he was so familiar with. Robert had pressed him about his people, had him force rank them, went through the exercise of listing what the risks were if the name forced to the bottom of the list, the person ranked last out of six, even though all six were valuable in their own ways, was no longer with the company. He gave his feedback. He knew what widening spans of control meant. He just didn't take his cynicism all the way down the path. Robert had sworn him to silence until he could speak with Jen late Tuesday, and Wednesday was a blur of meetings and he never saw Robert all day. And then Tom's workweek was done. Or so he thought. Tom offered what he knew to Jen:

"Well, I already told Robert if you put a gun to my head and told me to force-rank them, which he then proceeded to do, that Jeff would be sixth, but I also told him Jeff does so much shit for us that no one even knows about, does it without being asked, does it because that's just the kind of person he is, that it would be a really bad idea to get rid of him. I told him I thought he would stay, even in a reduced role, if the offer was made in the right way. Christ, he's got like three more years to work and he's golden."

"I heard that you gave that feedback. I just don't know if that's going to happen. So how would you organize the rest of your world if you assumed you didn't have Jeff as a director or a manager?" Tom now knew there was more going on than Jen was explaining. He interrupted her, a little more agitated.

"Jen, excuse me, but what the fuck is going on? Why do you have to have this nailed by the end of the day?" It was a rhetorical question. The end of the quarter was coming. The end of the fiscal year. Tom's nose was working now. The smell of scorched flesh filled his nostrils. Not just reorganize, but shrink.

"Can I put you on speaker so Donna can hear your end?"

"Sure. Hi Donna." Poor Donna. Here she was again, helping Tom and the peers he's leaving behind downsize and reorganize, just 7 months after the last one. "So, no offense Donna, but to repeat myself Jen, what the fuck is going on?"

"All I can tell you is, Donna asked me to come down and help her put this together for Robert. He has to have it by the end of the day, with names, so he can review it before we turn it in to Dutch, tomorrow, so he has the weekend to review his entire team, before turning it over to Patton by Tuesday. Robert hasn't even spoken to me, so I'm just taking Donna at her word that this is how big my team's going to be, but right now I can't even get my head around it."

"They want names to the C-suite by Tuesday?" All the gears clicked into place for Tom, and he shot a glance at

Seaver sitting on his couch, and slowly shook his head at him, as if to say, 'Yep, this is exactly the shit I've been talking about.' Tom spoke aloud again.

"So, this is very clear to me now. This is pre-merger posturing in motion, so we can make an announcement and take a write-off by the end of the quarter, and there's basically two weeks left, so now this is super urgent. They need the names so HR and legal can run all the demo's and see how old, what gender, and what race we're all thinking we need to cut. It sounds like there are two components, just like last time: a dollar reduction goal, and a title reduction goal – fewer directors and up. Do I have that about right, Donna?" Donna cleared her throat.

"I'm not at liberty to discuss the details."

"Of course you're not Donna." Tom did not say this meanly, just an acknowledgement that he knew Donna's response was an affirmation that Tom was correct. "Okay. Listen, can I call you back in half an hour? I'm having coffee with a friend. No worries. I'll call you on this number?"

Tom put his cell down on the coffee table and looked at Seaver. "Well, I'm guessing this means the fuckers aren't going to put me down humanely. They're gonna make me do more bad shit, help identify more people to fire. Un-fucking-believable." Tom's mind began running again. Rather than a measured passing of the torch over his last six weeks, he'd be facing yet another trauma, more dead men walking, more dread, more rumors, a reduction event. They weren't going to wait for the merger to drive head count out, they were getting pre-emptive. Now they could say to the guys at Broadview that the cuts on this side have been done. All the blood post-merger would be theirs. And, it was slowly dawning on him, the impression outside the company would now be that Tom was part of the reduction. How ironic. The company could say it was "electing not to fill his opening", instead of "eliminating his job". But the cynical world would only read it as "Tom was pushed out". What would he tell people? How could he explain to his many professional acquaintances why he had decided to leave? They would never believe he was simply retiring young from corporate life. No one with any brain does that on this side of 55.

"Hey, sorry," he said to Seaver, thinking he'd just been lost in thought for several minutes, when in fact, all of that flooded through his brain in about 4 seconds.

"Don't worry about it man. I couldn't stay much longer anyway. Sounds like you've got some shit to work through, so I'll catch up to you again soon." Seaver got up and grabbed Tom's hand soul-style, like they might Indian thumb-wrestle, and pulled him in for a hug. "Be good, my brother."

It was 12:30 in the afternoon of what was supposed to be a slow, easy day off in mid-March, but deep in the earth's crust, a plate was crumbling along one edge, driving a fissure toward a fault line, preparing to rock the corporate headquarters of one of Tom's employers for at least the sixth time that he could remember over the last 30 years. He'd survived them all, and now he was going to step over the rubble one last time and walk away on his own terms. Even if the world would choose to believe something else. Alternative facts. A different narrative. Whatever the fuck the world wanted, because the world always gets what it wants.

"No man, fuck them, sit down, stay. I shouldn't have said half an hour. Just habit." Tom was in no mood to chase Seaver out – his old friend had driven nearly two hours to see him – so the half hour he promised Jen stretched to two. Seaver had been filling him in on his brood of kids, one at a time, and there were great stories to tell about each. Tom let the familiar voice of his friend wash over him like the ocean at low tide, his unique cadences coming in ripples. Tom relaxed and breathed and imagined that every day of his life could be filled with warm feelings like this, soon, so very soon.

After Seaver left, Tom called Jen back. He wanted to help her, he really did. She had a lot in common with Tom, had worked at a high level elsewhere before relocating here four months ago. Stover had brought her in and then of course he was gone within weeks, and Robert was in. Then the white paper broke. Then Hirschfeld took his own exit, and Tom announced he was leaving. She hadn't even moved her family yet, and now they were telling her she was getting everything Tom had as well? He couldn't imagine they would give her more money than they already did, to get her to come here in the first place. They were probably just leaning on her ego to suck it up and recognize this bold-faced golden opportunity they were handing her, the hell with the fine print of doing two high pressure jobs for the price of one.

Tom knew he'd primarily survived the last cut-down because he had such a strong knowledge of some arcane but very important pieces of the business. And now someone who'd barely had time to learn her own businesses had to decide which of Tom's people to keep around, to best run businesses that very soon, no one at the company would have much experience running. And people wondered how big companies fail. Tom hated the idea of leaving behind anything but a well-oiled machine, and up until a few days ago, that's what he thought he was doing, even in the midst of chaos.

Then Robert told him his job was going to be eliminated upon his leaving, and Jen would inherit his team. There was no ego involved in the long internal laugh that Tom experienced, but did not really enjoy, upon hearing the news. He'd looked at Robert, dead in the eye, and with a gas-pain grin and gentle shake of the head said, "Are you serious? Jen will be gone in 6 months." Robert had flashed some anger in his eyes and his jawline tensed and untensed, before he'd said, "I don't think so. But I understand it's a bear. I know you don't have much time left, but I would appreciate any help you can give her over these last few weeks."

"Of course."

And this was the help needed? How to take on the entire workload of another senior vice-president while simultaneously reducing the director headcount by two? For Jen, this had to be the corporate version of Dante's descent through 9 circles of hell. One, come to a struggling company to replace a rising star who'd just ditched. Two, recognize the absurdity of Dutch within a month (points for intelligence!). Three, lose the boss that convinced you to come. Four, see the company exposed by activists, pushed by hedge funds, and put into play for all manner of vultures. Five, lose a co-worker to suicide. Six, lose another coworker to what? Retirement? Seven, assume twice the work for the same pay. Eight, identify associates to be laid off and then let them go. Fucking Christ, she was one level from the burning fire in less than five months. Had to be some new world record.

But she was being strong, even as she said words that would sound like panic if they weren't delivered so calmly and matter-of-factly.

"Tom, I've been part of companies in the past that have gone through change, and I obviously know that the last few months here have not been normal by any stretch, but I have never seen anything handled as badly as this."

"Welcome, finally, to my nightmare."

"I mean seriously, I realize Robert is under a lot of pressure, but we didn't even have a discussion. He literally walked into my office, sat down, and said, 'I've decided I'm not going to fill Tom's job.' I said, 'Okay,' and then he said 'You're going to take his businesses. It's a lot of responsibility I know,' and then he gets up and says he's late to share his total plan with Dutch. I was speechless. I just sat there for like five minutes wondering what the fuck just happened? So, that was Tuesday, and I haven't even seen him since, until this morning, when he does the same exact thing, flies by, sits down, tells me I have to go down two directors when I take your stuff, and tells me Donna will fill me in on the details, but he's late to a meeting, and we'll talk later. And you know the rest."

"So, for you, on Tuesday, no mention of more money, a retention bonus, anything like that? Sorry to be so forward, you don't have to answer." Tom was still seething a little that Robert would just take everything he'd built and before he was even gone, squeeze it into a ball and stuff it into someone's else's hands. As if he had so little value to the company that his job didn't even have to be replaced. Now that he was realizing this was part of a mandated plan, he recognized how many jobs this move would save, worker bee jobs. Robert was sacrificing a queen to keep a bunch of pawns in the game. Not because that's generally how you win, but because it buys you time to fight a few days longer. Cutting an SVP head was a big chip, giving Robert room to get additional favors in this quick and nasty cut-down. That's what this one was. Not a reorg, although they'll call it that. This was just a sloppy, quick slice, decided upon at the last minute to dump all the extraneous shit they could into this quarter. Into this year. To make it look like Billy Baron was serious about his intentions. To signal Wall Street there really is a new sheriff in town. As if the smart money didn't already know that. You know, that money that somehow has sentient reasoning capabilities, anonymously, on its own. Not the collective, destructive assholes behind it. Just the money, doing what smart money does when it is free. Free to grow up and become Capital.

"I don't mind. The answer is no. No more money, no retention bonus, nothing. Like I said, I've barely had a chance to speak to him since he came by. And then this morning, Donna called me ten minutes after he left my office, and I was down there five minutes after that, looking at your org charts, with red outlines around boxes that had to be eliminated." Fucking Christ. Tom could put himself in her shoes, and she's right, even against the orgy of crazy that was his career, this would have stood out.

"Well, I'm sorry you're going through this, first of all. Now maybe you know partly why this was the end for me. I'll do whatever you want me to do to help you."

"Thank you Tom, I really appreciate that. I want to do what's right by your people, and I know you have some great people on your team. I just need to figure out how you would manage what you had if you had to go down one director." What would he do? Suck it up, that's what. Walk over to the next most talented person on his team and tell them their job just got more important because the company had fewer people to supervise everyone and the good ones had to start managing themselves. Turn back around and tell his boss, 'Of course we can make this work, we can make anything work, I just can't tell you it'll work as well as it could if you weren't forcing me to cut my fucking heads.'

"To me, it's not a question of what I would do, it's what is the company willing to live with? I can tell you that if Jeff is the guy that has to go, I would take his business and give it to Lisa, but then I would also tell you that you'd be missing critical expertise and industry connections that would take years to develop and that the business would quickly go from being one of our bright spots to just another train car wobbling down the tracks. If you told me that was unacceptable, and one of the others had to go, Lisa or Jose or Patricia or Jackie or Paul. You know I'd tell you we'd be crazy to send any of them home."

"So your answer is that there'd be risks, but you'd choose Jeff to go, give his businesses to Lisa, and leave the rest with what they have?" Tom knew there was a reason they'd hired Jen. She got it. She knew the game. She could listen through the venting and hone in on the only thing she really needed to know.

"Sure, but I'd say it's more than a risk, it's a horrible mistake."

"So what are you suggesting we do, because keeping all six jobs you had is not an option for me". There was a little edginess there, just a door-crack sliver glimpse of annoyance.

"I'm suggesting what I suggested to Robert, that Jeff get an option to stay at a lower position. I think he'd take it. It'd be a blow to his ego, but at least he'd still be in the organization, and I can tell you that he would be able to overcome that and do what's right for the company. He's got a ton of integrity. He also needs to work just three more years, he's been very upfront with me about that. This is just the right thing to do for every reason I can think of."

"I hear you, but I'm not feeling like that's an option for Robert. Jeff would get the same opportunity any of the displaced people will get, which is to post for open jobs in the company that aren't being eliminated, in the two weeks they have left."

Two weeks. Par for the course. That's always the way companies wanted it. No use keeping disgruntled people around. But the phrase 'two weeks' hammered home the rapidity with which his own exit was approaching, and with it, the feeling of finality, of dangling threads wrapping themselves back into a piece of rope, a strong thick rope to hold his weight as he climbed out the window of the tower and shimmied down to make his escape. Only now, as he passed the rope from hand to hand on his descent, bodies would be falling from the windows above, hurtling down to earth ahead of him, covering the ground with their fallen forms, part of the rubble Tom would have to navigate. Six weeks for him. Two weeks for Jeff. Jen's voice cut into his brief reverie.

"That's what the meeting's about tomorrow, the timing of all this. Did you see the meeting invite? Are you coming in?"

"Yeah, I'm coming in." Resignation in his voice. Resignation official. Resignation decision resoundingly confirmed.

"I'm sorry this is how you're going to spend your last few weeks. You deserve better."

"Thank you Jen. Sorries all around, I guess. Sucks to be us."

March 16, 2016

By the time Tom got in on Friday, the rest of Robert's team had assembled in his conference room, minus Robert. Jen was there of course. So was Pete Hamilton. Or as Tom kept calling him, Next Man Up. Pete was one of Tom's favorite projects. When he'd come to the company he was viewed as talented but prone to be an asshole. He was passionate and too often that spilled over into anger. He got a bad reputation as someone who was difficult to work with. It was a red flag holding back an otherwise bright, strategic, hard-working, and as Tom had found over time, ethical and generous person. Tom made Pete a personal mission. He'd taken him back from the brink first, then on to the radar screen again as a future leader, and finally, back on to that leadership track. Now he was the Next Man Up. After the hot shots left, Stover took the first whack at the senior tier of his organization by electing not to fill one of the seats with an SVP. Instead, he shrunk the job a bit, hired Jen for the bigger piece, and promoted Pete to VP for the rest. Tom was happy for him, and proud of him and afraid for him. He'd been invited into the wolf's den, but given a foxes' credentials. He had to go toe to toe with Dutch and Patton and not be afraid to stand his numbers up to the CFO's scrutiny. Tom was concerned it was too much fire, too soon. What if Pete's old habits came back under duress? He could explode the way Tom feared he was capable of himself.

But on this day, Pete simply sat quietly as Tom came into the room, looking down at a pile of papers in front of him, somber. To the right of Pete was the Next Woman Up, Hirschfeld's replacement, Sara Hufnagel. She looked up at Tom as he entered the room and gave a grim little smile and said 'Hi'. Sara, like Pete Hamilton, had not been promoted to the exact same job even though it was essentially the same accountability as Hirschfeld's, and she was getting there ahead of her experience and skill level. Tom smiled back, but even more to himself. As he was lame-ducking his way out of here, he realized the rest of the room was essentially full of Next Up people, and he included Robert on that list, when he came in just behind Tom and closed the door. Robert had been in the organization a long time, and had seen a couple versions of Stovers come and go from the outside. Dutch had tired of the inevitable tug of war that had come with his last two lieutenants. Each of them was much smarter than Dutch, and therefore came to despise him over time as they realized it. The first one, the one that hired Tom into this frozen circle, was professional about it, but Tom could see it eating him up inside, and he eventually bailed. Stover was far more overt in his disdain, at least to Tom, and he'd been shown the door. Robert had come up the ranks with Dutch. It was finally his turn. To the rest of the organization it may have looked like a well-deserved promotion, but in Tom's mind, Robert himself was no more than a Next Man Up. He was not the visionary needed in his spot. He was the safe choice for Dutch, someone he assumed he could control. And lastly, there was Jen, now taking on all of Tom's shit for no additional money, the ultimate Next Woman Up.

There were a couple people missing, slightly more junior members of the staff. Tom didn't want to consider what the implications of that were so he didn't ask. He felt a little outside his body again, for about the millionth time in the last seven months. He felt like he didn't really want to plug into the details of this thing. Somehow float out without dealing with it. Donna was there too, of course. That brought it back to real. She looked like she'd been crying. Tom momentarily flashed back to the Hirschfeld suicide announcement meeting and got a little confused in his head what this meeting was about.

Robert nodded at Tom.

"Thanks for coming in Tom. I wish it was a better meeting." Robert sat down.

"As you know, with the board's decision to accept a substantial private equity partner, and now the merger, there's a lot of pressure to reduce our expense base going into the new fiscal year. We've got to get real about spending because we just don't have visibility into a turn in revenue growth. Every member of the EC was given a new lower target to hit, and we were no different."

"Robert?" Tom knew it would piss him off that he was already jumping in. Robert liked to execute his responsibilities perfectly, and this was obviously a prepared opening that had more to run, but they all knew the punch line, and Tom had context he wanted his peers to have. "My understanding from Stover was that every member of the EC was already working against a two year targeted reduction when we slammed everything together back in September, and that he took most of the cut in year one. So, do you have a less aggressive target this time around than other groups?" Tom wanted to understand, wanted his peers to fight, wanted Jen to demand that Jeff not be sent home.

Robert sent invisible lasers of anger across the table at Tom, in his inimitable, 'how dare you challenge me' way. Another reminder that after all this time, eight years together as senior vice presidents in the same small club, the last couple months as manager and associate, they really had no affection for each other. Robert saw Tom as a rival when he was brought in, much the way Tom saw Hirschfeld when he arrived a few years ago. Robert never went out of his way to be welcoming or helpful to Tom. And Tom paid it back to Hirschfeld, just because he found him annoying. How very fucking sad it all was. Now Robert had put his fingerprints arbitrarily on a reduction plan and somehow, six weeks before the end, Tom was still in the arena, locking horns with his own team, fighting over human flesh.

"I can't answer for what Stover was thinking when he created the current organization. I had a goal that came from Dutch, and I had to hit that goal. I know this wasn't easy, and I thank all of you, particularly Donna, for the work that went into this. I think you each know pretty much who this is going to impact, but before we leave this room today, Donna will hand out the go-forward org-charts and you'll have the full picture. Dutch has my plan and will take the weekend to review, along with the rest of his world. But I've given him the high level and I wouldn't expect it to change. He meets with the rest of Patton's direct reports Monday afternoon to go over the whole thing, and we expect to have the go ahead to conduct conversations by Tuesday, to be completed by Wednesday. Impacted associates will be able to review open job listings in the company and elect to post for any they are qualified for, but if not offered a position by the following Friday, the end of the quarter, that will be their last day." It sounded like a press briefing at the Pentagon, coldly, bloodlessly discussing body counts and civilian casualties. "Donna?"

Donna cleared her throat to speak, her mouth opened slightly but no sound came out. She was holding a piece of paper up a few inches above the table, gripping each side of it with just a thumb and middle finger, in the middle. Her hands were trembling, so the paper fluttered, bending backwards at the top like a rag doll. Tears welled up in her eyes. Tom began to have an awful realization.

"I'm sorry." Donna gulped once and sniffed, and let a couple of the held back tears pop free. "HR was not immune from this, and I found out before the meeting that I'm being impacted." Tom flashed to the family photos in Donna's office, a couple of kids that looked about college age. He wondered if the husband in the picture was a good earner, or was Donna's job the primary family income? He searched his memory for Donna's history; fuck, she's been with the company probably twenty years. Donna sniffed again, exhaled fully, sat up straight and smiled wanly, looking everyone in the room in the eye.

"But for the next two weeks anyway, I'm here to support this team through the conversations that I know are going to be difficult, and to have HR support available to you for any discussions where you feel you want us in the room. Once I get the go ahead from Robert that his plan is approved, I'll get packages prepared for each of you, and for the people on your team that will be conducting conversations. We'll have to coordinate timing, because even if you swear them to secrecy people talk, and we want to make sure we're not telling someone they have a new job, and creating rumors about who's being let go, before those people are told. As Robert said, the conversations with impacted associates all have to happen by next Wednesday, with last day worked the following Friday. We'll be making an announcement to all employees on Thursday, when we also have to go public with our impact statement because it's more than 200 jobs. And, also as Robert said..." Tom stopped listening. He'd heard the logistics speech before. He'd have a calendar to follow, he didn't need to listen any more now. He turned a dead gaze to Robert and just poured all his hatred for what he'd spent the majority of the last 32 years of his life doing into the only person in the room more senior than him. Not in age, but in rank. And corporate life was still all about rank, wasn't it? Robert had been promoted to rarefied air, air that Tom had decided was toxic. He was sitting there, stone-faced as Donna managed the composure to speak, complicit. Tom let the last strands of respect for a long-time coworker and fellow human being he'd been holding onto go. He allowed Robert's form to become the embodiment of all the evil that had taken up residence in his head. He stared at him hard. These fucking fuck fuckers. Telling this poor woman she's going to lose her job, and then making her stay for two weeks helping other people lose their jobs? This was it. This was so far the fuck over the line. How could Robert just sit there and let her spill her entire emotional life onto the table? He looked back over at Donna, who was still going through the process and calendar, and noticed that Jen was gently rubbing her back. Sisterhood was alive at least. Tom turned back to staring deadly at Robert. He began to recount the various conflicts the two had had over the years, and let his anger build about Robert's condescending attitude when Tom first arrived, the lack of collegiality and help. He hated how he himself had reacted, at first kicking himself for not being confrontational enough, and then for how he'd allowed it to become a cultural trope he passed along. This is a company where we don't help our peers. It's a tough place. Stand and deliver. Tom had let himself become a part of it. Not all the time, but he felt freer to pick and choose whom to ally himself with, whom to help. Just another coin flip executive. Bastard to half, good guy to half. Happy with a 51% approval rating.

You know what? Robert could fucking fire Jeff himself. If he's so sure he can do without him, let him try to explain it to the guy. Let him stumble over the words because he'd know there was nothing that Jeff had done wrong. Nothing that was his fault. Plus, he really didn't understand what Jeff did, so he'd look and sound like an ass, and Jeff would hate his guts. Would that hurt Robert, to know that? This was the company's fault – they didn't make earnings for too many years in a row. They let sales fall. Now they had to put expenses in line with sales. Except a really expensive executive was going to have to tell Jeff it wasn't him going home, but Jeff. Because those less culpable are always the ones let go first. It takes the big ugly shit like shareholder revolts or corruption scandals or spectacularly bad decisions to root the senior leadership out. And even with all of that shit going on here, minus the corruption anyway, this group somehow managed to hold on to their power positions even when the smart money says they've royally fucked up. That was the case here, wasn't hit? Fucking Patton and Dutch still hanging on, like barnacles, to the busted, rusted hull of this company, while good people like Jeff are going to be sent home? Sure, Robert can have this one. Maybe there's a vein of humanity left in there that the experience can prick and make him taste the blood that Tom had tasted too often. And then Tom remembered Donna again, who was still droning on about how to conduct difficult conversations, and his anger turned to the head of HR, to Perry Chin. The anti-human human resource chief. Great fucking timing Perry. Great fucking scheduling. Tell a director she's going to be terminated unless she's lucky enough to find an opening that's not been eliminated that she can live with, and then send her off to a tough meeting with a bunch of emotional executives? What the fuck is wrong with these people?? Tom wanted to shout at Jen, Pete, and Sara, "Run! Bolt! Fucking get out! Any way you can! Don't accept this! This is not your fate!" He'd never been happier about his own decision to leave, but was now overcome again with the kind of anger that had been tying him up in knots inside for far too long. The kind of hate he thought he was expunging on the ride home the night he knew he was leaving. With Frank on the iPod. He wanted to quietly get up, leave the room, go up to six, walk into Perry Chin's office, and sucker punch him in the jaw. Then he'd walk on down the hall, and he'd come to a door, and he'd look inside. And he'd say, "Patton, you're a pathetic motherfucking excuse for a human being and I hope you rot in hell for everything you've done in your entire miserable fucking life." And then he'd walk back down the hall, and come to another door, and look inside. And he'd see Dutch behind his wide desk in front of the windows. That ostentatious, old-fashioned asshole's desk that probably weighed half a ton. And he'd rush that desk with superhuman strength fueled by hate, and drive that fucker into Dutch's chest, pushing his chair into the credenza under the window so hard that it splintered on impact, while the heavy desk fractured several of his ribs and punctured a lung. Injuries to cause every breath to be a shock of pain for months. A little taste of hell. Hell, an IV drip bottle full of hell. That's what Tom wanted to do, and the only thing he was confused about was why he'd just spared Patton physical harm in his manic daydream.

"Tom?" It was Robert's voice. Tom suddenly became aware that someone may have asked him a question just a moment ago.

"What?"

"Donna needs to know if you're okay having the conversation with Jeff." Tom stared at Robert, knowing what the answer had to be, already formulating how he would spin it for Jeff, deciding now how to take it off Robert's shoulders in a way that would give Tom some measure of juvenile satisfaction.

"I think it needs to come from someone who actually knows him and knows what he does for the company, so obviously that has to be me." Tom continued to stare directly into Robert's dark brown eyes, even though he was essentially answering Donna's question. Robert was now giving him a look back that said, 'I know you're leaving, but don't fuck with me right now.' Were they going to throw fists right here in the conference room? Tom turned to Donna, but now was speaking more to Robert.

"I'll do it, but I'll do it myself. I don't need HR support." Tom looked back over to Robert. Yes, I'm going to throw you under the bus, you mother-fucker. And Patton. And Dutch. I'm going to steer Jeff to a couple of the good guys, assuming they're still going to be here. I'm going to save him somehow. And you're still going to be here, drowning in shit, and walking around a building where people hate you. How's your slice of hell, Robert? Robert stared back at Tom. Tom knew he heard every bit of his telepathic rant, loud and clear. He knew he wouldn't challenge him. He knew the other road for Robert was worse, firing Jeff himself. Awkward to say the least. Barely knows him. There was some tiny satisfaction watching another denizen of purgatory struggle between hot pokers and sharp needles.

March 20, 2016

Jeff Minor never knew his biological father, and when his mother had her fourth child, he went to live with his aunt and uncle until he finished high school. He went to two years of community college in California before taking his first sales job because he had met his future wife and he wanted to show her parents he could support them. Tom knew this part of Jeff's story because it was the backbone that Jeff built his life around, and he came back to those key details, including the numbers – one of four kids, two years of college - often. The factoids stuck in Tom's head because they were the reverse of his own experience, one of two kids, four years of college each. In the rigid world of Corporate America, four years of college was a price of entry today. And Tom's fellow generation of professionals seemed to be controlling the population by limiting themselves to a maximum of two children. Jeff Minor had become an anachronism. He's only a two year grad? He was part of a brood so large he was sent to live with relatives? That was how people lived long ago, but not today. Not the people in Corporate America. There were some clear rules of admission to this club. Jeff had become an interloper in his own world. The executives above Tom, even his own peers over time, saw Jeff as inferior. To make matters worse, he had a chipped front tooth that he'd never bothered to fix. Who does that in Corporate America?

Jeff's first company had been acquired 21 years ago by the company that was then acquired by this one, just before Tom arrived nearly eight years ago. All in, including his service with his first employer, Jeff had 41-years of service. He had survived the acquisitions the same way he'd pulled himself up from the challenging upbringing he'd endured: by outworking other people and being ceaselessly nice. The way Jeff manifested his work ethic, he naturally gravitated to complex but not insurmountable problems, and then plowed into the details with a vengeance. The killers above Tom tended to see it as an unnecessary focus on small things. 'Where was the strategic thinking?' they wanted to know. The ceaselessly nice part, the gentlemanliness he exhibited that definitely seemed of another time, only made those killers more suspicious of Jeff's capacity. And of course, Tom saw some of those same things. He was too attuned. He knew Jeff worked as hard as he did because he recognized long ago he'd have to. He didn't have a pedigree. He didn't get straight A's. He was grateful just to get those two years of college. He must have been smart enough to know his work ethic and good manners would win for him, because that's what he built his career on. He was also smart enough to know now that his white hair, broken tooth, and folksy persona were increasingly putting him at risk. Tom had already gone to bat twice in the last six years to keep Jeff on the team, to keep his run alive. He was valuable, first and foremost, but beyond that, he was just a really good man, loyal to a fault, and at the end of that proverbial fucking day that never really ends, he got shit done. As long as Tom still planned to be there, he had planned to have Jeff on his team. All those talent management sessions and those crazy assessments about vision and agility, Jeff was in play, his continued employment batted around by people who could only see what they thought was obvious, putting Tom on the spot to defend, deflect, and save. And that's what he'd done, as he suspected other bosses that Jeff had had over his 41 years inside successively larger fish had done. But the smartest dumb fuckers of them all had taken over the world, and Tom no longer had the will to fight them, and had decided for himself that he could not work for them any longer. Unfortunately for Jeff, that meant strike three had come. Tom was no longer in a position to handle the fastballs. All he could do now was put his arm around Jeff's shoulders and walk him back to the dugout. If he'd let him.

Tom was sitting at his desk, waiting for Jeff, drowning in sports metaphors, twisting inside, thinking about his first words, the ripped-off-band-aid of the conversation. He had already put in a call to a good friend in another part of the business. Might there be something for a guy like Jeff? A very good three years of work he still wanted to offer us, tons of experience, work ethic, gentlemanliness. He'll be a pleasure to be around and get shit done at the same time. There was receptiveness, even potential opportunity. Tom was encouraged. He felt like he perhaps had one more save in him. But he also realized the price to be paid. He didn't have the words yet after those first ones. He knew Jeff would be stabbing him with his eyes as a betrayer, a failed champion, a bystander who failed to stop a brutal attack. Mopping up with an olive branch of hope for a different assignment would not grant him hero status. Jeff may never speak to him again starting in about an hour. A man who gave him his all, including personal support and encouragement, for the better part of seven years, was going to walk out of his life in disgust.

How is that part of the plan? Fucking Robert. Fucking Dutch. Fucking activists, fucking hedge funds, fucking everybody on Wall Street. How can all those smart fucking people have fucked up the world this badly? How is it that Tom has to sit in front of Jeff, and tell him that after 41 years, he's drifted down to the bottom 10 percent or so of the organization, and has thus been deemed expendable? When Tom doesn't believe it, and Jeff won't believe it, and together they'll know it isn't true? But they'll play out the conversation anyway. Two players in a farce. Forced apart by power structures they've both submitted to. Maintained by assholes that survive like cockroaches.

Tom realized he was pressing the palms of his hands into his eyes so hard that little droplets of water were now floating around his head, tiny enough to stay aloft. Through the mist, Tom saw the clock on the wall, saw that his prep time was drawing to a close. Jeff would be walking through the door in moments. Tom gathered up the documents he needed to hand Jeff, snapped a straight line across the bottom of the stack by tapping them on his desk, and laid them neatly inside a manila folder, which he then placed on his conference table. Hidden under the smooth yellow cardboard were words Tom knew would burn in Jeff's brain forever. The folder already looked radioactive sitting there on the empty table. Tom tried to take some comfort that Jeff had to have heard the rumors, which were rank. He had to have done some mental preparation for the worst-case scenario. He knew Tom was leaving, and that could be a problem for him. He had to be smart enough to suspect something, didn't he? But would that really make this any easier? And then there was no more time for angst. Jeff was prompt as always at eight a.m. sharp, and his still athletic frame had suddenly filled up Tom's doorway.

"Good morning." Jeff's voice and face were more solemn and tense than normal, but not so much that he completely lost the warmth in two simple words he actually and sincerely used to acknowledge he's happy that another day has dawned on their relationship.

"Good morning. Come on in, sit down." Tom motioned to his conference table, and he knew Jeff's eyes would zoom in on the folder, sitting there naked, all alone. He instantly regretted straightening up his table, removing the stacks of papers and folders except for the one containing the Kryptonite. They sat, and Tom unloaded those opening words.

"Jeff, the company has made a decision not to replace my job. The bulk of my responsibilities are going to fall to Jen. That decision is consistent with an effort company-wide to further flatten out the organization. As Jen is absorbing everything, she also has to flatten out her leadership structure, and as a result, Jeff, your current role is being eliminated." Tom watched Jeff's jaw set as he tightened the muscles around his closed mouth. His deep smile lines creased down rather than up. Tom imagined he saw the last bits of warm light disappear from his eyes as he stared back at Tom. Tom did not look away. He never looked away. He hated when people did it to him. Cowards who don't know how to look someone in the eye when delivering a challenging message. But it was painful too. To see that draining of friendship and respect so quickly. It was like penance for Tom. If he was willing to do the evil, he had to endure the pains of hell. Jeff stared right back at Tom, jaw still twitching, the motion extending down the veins of his neck. Now his eyes began to narrow as the words just spoken sank in. Tom knew he was formulating his immediate response, and he wanted to make it easier for him.

"Jeff, in that folder are papers that I have to give to you, and normally HR would be in the room, but I told them that wouldn't be necessary. I want to be able to speak to you man to man, just us in the room, I thought I owed you that." Jeff inhaled, and as he began to speak, it seemed to dawn on him that not only was his job being eliminated, but he himself.

"How can my job possibly be eliminated? I don't think we're getting out of the business."

"No we're not. And you and I both know that there's no one in this company that can do what you've been doing better than you. When I was presented this, believe me, my first reaction was that it would be a terrible decision and I still feel that way."

"So why was it made? Who made it?" Jeff's steady stare had not wavered, his eyes were accusatory, knowing Tom had to have been able to give some input, had to have ranked him behind everyone else on some secret list.

"Jeff, I've been pretty open, I think, these last few months, about how I feel about this company. There's some hope, and some bright spots, but overall, I think it's a fucking shit show. And now that we know we're not going to be acquired, and we're not going to go private, and Armistice is involved, it's pretty clear what's happening, to me. They're going to turn the place into an ATM. Once they merge us with Broadview, this company will be a cash-generating machine. So, if we stop spending to grow, stop wasting money on consultants, cut the shit further out of staff, we can still grow earnings from here, even as we shrink, for a few years, anyway. And then who knows? Maybe we level out, turn into a dull widows and orphans stock. Maybe we get broken apart again then and sold off. The point is, any and all of it could happen, because there's cash flow, and everyone loves cash flow." Tom realized he had wandered way off topic. Jeff was squinting now, wondering what the fuck this gibberish had to do with him. "Anyway, what I'm trying to say is that there obviously wasn't much thought put into this, because they wanted to get a jump start on a new lower cost structure in time for the new fiscal year. To answer your question directly, this was Robert's call. I was asked very late in the game for a limited amount of feedback. I told you what I said. A terrible decision. A ton of specialized knowledge lost."

"No disrespect, but Robert doesn't know me from a hole in the wall." Tom giggled a little deep inside. That was Jeff, begging forgiveness for harsh words that to all other ears were tame as little kittens. But there was also in those words, Tom knew, an accusation, that Robert still had to have had some help from Tom to make this move.

"That's why I felt this should come from me. I'm not just trying to be professional here, Robert's not a terrible person. I can understand how much pressure he must feel dumped into this impossible job, and then having to downsize the team again, just seven months after a pretty major re-org. I gave him what I thought the risks were, and I also told him that I thought if title and level were the issues, you might be open to stay in a different role, but one that still leverages all the things you know. I was hoping he would take that idea and run with it. When I saw his final plan last Friday, he hadn't."

"Who else had their job eliminated, am I the only one?"

"No, absolutely not. I mean, really, mine was eliminated too, as far as the public is concerned. But there were others as well."

"In our world?" Jeff was now in ego-self-protection mode. Forty-one years. Never been fired. How was it him this time? Had the world really passed him by? This was worse than recognizing your mortality. This was a little death you survived. It wasn't inevitable. Or was it?

"Yes, in our world. You know I can't tell you which jobs but of course I expect that by the end of the day today, you'll know. But I need to tell you something else as well. It's in the folder, but I'll just tell you that all impacted associates can post right now for open jobs in the system, and if chosen to interview, you'll be given that chance before the end of next week, when your official termination date would fall."

"I'm sorry, but I just can't get out of my head that if this reduction is the normal 10-15% cut, that I'm ranked so low I didn't make that cut. Is it a lot bigger than 10-15%?" Tom could feel the rush of guilt of a defendant on the stand with something to hide. Of course, the record would show that in the last reorg, even though all his people survived it, Tom had rated Jeff the lowest on the infamous AGILITY/VISION/ DISRUPTIVE scale. That rating corroborated all the preconceived notions that had now doomed this fine man. STEADY, RESULTS-ORIENTED, SAFE. In other words, to the smartest dumb fuckers, expendable.

"Jeff, I've been honest with you all these years we've worked together, all the talent management sessions I've gone through. I've given you the impressions people have, the feedback I've gotten from others. You know what I think of most of that shit. But the world is competitive. This company is competitive, internally, for sure. You've done a great job for me, and for this company and you absolutely do not deserve to be sent home. But I know for my team at least, there's not a single one of you who should be sent home, no matter how deep a cut they're being asked to make." Well, that was pretty much an admission, wasn't it? Tom was culpable somewhere along the way. Robert must have asked him about each of his people, not just Jeff, right? And Tom just said he'd fight for all of them. So he must have fought weakest for Jeff. Because that was the result, wasn't it? Jeff had finished last, Tom had ensured that.

"Who's going to take my team?"

"I can't tell you that right now."

"Are all of them safe?"

"All of them are safe."

"Do I have the opportunity to speak to Robert directly, and ask him what it is I'm not doing that he needs me to do?" Tom wasn't sure Jeff really grasped the urgency of the timeline and the finality of it.

"I would certainly encourage you to confront him if you thought it would make you feel better, but I wouldn't want you to think it would change anything. I want to tell you that I did put in a call to Larry Zepp in Albuquerque, because I know he values you and I know you'd said you wouldn't mind getting back west someday. He might have an opening that's still part of the budget." Jeff perked up just a little. His eyelids opened another millimeter and a tiny spark of hope caught the light just right. Tom didn't always remember the little things, like the names of Jeff's kids, but he knew the west was the best for Jeff, his roots, his once and eventually final home. Albuquerque was its own little pearl in the four-days-in-the-sun oyster this company had become. It would survive nearly anything intact – a sale, a break-up, a chapter 11 – that's how solid the business was. It was just small. Not a ton of room for growth. Too little to move the needle for the whole ship. Just a nice tidy business run by nice people out there in the high desert. Of course, Jeff would have to move, but it was west. And it might not be a director's job. And it might not be exactly what he likes to do best. And it won't salve his ego. And it won't make Tom a hero. But as they say about growing old, it beats the alternative.

Jeff shifted slightly in his chair and the hope light seemed to go out, the smile creases were still fixed in the opposite direction, and he continued to hold his gaze on Tom, and Tom absorbed it, staring directly back at the Medusa, feeling himself calcifying further into stone inside.

"Am I supposed to look on the portal for this job that Zepp might have, or am I supposed to call him…?"

"I told him I would make sure you were interested first, it's something he hasn't posted yet."

"Is it at my level or not?" Jeff had convicted Tom and now he was in the sentencing phase. How much had Tom mitigated his sins of the bystander? What kind of soft landing had he negotiated to ease his guilt?

"I honestly can't tell you Jeff." Tom hated himself for the short lie that actually included a form of the word honest. He *could* tell him that Zepp had asked if Tom thought Jeff would accept a manager's role. He *could* tell him that he told Zepp that if it was something that got Jeff closer to the west coast, and it was secure for the next three years, that Jeff would almost certainly take it. He could tell Jeff those things because they were true, but he could also lie because he didn't know for sure where Zepp would end up leveling the role. So he chose the slightly kinder lie. Kicking hope down the road.

"Well of course I'm interested in hearing what he has." Jeff intensified his gaze deep into Tom's expressionless face. "You know I really just need these last three years." Of course Tom knew that, it was another factoid Jeff referenced often. Two years ago it was, "All I need is five more years," last year, "All I need is four more years," this past year up till right now, "Three more years." Jeff was nothing if not consistent. He was a marathoner in sight of the finish, even as the grade began to slope gently up. And Tom had held out his last cup of water for one of the runners just ahead, and now had nothing but a slow clap of encouragement for Jeff. Jeff, who would stagger on, desperately trying to get to that finish line, while Tom turned away from the race and blended into the crowd.

"I'll call Larry and let him know. Believe me, he'll be thrilled." .Tom tried a friendly smile. The warmth hit the air between them and frosted into a small cloud that drifted away before ever reaching Jeff. Jeff nodded over at the folder.

"Is everything in there pretty self-explanatory?" Tom looked over at the damn folder sitting there on the pressed-wood table top holding its indictments and penalties and partial remedies, and reached over to put a hand on it, touching it only with his fingertips, like it was indeed radioactive, and slid it across the table in Jeff's direction.

"Yes….but I really believe it will be moot, because things are going to work out with Zepp."

"Can I be the one to tell my people? And what am I going to tell them about who they're going to be working for?"

"For now, you can tell them what you know – that your team will be part of Jen's team, but that your specific role is being eliminated. And of course please tell them none of their jobs are going away. It sucks, I know. These things always come out in pieces, and then, you know, the email will come from Robert announcing the new org, and everyone will look for the names that aren't there, but they'll already know who's not there, because of all the hallway chatter. Their new boss will gather them at some point and introduce themselves, but you're free to tell them what you know now. All of the conversations with impacted associates are today, and like I said, meetings with new teams and new leaders will follow. It's not exactly being synced up perfectly by HR, because they're impacted too, and folks are a little distracted."

Jeff said nothing, just continued to hold his eyes on Tom's and slowly but perceptibly shake his head. Tom had never seen Jeff look so angry, so devoid of light and life and good humor. It was physically painful to look back at a face that was usually so warm and kind and see just disdain. And Tom felt himself begin to slowly shake his head along with Jeff. Yep, the last shred of unspoken communication between them was a mutual acknowledgement that this place to which they'd each devoted years of hard work, had become a sloppy pile of burning garbage. And there was nothing ironic or even absurd left in that to grimace and laugh about. It was just an ugly fact, and here were two of its victims, doing double penance, each individually beaten, and their personal bond fractured in the bargain. Jeff finally reached out and put his hand on the folder, drawing it to him as he stood, picking it up without looking inside, and tucking it under his left arm. He reached out his right hand, which Tom shook, a tepid grip.

"Thank you for everything you've done for me Tom."
It was perfunctory, as if literally everything Tom had ever done

for him was deserving of simple gratitude. Miss Manners thankfulness. Thank you for being my boss. Thank you for not firing me until now. Thank you for trying to find me something that at least keeps me employed. See you later.

"I hope things work out with Zepp. If you still want to be here, it's not a bad option."

Jeff inhaled and then let out an unenthusiastic, meaningless, "Yeah.". And then he turned his back on Tom and walked out. Tom looked up at the clock. It had taken all of fifteen minutes to undo a personal relationship that had been one of the little puzzle pieces of his life for several years running. That's what it's always been like in this life. Every day you're a changing mosaic of tiles, old ones falling off, new ones being glued on, people coming in and out of your life, in and out of your daily sphere of existence. So many hours spent attached to these strangers, and yet the glue is always coming unstuck. They say families should always stick together, but in this corporate hell, you can't stick, you're not family, you'll always be pulled apart, you'll always be mutating into something else or someone else. At some point, don't you have to get out, just to let your own pieces come back together and stay whole? For Tom, the answer was indeed.

April 4, 2016

Tom opened up his email first thing Monday morning in his best mood in months, maybe years. The past Friday officially marked the end of the fiscal year. Tom was still there. He was bonus-eligible. 9,000 more shares of the company stock were now officially his, free and clear. As Tom calculated their value at the recent closing price, he realized that for all the agonizing he'd done about being there to get those shares, they were only worth about as much as three years of student loans. For one child. Or expressed a different way, it was enough money to pay his monthly living expenses for 10 months. Not even a year of freedom. As he contemplated those hard facts, Tom realized he'd been overly-focused on getting to a date, to get to a number, that at the end of the day, wasn't that significant a number. Which pretty neatly summed up his entire career didn't it? Every number was made to seem like life and death - every quarterly report, every annual report, the number had to be hit or the world would quite possibly come to an end. That's how the CEO always saw it, and therefore, that's how Tom always saw it. And now the single biggest number in Tom's own little universe for the last few months was secured, and in reality, while it was quite helpful, it was not going to change the long-term trajectory of Tom's life.

And yet.......Tom was in a very good mood. Because the larger point was that he'd achieved a goal that was his, not somebody else's. And that was worth the little mental celebration that manifested itself in better than average sunshine and light. Perhaps that was why he reacted to a dinner invitation from Steve Light the way he did. Steve was retiring soon as the President of one of Tom's larger suppliers. He was the one Tom lit up back in January, securing incremental profit that might just be partially returned to him in his year-end bonus.

Considering that was the last time the two men had spoken, it did seem a little odd that Steve was asking for a dinner, but he couched it as a way for him to gain helpful insight into how his team could work more effectively in the future with Tom's team. Tom had not made his own departure public. Steve didn't know how little Tom cared about how their two teams worked together once he was gone. But since Hirschfeld's suicide, Tom had felt little pricks of guilt for the way he'd behaved toward Steve, and many others. He felt he owed it to Steve to say yes to dinner. Since he had cleared his calendar pretty effectively for his remaining month of work, he replied in the affirmative to the first available date in Steve's email. Wednesday night this week.

April 6, 2016

Steve and Tom met at the hostess stand. They shook hands cordially, both of them dressed nearly identically in khaki pants, plaid shirts and quarter-zip pullovers. They each had that sheen of successful older men – a well coiffed salt and pepper wave of hair, a not-too-thin, not-too-fat all-American dad build, worry lines and smile creases in all the right places. They were the same person, only Steve was ten years older and half a head taller.

Once the hostess had seated them, the exchange of pleasantries ensued.

"Well Tom, I really want to thank you for agreeing to get together. I always find that getting out of an office setting is the best way to have an honest conversation."

Tom smirked a little and said, "I'd like to think I'm pretty honest in the office, but I know what you're saying."

"I think you do; I hope you do. You know, shame on me that over the few years we've known each other we haven't done this, haven't taken the time. Kind of ironic that now that I'm retiring we're getting around to it." Steve had a slight hesitation in his speech, not quite a stutter, just a momentary gathering of the muscles in his face to form the next word. Tom had picked up on the tic in their very first meeting, and he'd seen and used the opportunity to easily interrupt Steve when it suited him. Now, looking across the table at him, it was a small piece of who Steve was as a person. Perhaps it was a stutter that he'd overcome, after long work, maybe in his adolescence. Maybe he was bullied over the stutter and dug deep and took the speech therapy he initially balked at. Maybe all that remained of that Herculean effort was this slight hesitation tic. So much is never asked when it came to other people.

"Yeah, tell me more about that, I'm jealous. I know you told me you were 65, but you don't seem like the kind of person who looks at a number and says, 'Well, that's it then.' What's your next act?" It was a natural, polite question, to assume someone still has the drive to do more than just putter around the garden in retirement, but also a probing, for Tom to decide whether this preamble to their business conversation should go on for a while, or be quickly shut down to avoid the tedium. A strong bias for forcing someone to get to the point and move on as quickly as possible had by now become an ugly character trait for Tom. There was simply not enough time to waste in business. But like many of the bad habits he'd picked up along the way at work, the same bias didn't work so well in personal relationships. Sometimes you had to just take a calming breath and listen. Tom had to constantly remind himself of that, though his family did it for him with great regularity.

"Well, first of all, I've got two little grandchildren that live nearby, and my wife sits for Melanie, the four year old, so I'm looking forward to some serious grandpa time. I spent a lifetime on the road, you know? I was in sales my whole career, with bigger and bigger territories, more and more travel. I have a great relationship with my two kids, but you know, I missed a lot. Now I'm lucky to have one who lives close enough for me to be involved in a different phase of her life."

"I get it. My kids are out and just finishing school, so no grandkids yet. But I get it." Tom nodded as he said it. A reflex demonstration of empathy.

Steve continued, "The other thing I plan to do is go back to school, so to speak. I had a boss I really admired who picked a different topic every year that he was curious about, and then spent the year reading books on the subject, watching documentaries, even going to lectures at local colleges. I'm going to try the same thing."

Steve paused, and Tom thought it was his tic. It forced Tom to look directly at Steve's face, to notice the muscles weren't working to form the start of the next sentence, to realize he was being invited to follow up with the natural question of, 'what are you thinking about tackling first?' Being forced to look directly at another person like that, another human being's face, just a couple feet from one's own, was the secret behind why the world still worked, wasn't it? All the wariness, distrust, fear – they were hard to maintain at close quarters, looking at another person, with a life like yours, breathing in and out, trying to make sense of everything else that sat on top of that one common rhythmic movement we all share. Tom thought about all the times he'd used his eyes to penetrate, to intimidate, to wound. This was a better use of those spectacular little gemstones.

"Okay, I'll bite. What are you going to study first?"

Steve hesitated, then leaned forward conspiratorially and said the words, "Income inequality."

Tom almost laughed out loud. He shifted his butt cheeks in his seat. How could this be a comfortable topic for either of them to scrutinize? A couple of old white guys from Corporate America were going to talk about income inequality now? Would their conversation meander to home size, retirement property, boats, cars, golf club memberships? Would the income inequality be the gap between one privileged man's success and another's? Of course Tom was sure that was not what Steve meant. Just the word "inequality" was enough to get Tom's attention. It was a buzz word for him. Right up there with injustice and hypocrisy. They were the axis of evil and too abundant in the world. There needed to be more defenders of righteousness, equity and truth Tom had the sensation of slipping further back, away from who he was at that moment, to someone he recognized as himself, but from a long time ago. Maybe Steve had more to him than he'd thought. Was he as itchy as Tom?

"That's quite a subject to tackle. I'm assuming you don't mean the difference between the super-rich, and the merely well-to-do?" Steve laughed and his eyes crinkled up warmly. Tom had never noticed such warmth in Steve's face, but then again, he'd never looked for it.

"No I mean the real deal. I myself came from very modest means. My father sold TV's at Sears. My mother was a school admin. I mean, it's not like we came from extreme poverty, but I think about how small our house and yard were, our whole lives, the single full bath that five of us ended up sharing, and compare that to the house my kids grew up in, and it's clearly night and day. But back then, I don't remember thinking that there was this crazy gap between what we had and the richest kids in town. And I was encouraged by my parents that if I went to college I could get a good job when I got out, and I could be anything I wanted to be. And they were right. But today's kids don't believe that when we tell them that. They talk about the 99% as if they'll be forever poor and only one percent of Americans will control all the wealth in the country."

"There's some truth to the math," said Tom.

"Yes, but also truth in this math. There's a one percent, but there's also a two, three, four, five and ten percent. I mean there is a lot of money in this country. I don't like being assumed to be a "one percenter". I might only be a five percenter, and that's not so elite, that's 15 million people. I just can't believe that 15 million people can conspire to do anything, let alone create income inequality all by themselves. So that's why I say I want to study the issue, because obviously there is a lot of anger out there, in our kids' generation."

"I came from modest means too." Tom thought about his parents, and that too brief moment when they tasted the good life. Country club membership, golf lessons, a big grassy backyard. Then everything went sideways. The business his grandfather had started went under, and Tom's father had to swallow his pride and go to work packing trucks. They moved from a house to an apartment, and Tom never knew his own backyard again. His father, to his credit, went to school nights and got an accounting job at a manufacturing concern, but he was fired for not getting along with the woman who was his boss. A long succession of jobs followed, boring shit Tom could barely understand. He was too busy struggling through adolescence and the unkindness of strangers in junior high and high school by then to care.

When Tom turned 11, he got a newspaper route. At 13, he babysat for the people next door, at 15 he washed and waxed cars in the apartment complex parking lot and did odd jobs for the residents, and at 16 he started cleaning factory bathrooms at night. The world had seemed to wash over his father, and he'd never recovered. Tom wouldn't, couldn't, let that happen to him. Steve had managed to get Tom into a sharing mood, and as the memories flooded his brain, one particular story from that time stood out.

"I saw a family business collapse, in the early 70's. We moved from a house to an apartment complex. There was one day around then I can remember my father gathering up all these silver dollars and half-dollars that he had in a big coffee can, and some silver spoons and stuff that must have been wedding presents, and taking it all down to this place that weighed it all and gave him like $700, and I thought it was the coolest thing, that we could have that much valuable stuff just lying around the house. But, now, I think, wow, things must have been pretty desperate. But I'm like you, I don't ever remember thinking to myself that I was poor. And there were other people in the family that were successful – doctors, dentists, businesspeople. I always felt that my parent's circumstances didn't have to be my circumstances, that I could do better, if I put my mind to it. I guess just like you, but for more negative reasons than positive ones."

"And you have." Steve gestured at Tom with his palm extended and facing up, sweeping across his entire persona, as if to say, 'Look at you, a senior vice-president at a big company, nice sweater, expensively comfortable shoes, crisp dry-cleaned cuffs shooting from your sleeves, a comfortable confidence that says you've got it made'. And Tom smiled right in the teeth of that lie, wondering if any of the irony of it was seeping out of his eyes or turning the corners of his mouth up wryly without his realizing it. Tom returned the compliment.

"And so have you. So why does it feel like it isn't the natural way of the world anymore?" Tom asked.

"I don't think it's really about us, but we're caught up in it. Look, I don't know your personal financial circumstances and you can only guess at mine, but I think we both know that for most people in the world, what we have is an astonishing amount of wealth, even though we know that it's not even close to real wealth."

"Exactly, it's nowhere near 'fuck you' money." Tom's vulgar sense of humor once again induced a chuckle out of Steve.

"That's funny, I've never heard that."

"Seriously? That's what I've been working my whole life for. Until I realized it was never going to happen, so then I started buying lottery tickets."

Steve laughed again. He was making Tom feel like a comedian. The waitress came over and looked down at the closed menus on the table and asked if they'd like to order a drink. Tom could see the time ticking from 90 minutes to the full two hours or even longer, but he was starting to think he didn't mind. Steve asked if they should order a bottle of wine. Tom shrugged in agreement and Steve quickly identified a bottle. Such a civilized world. Except for the ants crawling all over it, making it uncomfortable. Tom wasn't done digging into Steve's interest in income inequality. Or more to the point, justice and a remedy for it.

"This is what gets me," Tom started once the waitress departed. "It's no secret my company hasn't been doing so hot for a few years now, right? I mean, why do you think I was so mad about the whole Pyramid thing? They're kicking our goddamn ass. But do you know how much money Patton's made over the 11 years he's been the CEO?"

"Oh, I'm sure it's a lot." Tom noticed that Steve didn't swear, even when he had an easy opportunity. The man was a gentleman. Tom would have answered 'a shit-ton'. Although to be fair, until the last six months, Tom didn't naturally curse in a work setting either. The demon was loose.

"He made $110 million dollars. And do you know how many layoffs we had just in the last eight years? I can count 4 major ones, with corporate-wide impact. And he's not done making money. Whatever ends up happening with Billy Baron and the merger, Patton's got a shitload of shares, and he's just going to get richer, even if they kick his ass to the curb."

"I can only imagine how challenging it's been there the last few months."

"Well here's the thing, back to income inequality. When's the last time you heard a public company say that their mission is to raise the earnings of their lowest paid employees and help them achieve their financial goals in life?" Tom shook his head vigorously to emphasize the point. "No. Every public corporation only has one mission – maximize return to the shareholders. And how do they do that? 'Align the incentives of management with the return to shareholders', or even better, 'Make management big shareholders too, so they'll also act in their own self-interest'." Tom threw proverbial air quotes around his little shareholder capitalism word balloons. "Brilliant fucking plan for everybody else, when the quickest way to improve returns is to cut heads." Tom took a breath. Cutting heads was what he really hated the most, with all the times he saw it happen to his father. Was he really talking about this to a C-suite executive? How did they end up here again?

Steve responded, "Yeah, I've seen it time and again as well, although your man Patton is pretty unique in being the CEO in one place for so many years. I've seen the other side of it, when a CEO comes in and flames out in a year, but still walks away with millions."

"Oh yeah," exclaimed Tom. "The golden parachute. Funny that you never hear the phrase, 'He jumped out of an airplane with millions.' The bad guy walks away with the money. You'd think they'd at least have the decency to run away, seeing as how they did just rob a bank." Steve chuckled again, as did Tom. The wine came, and with it the obligatory pretentious first pour, the swirling in the glass, the sip, the thoughtful expression while tasting, and then the seal of approval for the server to pour for others. When finished, Steve raised his glass in a toast.

"To balance. And thank you for coming out to dinner."

"Thank you Steve. I have to admit I was a little surprised to get the invitation, given our last meeting, and your retirement."

"Tom, you were right to be angry with us. And I understand this business well enough to know when someone is putting on a show and when someone is legitimately upset, and I could tell you were coming from an authentic place."

Tom nearly blushed. Had he become that good an actor? Maybe that should be his life's act two.

"It's the job, right? Nothing personal." The trope rolled out of Tom's mouth automatically. It was the short cut justification for his entire career.

"Of course. Nothing personal taken."

Tom was almost overwhelmed with how much decency he was discovering in a man he'd considered just another one of the black knights inhabiting the upper echelons of every corporation in America. He wanted to know more about Steve. By the time Tom had reached his late 20's, he was harboring doubts about his career choice. What about Steve?

"So, this education on income inequality that you're going to go get – is this something new, or is it something that you've been thinking about for a while?" 30 years, maybe?

"I'd say it's something I've thought about a lot more over the last few years. Certainly, when the Occupy Wall Street group was out there, and everyone was talking about the 1%, I started to take it to heart. I'm very grateful for what I have in life, and I'm proud of how hard I worked to get it. I was raised to give back to those less fortunate, and my wife and I do that. I feel a little persecuted, to be honest, to be labeled some kind of capitalist monster."

"Did you have to do a lot of layoffs over the years?"

"I didn't. I mean, yes, if you include firing salespeople for not making their goals. But I always saw that as part of the deal. You know, pretty black and white, you have a quota, you know what you sign up for, that's the job. I'm not saying it was easy. I always told myself it was just the business."

"But every one of them had that job because they needed it right? And if they were still in it, it was because there wasn't a better one out there for them. So to take it away, that's pretty brutal for anyone."

"Yes it is." Steve agreed. Tom could feel Steve looking at him in a different way, almost like he was trying to see past something into a place further back.

"So what do you think will come of your studies? Will you be in a tent on Wall Street next time there's an action?" Tom returned to humor, another tool, another deflector. And again, Steve chuckled.

"No, no. No tent on Wall Street. I just want to be better-read on the subject. I want to see what economists are saying. I want to really understand it. I guess I want to know more so I can have an opinion and maybe see a way to have an impact."

Tom admired Steve's bias for positive movement. He just wanted to run from it, from everything, every responsibility he had, everything he had to think about, all the noise in the world. He felt defeated and had come to the conclusion that there was nothing that could be done. As long as there were hyenas and crows and other scavengers, there would be companies picked apart and workers discarded. It was the way of the world. But...

What if there were thousands upon thousands of Steves and Toms out there? What if there was a movement? The broad base below the one percenters. The two, three, four, and five percenters. The merely comfortable. The ones that fought their way to what they have in a mostly honorable fashion. If not examined too closely, their success was the American way. Get a job, do good, get promoted, learn and grow. Compete to win. The only bad deeds they committed along the way were compelled by the system, in Tom's case, ordered by his inner CEO. If they could be given a pass, forgiven their biggest sins, they could be the knights of the round table overthrowing the kings and queens! They know where the real wealth and the real evil lives. It's just above them, mocking them, laughing at them, brutalizing and tantalizing them. The CEO and those aspiring to be one, the high-stakes gamblers running hedge funds, the activist investors flushing costs away and showering in dollars, the retired gentlemen and gentlewomen of privilege getting richer in their dotage sitting on corporate boards and nodding along like slinky dogs.

That's the group that's done the real damage further down. That's the group that dismantled the economy that gave people who worked with their hands a good living and shipped it overseas. That's the group that is constantly cheapening the quality or shrinking the value of the basic necessities of life so that modest income people bear an unending cycle of replacing cheap shit that breaks and buying 12 ounces of food for the same price that used to get them a pound. That's the group that's wrenched the American Dream away from middle class families who mortgaged their future to send their kids to college, only to see them constantly downsized and restructured out of those formerly secure jobs at the country's biggest companies. Yeah, that's what the masses need: champions with real knowledge of how the game is played, who can't be bullied away or waited-out. They're out there, hiding in their McMansions in ring cities and close-in suburbs, right under the noses of the killer elite. Just down the road from the gated communities which are just a few miles from the private enclaves which are just a stone's throw from the playpens of the super-rich. They've got resources, these potential knights exemplar. A million here, a couple million there, and what's that they say? Pretty soon you're talking real money. Not that money alone makes everything happen, but money is the shield and the safety net. Money buys a microphone. Money buys a ticket. Money well-organized can usher in change. It was almost romantic to think about it – that all these resources could be mobilized for some greater good, that they had a common soul that could be found and activated. Tom knew that you couldn't just get rid of the profit motive and tell people to stop loving money. Hell, he'd met brilliant young Chinese entrepreneurs - expert Capitalists - who had been born and raised in a communist system. There was a human need to build things, to solve problems, to change circumstances. But as it was currently practiced in this America, something had gone terribly wrong with the system. All the rewards were going to those who risked their money, mostly in the short term. People who devoted lives to building the enterprises from which those rewards flowed were being discounted, if not ignored. There had to be a change in attitude. There had to be a new mindset. People had to step up and speak up, not in the streets, but in C-suite conference rooms and board rooms. Demanding balance. Demanding meaning. Demanding that shareholders be redefined as stakeholders. Demanding that all stakeholders, including the employees, be treated equally. That's how you got balance. It wasn't socialism, damn it. It was common decency!

It was also preposterous, right? Who would actually lead this revolution? Oh what a fucking idiot Tom was. What a gang of two at the table right now! Steve was retiring and all he'd said was he'd be embarking on an academic exercise. And in less than two weeks, Tom was dropping off the grid into the void of the unemployed; invisible. And even if there were thousands and thousands of Toms and Steves out there, people with that kind of privilege just don't go grabbing pitchforks to shake at their even more privileged cousins. Do they?

"Well, I admire you for it" Tom said. "I wish more people would stop and think about what they're doing and question it." Tom thought about telling Steve that he was also leaving the corporate world, but he really didn't know how to put into words for a relative stranger why. So he kept it quiet, and the two men eventually discussed how Steve's sales team could work better with Tom and his company, and Tom did his best to give thoughtful responses that showed how much he still cared about the business going forward, though he couldn't give two shits, even if he were offered a pot of gold for each. Inside he kept mulling over the idea that Steve was a less troubled version of himself, just as he'd come to see Hirschfeld as a more deeply troubled version of himself, and come to think of it, just as he'd come to see the version of himself that was walking away with no plan as the dreamily unbalanced version of his own self. How many other versions were out there? How many victims of long-term exposure to corporate capitalism? How many different exits? If Tom was far from the only one, if Steve was evidence of more, wasn't there something good that could come from all that? All that what? Angst? Uneasiness? Unhappiness? How do you turn those positive and start a revolution?

In the end, there was no sharing of that next level craziness that pinged around inside Tom's head over the course of their two hour dinner. There was no revelation of the misgivings in his journal. Steve would not get to know Tom another level down. Whatever he seemed to be looking for in Tom's eyes earlier had been deflected away, another easy save for the goalie. Tom knew in a month or two, Steve would run into someone and they'd say, 'Hey, did you hear Cooper left?' and Steve might remember the details of this conversation, and if so, most likely not be surprised. But he wouldn't know what was really behind it, and he wouldn't stay curious long. Not that unusual, happens every day. Corporate burnout. The common cold. Nothing to see here. Nothing to be concerned about.

"Hey, if you learn something really insightful about that whole income inequality thing, drop me an email," was Tom's parting line, as he gripped Steve's hand in an authentically friendly way and made sure to look him in the eye. It was about as close as Tom could come to telling a relative stranger he appreciated them. Literally at arm's length, but still connecting, however tenuously.

From Tom Cooper's private journal. March 2001. Age 39.
Employer 4.

I don't know if this is really an indictment of our public schools or just the nature of children, but there are very few days my seven-year-old daughter can answer the question, 'What did you learn in school today?' with anything other than, 'I don't know' or, 'I don't remember'. But the other day she did give me one of those rare opportunities to speak with Solomonic wisdom, like the dads in Fifties sitcoms.

There was a holiday party at school, with a pinata. When the pinata was broken and goodies were spilling out over the floor, there was a lot of pushing and shoving. She needed to say no more. Allie hates pushing and shoving.

"So, what happened?" I asked.

"I got a broken party horn and two empty candy wrappers." Accompanied by the saddest little face, the image was pretty pathetic, and I wanted to cry for her or go out and murder those damn pushy little kids. And that, I thought, was precisely the duel reaction that inspired cartoonists to pop little devil and angel souls on to the shoulders of lead characters. I chose the angel's advice to teach a lesson!

"Because you waited your turn?" She nodded. Allie always waits her turn.

I told my daughter that she could look at this a couple of different ways. One is that often in life, if it's goodies you're after, you have to push and shove. It's the American way of every man (or woman) for himself Capitalism. If you really want something, and not having it will make you crazy, then push, shove, do whatever it takes, to get it. Those are the rules of the game, criers go home. On the other hand, you could say that personal integrity and being happy that you are the way you are, are far more important than the goodies. There is nothing wrong with someone who waits their turn. In fact, such people are always better loved and admired than those who push and shove. The only caveat to this is that you can't complain about goodies you don't get. This is still America, people push to get goodies, criers still go home.

Of course, I presented these two scenarios at a level more suited to a second-grader than that which has just spewed forth, or so I thought. Later on in the morning, she could recall neither of these lessons in great detail, even though my wife had also answered this call to parenting in a similar vein. Ah well, hopefully some little nugget of it burned into that crazy mind of hers, and in the meantime I, Ward Cleaver, can perhaps learn something from my own wisdom.

This is the time of year when all the executives at my company receive their Peer Review report cards, or 360-degree feedback. People who work for you and with you rate you anonymously and can make anonymous comments that are fed back verbatim. It's meant to give the company and the executive a more well-rounded picture of their performance, but because it focuses on behaviors more than results, it can feel very personal, and in fact, some of the comments can be pretty tough. It strikes me that I do get the results I get at work primarily by pushing and shoving. What's really interesting though, is that at the first level of jobs that receive these peer reviews, you're encouraged to develop better people skills if the feedback indicates there's a little too much pushing and shoving going on. Move a little higher in the organization and there seems to be a don't-worry-about-it' attitude that says, 'Hey, if the worst thing that people say about you is that you're aggressive or demanding or tough or you push them too hard, you're doing fine. You wouldn't be successful if there weren't a person or two or three who thought you were a complete bastard.' Though we are not supposed to share our personal results with anyone other than our boss, you do get the feeling that some tough scores on playing well with others are sort of a merit badge in the executive ranks.

I have a hard time being proud of that, but at the same time, forced to look in a mirror, I recognize myself in even the harshest comments; or at least I can understand how someone might perceive me that way. I can pervert the lesson I gave my daughter and say to myself, ' You are who you are at work, you do push and shove, be happy with who you are, accept the fact that some people won't like you, criers go home.' I can tell myself that the goodies at stake – the job that is the lifeblood of my family's well-being and security – are so important to me that I will push and shove if I have to, to get those goodies. And I'll have to, because I'm in the business world, and there are lots of people in it who push and shove pretty good. The ones who wait their turn almost invariably wait their turn for their entire careers. They are the ones who are more popular and well-liked partly because they are non-threatening to those who are doing the pushing and shoving. One less obstacle, nice to meet you!

I could tell myself those things and believe them, but I can't feel good about being who I am. I'm human. I don't want to be unpopular with anyone. I want to figure out how to get the goodies without pushing and shoving. How to be resolute and competitive and still much-loved and admired. I want to, but I don't know a single executive in the company to role model. I could try to make it on my own, but I don't know, there's an especially active period of pushing and shoving going on at the company right now, and the economy sucks again, and those goodies are awfully important to me. I can't afford to stand on the sidelines holding a broken party horn and two empty candy wrappers. My daughter is a golden soul who will always wait her turn. Don't they say good things always come to those that wait? If it gets her naught but loved, I want to be there for her, to have rewards that are far better than the horn and wrappers, the kind of goodies that you get when you're aggressive in America. The goodies you get when you want them, not when everyone else is done with them. Criers go home.

April 27, 2016

This was it. Last day. Tom had read a ton of goodbye emails in his career, and had always thought when his time came he would just leave something short and sweet for the people who worked for him to say thank you. But over the last few weeks since his dinner with Steve Light, he'd thought that maybe he should try to pass along some gathered wisdom that might actually mean something to the younger people on the larger team he managed. Tom couldn't bear it if there wasn't something positive that could be learned from his experiences. Isn't that all any of us have left at the end? Our life experiences to share? He mostly wanted to talk about leadership. Ironically, it's the quality he found most lacking from the people he most wanted to have it from, the CEOs of his various companies.

While nature abhors a vacuum, leadership craves one. When you see a need, step up and meet it. That's leadership.

Get Shit Done. Tom's first commandment. Work hard to understand what needs to get done and then work hard to get it done. Tom had been through so many transformations, restructurings, and downsizings, and had always raised his hand for the tough assignment or the extra responsibility. And then he calmly stayed focused on the right priorities, doing what the CEO would do. Eventually that meant he fired poor performers, trimmed his staff without being asked, managed hard to a bottom line, and negotiated tough with suppliers. Yes, Tom was showing leadership the way it was shown to him. He was sad that it was empty of virtue. It was a good message about leadership, but it was often ugly in its execution.

Leadership is not bestowed by title; it is earned by your actions. Teach someone a new skill. Lend a struggling coworker a hand. Speak up when you have a good idea. That's leadership, too.

Tom wanted young people to know that they should help each other, that they had a voice, that kindness to others would be recognized as positive. But was it true? This place bitch-slapped him when he first came 8 years ago. Robert dumped shit businesses on him and ran. Dutch tormented him from day one. Patton snidely threatened him with replacement whenever results were tough. And Tom absorbed the culture and was truly no better to Hirschfeld. When Hirschfeld seemed like an annoying dork, Tom was short with him and took pains to avoid him. When he passed him in the hall that last time, Tom essentially averted his gaze. Or ignored what it saw. Was Tom a good leader or not by his own departing wisdom? Or did he just recognize that he had to get out before he did more damage?

Always take the high road. Sometimes the journey is longer, but the view is always better.

Tom admired the poetry of the line, but immediately began to feel sickened with internal remorse. He remembered things he'd done, too many and rushing at him all at once, times that he didn't even consider taking the high road. He did low-road things consciously, eyes open, and with the intent to gain some advantage he felt he desperately needed. He did it only when he truly felt his survival was threatened, when he was consumed by stress. But he wanted his legacy to be "always". Or at least his advice. Was that fair? Shouldn't others feel free to wallow in the depths if they felt threatened? And wouldn't they at some point? Tom was leaving but the world wasn't changing.

> *Try not to waste time 'managing up'. Try this instead: lead with confidence, execute to high standards, communicate the important stuff, own what you do, act like you belong.*

Tom wanted to warn people away from the bullshit politics of the corporate world and just be good citizens and -- yes, again -- Get Shit Done. But Tom did more than just get shit done over the years. He managed up with the best of them. He seized on opportunities to be noticed by very senior executives, if not the CEO himself. He knew if he could show off his thinking skills, his 'get to the heart of it' skills, his 'no fear of difficult conversations' skills, when he had those brief exposures it would work for him. He knew it intuitively because he watched how they responded when he used the right strategic buzzwords or concepts for the time. He parroted their speeches back to them. He was purposeful about it. Tom's mother always encouraged him to 'brown-nose the bosses.' She was scarred by Tom's father's serial job losses. In a sense, Tom took her advice. He turned himself into a generic American - responsible husband and father, Christmas celebrant, hard worker. Add in 'white' and Tom knew he had a package he could sell all the way to the top. Sometimes he thought the only thing that might keep him back was not being six-foot tall or better. Was it a sin to recognize the world for what it was and take the most advantage from it that you could? Wasn't that the heart of Capitalism?

Never forget to manage with your head, but lead with your heart. The heart is a muscle. It gets stronger with use.

Tom most hoped he would be remembered for this. You have to perform, you have to run a business, yes, so you have to make a good plan in your head to do that. But you don't inspire anyone with a plan to execute well. You inspire people with a vision of what a better future could look like. How the team can grow to address their challenges more easily, achieve their goals, improve their pay and career opportunities. And to do that, you need to appeal to the team's heart, you have to see them as humans, not resources. People were capable of growth and change and improvement. Resources were simply used and eventually dwindled to nothing.

Tom felt tears drop from his lower lids to his desk top. He was thinking about Jeff Minor and his broken tooth and his gentlemanly charm and the unfaltering loyalty he'd shown Tom. Jeff had taken the job with Zepp in New Mexico even though it turned out to be a two-level demotion in title. He hadn't stopped to say goodbye before he'd left. Tom had Jeff's heart, until he broke it. And yet, Tom's heart had gotten stronger over the years, hadn't it? Isn't that why he could feel the pain so acutely?

Tom looked at the words he'd written, desperately wanting to own them all completely, to feel like he always rose above the impulse to lead by intimidation, to feel like he never got seduced by the machine into believing other people were his bitter rivals, never intoxicated by the possibility of retiring wealthy and respected from a big corporate job, maybe even as a CEO. He wanted to feel like these lasting lessons he was leaving were lessons he'd lived by, but in truth, they were lessons he could only learn by living through, imperfectly.

Tom's youthful experiences had made him hard-headed and tough-minded, with a will to overcome whatever was thrown in his way. But his heart was not penetrated. He could open it up, first to Seaver as a friend, then to Michelle as a lover. He could expand it to his children and to the people who worked for him that gave so much of themselves. But once out there, that heart got pierced every day. Tiny, daily piercings, for 32 years. Until enough was enough. It was time to plug the holes. It was time to get a full-blooded heart again. Leaving was for Tom. Leaving a legacy behind in a long email was for Tom's ego. Maybe his first instinct was right. Maybe just say thank you and goodbye and ride off into the night, never to be heard from again.

But we can't be totally insignificant, can we? Don't we all have meaning? Doesn't what we choose to do and how we choose to do it, have meaning? Tom already had the evidence of that. As hard as it was to part with Jeff the way he did, there had been others on his team who had stopped by to thank him and tell him what he'd meant to their careers, and how they enjoyed working for him. He was leaving after these eight difficult years with some impact. He took justifiable pride in that. So why float this poetry about leadership that he couldn't completely own? Tom realized then who the messages were really for. They were a model for himself if he ever came back into this world, or for whatever next life he decided to live. He looked at the email one more time and entered his home email in the address line before pressing send.

It was still his last day though, and Tom was desperate to share something. He hit the compose button and entered his full team distribution list in the To: field. He tabbed the cursor to get to the body. He closed his eyes for a moment and looked for inspiration to find as few words as possible to sum up the whole of his corporate life. The effort spilled over to the whole of his existence instead. He typed two sentences. Paused and reread them. They felt like enough. He signed off "all the best". Cold and distant. He backed the cursor up, changed the little word, read it all together once. Pressed send. Left the building.

Dear Team,
Life is hard for all of us.
We should help each other.
All my best,
Tom

Made in the USA
Columbia, SC
22 January 2020

86984952R10200